The Bell Tower at Ladysmith Town Hall, 1900 following the shelling

*The Queen's South Africa Medal for service
in the Boer War*

i

THE AFRICAN MIRAGE

The Sequel to The Yukon Illusion

By Robert Davidson

First Print Edition

ISBN: 9798551920427

The African Mirage

©2020 by Robert Davidson

Dedication

To Janet and Flora

To Janet for her belief all should end well and to Flora for the selfless gift of love and affection of a true and loyal friend.

ACKNOWLEDGEMENTS

For fiction to be credible there must be truth in the equation. I have used the period of the second Anglo Boer war as a frame on which to drape this novel. I am grateful to established authors for their work on that conflict. While there are too many to mention the list includes Chris Ash, Ernest N. Bennet, Owen Coetze, Sir Arthur Conan Doyle, Anthony Jordan, James Mace, Donal McCracken, Thomas Pakenham, Geoffrey Powell, Deneys Reitz, Hugh Rethman, Roy Digby Thomas and Dr Frederick Treves.

I thank my friend of many years Richard Sutton of Saille Tales Books Design who prepared the cover.

I would especially like to express my appreciation to Desmond Latham, the writer and presenter of the Anglo Boer War podcast. It is researched in depth and makes for interesting listening. Des was extremely forthcoming with help and advice. The series is available on Podbean and https://www.abwarpodcast.com/.

Generous to the nth degree, John Fawkes the owner/curator of a website that comprehensively covers all British battles at http://www.britishbattles.com/ gave permission for his artwork and maps to be included in this book.

CONTENTS

ACKNOWLEDGEMENTS vi

PROLOGUE..1

CHAPTER ONE 4

CHAPTER TWO 11

CHAPTER THREE 20

CHAPTER FOUR 26

CHAPTER FIVE 28

CHAPTER SIX...35

CHAPTER SEVEN..45

CHAPTER EIGHT 48

CHAPTER NINE 59

CHAPTER TEN 65

CHAPTER ELEVEN 74

CHAPTER TWELVE 82

CHAPTER THIRTEEN...88

CHAPTER FOURTEEN 94

CHAPTER FIFTEEN 99

CHAPTER SIXTEEN 102

CHAPTER SEVENTEEN 110

CHAPTER EIGHTEEN.. 122

CHAPTER NINETEEN.. 129

CHAPTER TWENTY 142

CHAPTER TWENTY-ONE 155

CHAPTER TWENTY-TWO... 160

CHAPTER TWENTY-THREE 169

CHAPTER TWENTY-FOUR 179

CHAPTER TWENTY-FIVE 195

CHAPTER TWENTY-SIX 219

CHAPTER TWENTY-SEVEN 224

CHAPTER TWENTY-EIGHT 231

CHAPTER TWENTY-NINE 237

CHAPTER THIRTY 253

CHAPTER THIRTY-ONE 260

CHAPTER THIRTY-TWO 273

CHAPTER THIRTY-THREE 293

CHAPTER THIRTY-FOUR 300

CHAPTER THIRTY-FIVE 308

CHAPTER THIRTY-SIX 315

CHAPTER THIRTY-SEVEN 323

CHAPTER THIRTY-EIGHT 328

About the Author 332

Other Books by the Author 334

MAPS

NORTH NATAL 3

THE BATTLE OF HLOBANE 109

THE BATTLE OF TALANA HILL 141

BATTLE OF LADYSMITH 156

BATTLE OF MAGERSFONTEIN 225

BATTLE OF COLENSO 238

Robert Davidson

PROLOGUE

The haze cleared. The plateau with its miles of plain, interspersed with rocky outcrops and patches of thick bush lay before him. A rapidly rising sense of premonition took his breath, followed by the ominous dread, pushing to the forefront. "God no! Not now!" He struggled to remain calm and restrain the panic. It would overwhelm him if allowed.

The others cleared the edge and were leading their horses close behind to join him. The taste of iron was strong from blood flooding his mouth. He struggled to unclench his fists. He could barely trust himself to speak. Half-turned, and over his shoulder, he attempted to give the order. He tried but couldn't. He couldn't breathe. He tried to get air. He couldn't. He strained to shout the command. From a distance he heard his own silent whisper of an echo.

Trying again, it remained inaudible. He strained but only a faint gurgle emerged. The others appeared unconcerned and obviously could not hear him. Standing in the stirrups he tried to wave his sword arm above his head. It flopped uselessly by his side. He heard the growling roar which increased and rose to a crescendo pounding his ears. The Zulus were coming in waves at an incredible pace across the plateau. Every sinew strained as he forced the words to come out. This time with success he gruffly called out the instruction for all to mount.

NORTH NATAL

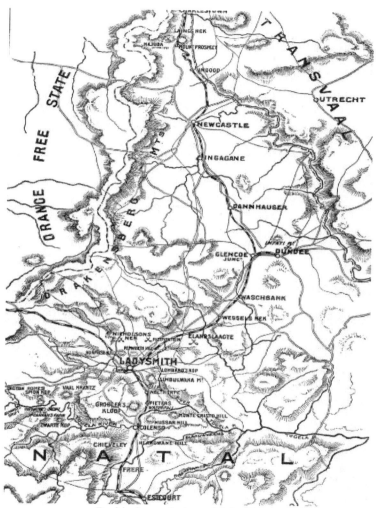

By kind permission of John Fawkes of
https://www.britishbattles.com/

CHAPTER ONE
Nicholas, Viscount Haddington

His journey in the railcar from the West coast had been no imposition. Plush velvet seats converting into a comfortable sleeping berth, steam heating, linen changed daily and attention from well-mannered attendants catering to his every whim, eliminated all discomfort. Meals on board equalled those of the Savoy. After the rigours of Dawson City it was idyllic. Despite this he was glad to be in New York embarking on the last leg of his return. Major Nicholas Craven booked a Saloon Category passage on the White Star Line's SS Cymric to Liverpool. He sent his recently purchased luggage ahead to the ship. After a night and breakfast in the newly opened Astoria he took a cab to the docks. He expected to be in England and back at White's in St James's after seven and a half days at sea. During the voyage he'd hone his skills at the card table in readiness for the sessions in the gaming rooms.

As heir to the Haddington estates, Nicholas Craven carved his own way in the world without undue recourse to his father's wealth. The Earl was rich, with coalmines in the north of England, two in the Midlands and an extensive one in Fife. There was an impressive stately home in Wiltshire, a vast estate in the Scottish Highlands, and twelve factories throughout Great Britain. Four newspapers, one of which was American, completed his inheritance. Lord Haddington, known to the Press as Croesus, did not have a close relationship with his only son. Neither made any attempt to change the status quo. His Lordship was disgustingly hale and still hearty with no concerns for his legacy or his mortality.

The return of the Earl's heir to civilisation since leaving Dawson had been uneventful, compared to the shooting on his last night in the Yukon. He doubted there would be repercussions. He would take any in his stride. However, having got this far, via Vancouver and San Francisco, with a border and the width of a continent between him and the defunct township, adverse consequences were unlikely.

Craven possessed an unmistakable military bearing. Erect, he stooped when passing through most doorways, but never suffered embarrassment because of his height. At six feet seven inches, with a muscular physique that was symmetrical, he was an imposing figure. The added panache of a black patch contributed to his air of élan. Not quite blind in the impaired eye he wore the covering to prevent the automatic rapid blinking and watering which could occur from strong direct light. The damage resulted from the severe beating administered in Conway's saloon. The bar owner and four henchmen ambushed him, hogtied him with leather belts and after a prolonged barrage of blows from a baseball bat wielded by the Irish gangster, threw him unconscious into the Yukon river. Days later he

5

surprised the five thugs during their attempted robbery of the town's Bank and shot them all, except the whelp, Fergal Boyle.

On entering his cabin he found the list of saloon passengers on his pillow. His eye was drawn to the entry showing the names of two lieutenants in the British Army occupying the suite two doors down from his. One was of special interest. Craven had served for a brief spell in Afghanistan under a senior officer called Frederick Roberts. Of course, it could be coincidence, but it was unlikely the listed officer was no relation to General Roberts.

While he was leaving his suite to go on deck next morning the two officers were leaving their cabin. As they came towards him both said, "Good morning." He responded then introduced himself. He wanted to confirm his earlier thoughts. The first soldier inclined his head slightly as he shook Craven's hand and said, "Roberts, Freddy Roberts." The other followed suit.

"Congreve, sir. Walter Congreve."

"Not Roberts as in—"

"The same. Only son of General Sir Frederick Roberts of Kandahar, Kabul and all points east."

They sat together on deck and had coffee while they chatted. The two had been on holiday in the United States and were about to travel north to Toronto when they received the telegram that called them back to duty. They thought, gleefully, that they would be under orders to go to South Africa. Craven enjoyed their company although he did think that only the young would blithely go off to war in such a carefree manner.

At dinner that night he dined in the company of two Belgian diamond merchants from Antwerp and three ladies. The darker haired woman of the trio had mannerisms which reminded him strongly of Belinda Mulroney in Canada. He did not think of her every minute of the day but realised too late, much too late, he had loved her. She had feelings for him but his respect for the hotel owner had prevented any attempt on his part to reciprocate, to his regret and chagrin. Paradoxically, this caused him to limit his conversation with the women and focus on the merchants.

One afternoon he agreed to play bridge. He was invited by a Texas oilman, originally from Ross and Cromarty, who was intent on touring Europe. He had left Scotland as a child with his crofter parents to settle in the one-star State. In his company was an American heiress. She was travelling to England for the first time to meet her proposed in- laws who were impoverished aristocrats. Her new on-board friend was an attractive beauty named Maud Gonne who agreed to complete the table. She proved close to Craven's ideal of a woman, having the unusual feminine attribute of height which, added to her attractive features and bearing, made her perfect in his eyes.

Until she spoke.

Her voice was pleasant, well-modulated but the opinions she voiced were radical and, to Craven's mind, seditious. She brought up the topic of the Irish question, always contentious even in the most non-partisan of company, and her views were extreme. She was English but took a supportive or even treacherous position of the resistance which, he thought violated acceptable behaviour. Gentlemanly mores and etiquette prevented him from openly criticising her behaviour but an unexpected and spirited intervention from the Texan halted her flow of vitriolic criticism.

The night prior to putting into Liverpool he took his place at the Captain's table. Freddy Roberts and Walter Congreve with Miss Gonne between them were sitting across from him. He smiled genially at the trio.

After dinner, the ladies excused themselves to retire for coffee. The men continued onto port, cognac, and cigars. The main conversational topic was the worsening of relations between Her Majesty's Government and President Kruger of the Transvaal. There had been previous conflict with the Boers lasting three months. Unrest, following a botched revenue collection, gave way to armed insurrection and the dissidents declaring independence from Great Britain. The antagonism started at the end of 1880 when the

Boers wiped out an Army convoy and blockaded British bases all over the region. Worse was to follow. Enemy fire killed or wounded a unit of one hundred and twenty soldiers of the 94th Foot within minutes of the initial shots. Boer losses totalled two killed and five wounded. The ante increased and the conflagration grew. Forces involved numbered in the low hundreds but a trio of resounding defeats, at Schuinshoogte, Laing's Nek and Majuba Hill brought the British to the negotiating table. The result was the young Zuid-Afrikaansche Republiek retained its freedom.

Craven did not serve in the First Anglo Boer war although he had fought in the Anglo Zulu War much earlier.

"So, Freddy what is the feeling in England now?" he asked.

"With the man in the street? Virtually none. The Press have yet to fully take part and there is concern in government circles a fresh intervention might prove difficult, because of events elsewhere. The Jameson Raid destroyed any trust built up over the years. Any further worsening of the divide could prove risky."

"Your opinion or your father's?" drawled Craven.

The younger man grinned unabashed.

"Pater's." He smiled broadly. "As you would imagine, he's well versed in all things war. He's pretty close with Lord Lansdowne. We dine frequently at his pile in Kerry. And as Secretary of War old Lansdowne's got to know what's what. So, I've no hesitation in voicing my father's opinion as my own."

"Touché." smiled Craven.

Later in the evening as he readied for bed, he reminded himself to seek an appointment with Redvers Buller, probably at the War Office, and offer his services in pursuit of a military resolution. He decided General Buller was odds on to become the Commander in Chief if the present furore developed into armed conflict.

CHAPTER TWO
Fergal Boyle

"Clench your teeth together and apply even pressure." The man had eaten garlic in a recent meal. Mixed with halitosis his breath was ripe and as he leaned in and spoke the warm moist drafts of each exhalation wafted onto Fergal's face. His was a strong stomach but it was difficult not to flinch. He complied and the dentist held his lower jaw. With a firm grip, he tried to move it, pulling, and pushing, side to side. Satisfied, he released it.

"Looks fine to me. How is it for you, Mr. Boyle?"

He ran his tongue over his gums and the new teeth pushing vigorously at them, but they remained immoveable. The sensation was a strange one, smooth, clean and solid. His original false teeth, cobbled together by a non-licenced quack in Dawson, were crude, badly fitting discoloured dentures which, for the past few months had deteriorated. It had been time-consuming replacing them. Manky breath and rank body odour aside this fella knew his stuff. Yes, different, definitely. And a vast improvement. But not cheap! But then he could afford it.

Now.

He was only a child when the man who shot his elder brother and ordered his father's transportation to Tasmania abducted him. As an adult he was accused of murder. The charge was erroneous. The person named was not the one he had murdered. He fled England. Penniless, he reached Canada. Financially, the time in Canada was well worth the short but action-filled period he spent there. He did not need false teeth when he arrived on the east coast of Canada and naively took on a land grant to make a start. The discovery of gold in the far-off Yukon had been the trigger causing him to throw off the bone-aching monotony of land clearance and set off across the dominion to make his fortune. It was an arduous, dangerous, and difficult trek of nine months to get there. Most of the time on his own in the wilderness, and with death ever close, never were nature's perils as severe as the dangers posed on those occasions he travelled in company. It appeared those desirous of fortune from the strike in the Yukon left all morality back in civilisation. Not that he wasn't ruthless. He had been, with success. Otherwise he would be a carcass, mauled and fermenting, somewhere on the banks of the Peace River. Losing his teeth was a direct effect of the scurvy developed on the trail to the Yukon. Although the magnetic pull of gold brought him to Dawson City, he never hefted a pick or turned one spadesful of earth to gain his riches. When one thought about it, most of those digging for gold saw none, while those in commerce, the victuallers, hoteliers, and saloon keepers, garnered so much they could hardly carry it to the bank. He had not a moment of joy in Dawson. He would lose the love of his life there, not to death, disease, or catastrophe but to the arms of another woman. He knew he was to blame but knowing did not make it easier. To compensate he devoted all his energies to increasing the ill-gotten gains and income from the unsavoury enterprises Conway's demise bequeathed him. A sixth sense had niggled at him when to all intent and purpose the untapped treasure still in the hills and rivers around Dawson was limitless. The same innate survival instinct channelling the efforts of animals into laying up food for the coming of demanding times, prompted him to prepare for a sea change. In four weeks, he sold all the property and holdings he had acquired. He got a ridiculously high price, even for the bizarre Paris of the North's boom-town values.

Then he made plans to leave.

The light of his life had departed with her partner. Within days the palace of cards collapsed when the news of another gold strike broke. The lifeblood of Dawson City haemorrhaged, flowing across the border to stream over Alaska to the pacific coast and the township of Nome.

He did not plan to return to the country he had not seen since the tender age of twelve. Not at first. In the absence of options, he decided he would leave Canada and go to the United States. Then the news focused on an impending war in

Africa. It didn't matter who was about to challenge the British, he would support Satan with life and limb, if he could fight against them.

Back in Dublin he checked into the top floor suite of the Shelburne overlooking Stephens Park.

"Excellent fit, sir," the tailor said whisking a non-existent mite of lint from Fergal's shoulders. Fergal said, looking closely at his legs in the full-length mirror, "For those other suits, I would prefer the trouser cuffs to be narrower."

"Yes, sir," the tailor responded, pulling his tape from his neck, and sinking to his knees. "Two inches? More?"

"No, two inches would be ideal."

With a last look at his image Fergal grinned.

Ye're the epitome of sartorial elegance, and no mistake.

In the cocktail lounge with coffee and a post prandial cognac he opened the Dublin Evening Mail and read four or five pages before lowering the paper to clip a cigar. He surveyed the room and watched as an elegant couple reached the armchairs on either side of the large ornamental fireplace. The man, conspicuously well dressed, was tall, wide-shouldered with a shock of dark grey unruly hair hiding his forehead and a sad, petulant look caused by the shape and set of his lips. She was equally tall but in perfect proportions.

"An Amazon," mused Fergal. When the recognition struck him, he put the cigar to one side and picked up the newspaper again.

"Yes!" he said to himself. This was the actress in the photograph accompanying the review of last night's play. The H. Uppmann lit, he leaned forward to better hear their conversation which was easy as they continued their discussion unabashed with animosity.

"It will never happen, Willy, so don't keep proposing," the woman said, but with a smile. "I would be a hazard to your inspiration over time and fail as the muse you so earnestly believe I am."

"But I am not whole without you!"

"Oh yes, you are, because you make beautiful poetry out of what you call your unhappiness and are glad. Marriage would be such a dull affair. Poets should never marry. Perhaps the world should thank me for not marrying you."

Fergal could see it was a poor effort as the man tried to smile and failed. The woman's response ended their conversation. The pair seated themselves, and as soon as the waiter arrived ordered before the man could ask. Both devoted their attention to the drinks and their surroundings. Fergal looked away, as the man caught his gaze, but focused instead on the actress. Initially unaware of Fergal's interest she looked at her partner and then followed his gaze back to her new admirer who raised his glass in tribute. He gave a wide confident smile displaying the gleaming whiteness of his teeth and inclined his head briefly. A stony returned look then turned into a spontaneous smile and she made a slight motion with her drink. She studied him enjoying a soupçon of empathy. There was an aura of danger around him, not overt but she detected its presence and willed him to approach her. He rose, deciding on the spur of the moment to introduce himself. The man got up as he approached. He was inches taller than Fergal, but this did not intimidate the smaller man.

"Not one iota," thought Fergal.

"Madam," he bowed deeply, "and sir," as an aside with a minimal inclination of the head, "might I say your performance as Cathleen ni Houlihan last evening at the Abbey was almost electrifying." With this statement, lifted directly from the piece by the Mail's theatre critic and changed by his qualification, he turned, pretending to leave, as the man sank back into his seat.

"Willy, invite my admirer to join us for a drink at least," the actress smiled at her partner's frown, reached forward to place her hand on top of his, "please?" After the briefest of pauses he stood again and made the introductions.

"Miss Maud Gonne you know sir. And I am William B. Yeats."

16

"Boyle, Fergal Boyle, late of Dawson City, at your service. It's a delight to meet both the author, William Butler Yeats, the Ould country's leading Bard and the personification of his heroine, one of our land's premier actresses, Madame Maud Gonne." He bowed slightly without turning his eyes from her. Yeats was perplexed and not sure if he detected a mocking note in the other man's delivery.

"And invited to share their company, however briefly. . ." Fergal grinned.

"Almost but not 'completely' electrifying," she said giving a rueful smile. "Ah well."

"I meant no disrespect," Fergal was quick to reply, "but to my mind you did appear rather distracted. Distant, from an aspect of reality in your day-to-day life, perhaps?" She stiffened slightly. It was true. She knew her performance had been less than perfect because of her impasse with William. Astute and attractive. She experienced the burgeoning of a deeper interest in this stranger.

His remark struck home. Emboldened by its success he turned his attention to Yeats.

"No one could improve on the play. Only an artisan of great merit could devise such drama." Mollified, Yeats beckoned to the waiter and ordered a fresh round of drinks.

"Dawson City, you say, Mr. Boyle?" she asked in a husky voice looking at him over the rim of her glass. "Were you part of the Gold

Rush? And successful?" she leant forward imperceptibly.

"Yes, to your first question, Miss Gonne and 'extremely' to your second," he smiled expansively at both. "As for my time in Dawson City, it represented a most interesting, and profitable, episode in my life." Boyle tasted his drink delighted his attention to Maud caused Yeats's unease to return.

"Are you a theatre goer, Mr. Boyle?" queried Yeats toying with his drink.

"Yes, would be an honest answer," Boyle continued his lie, "but opportunity has been lacking of late. Have you any new projects in mind?"

"Well, my poetry. . ." Yeats' dwindled into embarrassed silence as he realised Fergal was addressing his companion.

"There's talk of touring with the present production but I am of two minds and haven't yet agreed." This was news to William Yeats, and he gave a start of surprise.

"Will you be taking it to London?" asked Fergal.

"It is not my intention." Maud Gonne was short in her reply. "England and the English, play little or no part in my intentions."

"Not to appear in the Empire's capital would be to deprive the populace there of a theatrical experience of singular brilliance. You would appreciate appearing in the country of your birth,

18

surely?" Another telling snippet gleaned from the newspaper.

"Born there, yes, but I have no love of the English. My heritage is Irish, and my spirit will forever be Celtic. Tiochfaidh ár lá." Fergal mentally thanked the writer of the review for his accuracy in his reporting of the statuesque thespian's nationalistic views.

"Beidh do lá teacht," Boyle smiled, but your day as doyen of our theatre, has come, Miss Gonne." She smiled openly. Fergal stood then took out a small silver case from his waistcoat pocket and extracted a calling card.

"Miss Gonne. Mr. Yeats. I thank you for your hospitality and your company." He handed the card to Yeats, but Maud intercepted it, glanced at it, then gave him a dazzling smile. Yeats looked unhappy.

"We will meet again, Mr. Boyle. I'm sure."

He had arrived.

CHAPTER THREE
Greta Schopenhauer

Greta placed the wicker shopping basket on the well-scrubbed pine tabletop. The pristine whiteness of the worktop was one reason she insisted it should stay when they were deciding what to keep and what to dispose of after they bought the property. Another reason was its size. It had a surface area large enough for a person to work comfortably while preparing food. Since this was her area of expertise, and overseeing the household's finances, her friend put up little resistance. More modern in her outlook, and to be honest, more adventuresome, Aileen eschewed the mundane aspects of day to day living. She leaned more toward creativity than practicality. The younger of the two was adamant. It proved right to insist they be patient and not occupy the house before the installation of electricity and running water. The additional rooms, upstairs and down, gave them more space and privacy for their individual pastimes. The refurbishment included private apartments with bathrooms above stairs for each. There were no servants' quarters, other than Jenny's room, since the village was nearby, and their employees all lived there. Greta ran the household herself. As a child in her parents' house in Darmstadt, a full pension establishment accommodating students, she began learning her present domestic skills from the age of five.

All this was a profound change from the comforts, or lack of, they shared in Dawson City. There they lived in a shack, well insulated it was true, but primitive. Because of the hours of operation and the nature of their enterprise the interior of the shanty did not concern them unduly since they slept there but a few hours in any twenty-four. The saloon was taxing, arduous work, a labour of love for them both but not without an element of danger. The demand for protection money from the city's worst thug was frightening but was just one peril they faced. Without their time in the Yukon they would not have had the wherewithal to fund the undeniably well-to-do lifestyle they adopted here. She had her books and walled garden with both vegetables and flowers. There were apple and plum trees against one side. And Aileen had her stable and horses. Bliss!

She busied herself with the kettle at the sink before taking her coat off. The overcast sky threatening rain and hindering the passage of light through the window made the interior of the kitchen gloomy. Dim she could tolerate but sombre was an anathema. She had lived through more than her share of darkness in those extended nights in north western Canada. She switched the light on and immediately felt better.

They appeared as enigmas to the people of the town, two young not unattractive ladies living together. She and Aileen were not lesbians, but they loved each other in every other respect. Views held by outsiders of their togetherness mattered not one jot. Confident and capable they more than proved their worth together in the years they shared. Greta endured the hardships of the transatlantic crossing voyage in steerage to Halifax with Aileen, helping the Scots girl through the traumatic loss of her unborn child. They suffered deprivation in the New World, braved the dangers of avalanche, one of which took a dear friend, and endured the intense cold on the precipitous, arduous ascent to the Chilcoot Pass. Together, as members of a group of dancing girls, they negotiated the mountain pass littered with dead animals and survived the perils of broken limbs, awaiting the unwary on the long trek. They tumbled over hidden roots, clambered over rocks skirting lake after lake through the wilderness to the tents of Lindemann City. Doggedly they struggled on. Every day they endured severe cuts, broken bones, bruises and sprains but these did not deter them.

They reached Lake Bennett when the ice broke. Boarding an overcrowded low-in-the water decrepit steamer they travelled five hundred miles across lakes and down the Yukon River to their destination—Dawson City. Against the odds they opened their saloon. The Valkyrie provided honest female company and good meals, to miners starved of both. Unlike those unfortunates who had placed their faith in the discovery of gold, they placed theirs in arduous work. They believed in fair dealing, and undiluted liquor. Beyond their wildest dreams Greta's initial staking of the group increased tenfold, a thousand-fold and more.

On first landing in the country which was to shape their futures they went their separate ways. The callous and perverse nature of her uncle in attempting to force Greta to prostitute herself and service his friends drove her to flee. But not without first relieving him of a considerable amount of money from his cache in the barn. On renewing her friendship with Aileen this money gave them the courage, and means, to "go west" in search of adventure and fortune. They inspired other young women to join them in their venture. As the girls were dancers, Aileen an adept seamstress and Greta a no-nonsense jack of all trades, with the important seed money, all they needed was a venue to show their skills. A saloon fell into their hands when its owner overreached in a poker game and needed money to leave Dawson. Greta and Aileen obliged and so became joint owners of the Valkyrie in the Yukon. Fruitful as it was, the undertaking was to be short-lived.

The augurs were there for all to see. The light, and life, of Dawson, flaring then sputtering like a trail of loose gunpowder, was snuffed out by discovery of gold in Nome. Those astute enough to read the portends of what was to come had already made plans to return to a less frenetic pace of life in the actual world.

Aileen and Greta were among the first. Their group, comprising the girls who had not met men they wanted to marry, and Greta and Aileen, travelled together to Skagway, in comfort immeasurably more refined than when they arrived. They took passage to Vancouver where they spent a night in luxury in the Wedgewood and dined most elegantly before retiring late, and a little sad they would all part in the morning. They met at breakfast after which they made their tearful farewells. All promised to stay in touch.

Greta and Aileen sailed for San Francisco. Once there they held an in-depth discussion on whether they should make a fresh start in the United States or return to Europe. On deciding for Europe, the next decision was whether to sail around the Cape of Good Hope or go by rail to the east coast to embark. Both recalled how stressful their voyage across the Atlantic had been and how neither fared too well in rough seas. The discussion was brief. They booked a private railcar compartment to New York to depart seven days later. Meantime, they enjoyed the slower more leisurely pace of life in the City.

The crossing of the Atlantic, despite the luxury of their cabin, surfaced unpleasant undertones reminiscent of their coming to the New World. It seemed there was no clear weather or calm seas until landfall of the Irish coast came in view and then later the vessel entered port in Cardiff.

On board they socialised, at dinner and bridge, with a Welshman, who on becoming successful in business in his new homeland took American citizenship. He was silver tongued. His enchanting stories of the small town he left as a boy entertained his listeners. Both women, despite being in their early twenties, had met many male charmers but agreed his descriptions intrigued them. They would visit to see if it were as delightful as he made out. It might have possibilities. Neither had a place they were ready to call home.

The location, with a strong flowing river dividing the two halves and nestled in a steep-sided wooded valley proved to be all their fellow passenger claimed. And so, they came to own a sizable property in the township of Llangollen in the county of Denbighshire.

CHAPTER FOUR
Miss Aileen Maclean

The stillness, broken only by the sound of Garth's measured breathing, the occasional snort and click of his teeth against the bit, was integral to the enchantment of this part of the Dee valley. Aileen looked down at the picturesque bridge spanning the river which bisected the town since medieval times. On the far side, the trees clothing the hillside hid the aqueduct, carrying the canal to the next valley where it joined the Union Canal in Nantwich, across the border in England.

This view of Llety-cariad and its surrounds, their new home together, never failed to kindle a mood of fulfilment, something she had not experienced since her ill-fated teenaged relationship with Fergal when they lived and worked together in Haddington Hall. A lifetime ago. Strangely, he hardly ever entered her thoughts, now she was together with Greta. Their relationship created a sense of belonging and having roots, a semblance of home and family. She knew her friend shared this view as she had no kin in Germany other than an older brother who left home at fifteen, and she disowned her relatives in Canada. Aileen's family dissolved with the death of her father soon after he retired as the Earl of Haddington's gamekeeper on the estate in Scotland, followed all too soon by her mother's passing within a month of his demise.

Her sister Sheena, in service as an upstairs maid at Haddington Hall, married the senior footman and together the couple emigrated to New Zealand while Aileen was still in Dawson City. Jenny Moffat, two classes behind her in the village school in Perthshire, nursed both Aileen's parents following her father's stroke. The young woman travelled south to bring Aileen the MacLean's family bible and odd pieces of jewellery her mother left. Aileen felt honour bound to offer the young woman employment as compensation and they both welcomed her into their home. Greta appreciated the company when Aileen was not there, as she did when Greta had business with their solicitor and their bank in London.

She tugged lightly on the reins and Garth turned, breaking into a trot to take them across the side of the hill back to the track leading down towards their new home. As she rode Aileen reflected on what was yet to do in the way of improvements and conversion. With the completion of the Welsh oak panelling, the pointed arches, and the stained-glass windows there was little else needed in the main house. She would finish Greta's library then she could concentrate on rebuilding the stables, which would need enlarging if she were to get the second horse she wanted.

CHAPTER FIVE
General Sir Redvers Buller VC, GCB, GCMG

Mounted on Biffen, his favourite horse, they created a distinctive silhouette against the setting sun. He gazed across the parkland of the Queen's Parade. A large man and erect in his seat he valued these escapes from his desk and the humdrum day-to-day drudge of administration. The repetitive monotony of his daily life was, for years now, the norm. He swung out of the saddle to stand and ease the pain in his leg. The reins hung loosely in his hand.

At first, he welcomed his change of post in succeeding the Duke of Connaught, the Queen's seventh child, but the administrative duties of Commander Aldershot District were soul destroying for a man of his temperament. Evening was his favourite time of day. He would abandon the confining walls of the office, mount Biffen and together they would trot the length and breadth of the grassy expanse bordered on one side by the long avenue. The silence of the parkland recharged his vitality and encouraged reflection.

He had happily accepted this post would be his last. Retirement to his beloved estates in Devon would not have been unwelcome.

He had a varied and active career since the age of eighteen and the purchase of his commission as an ensign in the 2nd Battalion of the 60th Rifles. In the early days he was ruefully aware he made an unlikely officer. He gave the impression of a country boy with his red cheeks and speech impediment caused by the loss of two front teeth. His contemporaries considered him uncouth, but his immense physical strength deterred any open mockery. Nevertheless, he could feel its presence. It was there. The hidden derision made him argumentative in return.

Officially his first posting was to India, but no sooner he arrived there than he was sent to China as a participant in the Second Opium War. From there he served in Canada. It proved to be the making of him. For seven years, by experience and with guidance from an excellent Commanding Officer, he reached the maturity required of an officer. On his return to England he barely set foot there when off he went back to Canada serving for the first time under Wolseley. It was here his exploits became legendary. He played an important part in the expedition, especially on the trek to Red River, where difficult terrain and adverse weather complicated the passage. Fortitude and stamina were essential. He impressed those under him by example. Colonel Wolseley also noted his leadership qualities. When Buller and his soldiers entered the settlement unopposed the Red River Rebellion faltered and died without the necessity of force of arms.

Africa was to be his next destination where he was with Wolseley again, in the Ashanti War. When the 9th Frontier War against the Xhosa kingdom broke out, the War Department sent him there and afterwards he took part in the Zulu War where he won the Victoria Cross for bravery. He was so effective in his efforts against the Zulu they named him "The Devil's Brother" because of the amount of bereavement the Zulu families suffered. After a few years on staff duties he returned to South Africa at the end of the First Boer War and served again with Wolseley in Egypt. He commanded a Brigade in the Sudan fighting the Dervishes and distinguished himself in the Battle of El Teb by his active leadership. As Wolseley's Chief of Staff on the Gordon Relief expedition he excelled. Then it was back to desk duties for a time in the War Office. Subsequently, he served in Ireland "quelling disturbances." Sent back to the War Office he immersed himself in the establishment of what was to be an effective Army Service Corps. By this time, his status as a rising star brought him in to competition with his old patron General Wolseley for the post of Commander in Chief. The Government of the day would have appointed him had it not fallen. The incoming administration selected Wolseley for the position while he remained in his position as Adjutant General. Then came Aldershot and here he was, blissfully looking forward to a rosy after-life never to be.

His previous summons to London had dashed all hope of blissful retirement. It was highly likely he would be appointed Commander in Chief of British Imperial Forces South Africa.

Despite his protestations that he was a fighting soldier and would gladly serve in any supernumerary capacity, even as second in command, the plea fell on deaf ears. He pointed out his dismal failings in the recent Salisbury Plains manoeuvres in which he lost every battle he planned, and which highlighted what he recognised as his total lack of strategic concepts. He knew he appeared to be unshakeable, but he could be indecisive and experienced panic attacks which were the very devil to control. His much-vaunted personal bravery, recognised by the award of the V.C., lauded by all who served with him, and never disputed by those who had not, remained unused in any measure for years.

His courage was a fraud. There was nothing heroic about the motivation spurring on his actions then. The overriding momentum of his "valour" was fear, pure unadulterated funk, swamping and overwhelming his conscious thought. There was no way he could hold back the wave of overwhelming humiliation engulfing him.

The thought of commanding an Army in the field was paralysing and a burden unwanted at this stage in his life. He had never held a bona fide independent position of planning and directing the actions of massed troops He was now sixty years of age and about to leap into the cauldron of command; real, unrestrained hands-on command. He knew full well the ability to create battle plans abstractly for large numbers of individuals and units escaped him totally. He also doubted he possessed the ruthless streak allowing the sacrifice of hundreds of lives stemming from an order he gave. His sedentary way of life over the past decade aged him. The good things were no longer treats but necessities. He gorged on the food available at the luncheons and dinners, refusing no course served. His intake of champagne was prodigious. His waist thickened out of all proportion and he could not recognise the Buller of his early years. The change was not only in his appearance. He had become aggressive in his manner, brusque and overbearing. However, he was an exponent of impassivity. Outwardly nothing fazed him, but he knew, and dreaded that he would now need this attribute more than ever. This façade, which paradoxically helped saddle him with the unwanted assignment, must stay in place, constantly, to protect his reputation.

He broke his reverie as Biffen raised his head suddenly and pulled on the reins. He quieted him and the horse turned back to grazing after a loud snort and a vigorous head shake.

Buller, aware dusk was falling and that he was guest of honour at a Regimental dinner in one of the messes in Aldershot later in the evening, placed his foot in the stirrup and heaved himself into the saddle. He grimaced, never a facial expression he would use when not alone, as the pain from a severe injury as a boy flared through his leg. Accident prone, the carelessly swung axe caused concern that the limb might need amputation.

The distant bugle calling the troops to the cookhouse for their evening meal broke into his contemplation. With a grunt he turned Biffen in the direction of the Officer's Commanding Aldershot District living quarters.

As he was dressing for the dinner Beacon, his military batman, or valet as Buller liked to refer to him, summarised the various messages received while he was out riding. There were two of note. A request from a former comrade in arms, recently returned from Canada and a reminder of the meeting to be held at the War Office.

After the dinner and the speech from the Commanding Officer of the Regiment he made a brief speech in return. They drank the loyal toast and then retired to the lounge. For once he refused the after dinner cognac and sipped his coffee. He answered perfunctorily any questions in the ensuing conversations but spent minutes, while others spoke, in contemplation.

The knowledge he possessed of the character and temperament of his enemy, which would in any other case prove a distinct advantage to a commander, sapped at his normal optimism. Knowing their weaponry skills, dour dedication and will o'the wisp attack methods was a double-edged sword. He smiled grimly, recalling his well-publicised boast if he could not defeat the enemy with the number of troops provided, he deserved kicking. Behind closed doors at the War Office he repeated his conviction, numbers against the Boers would not be a deciding factor in pursuance of this war. What the Army needed was a complete change in training objectives and total re-arming of the soldiers called to serve in South Africa. He ignored the supercilious smiles and condescension because he accepted it was now far too late for change. Lansdowne and Wolseley appeared, or pretended to be, unaware of his deficiencies and remained immutable.

Soon he would leave for the Southern Hemisphere. The not unfamiliar veld, with its wide-open flat plains, dotted sparingly with clusters of hills, presented devilish topography which favoured an enemy well versed in defensive tactics. He knew too, the British battlefield tactics would be inadequate for combat against the old foe.

CHAPTER SIX
The Seed of An Idea

"Aileen?"

"Hmm?" asked Aileen closing her book but holding her place with a forefinger.

"This envelope. It has been everywhere." Greta passed it unopened.

"Well, it is for you, though it is difficult to decipher. When was it posted?" She checked the postmark. "It's been," she calculated, "four months in the mail. German stamps."

"Ja. Both the stamps and the writing are German. I don't recognise but . . . I have a feeling..."

Aileen sighed putting a hand on the other's shoulder. "Open it silly and reveal all." Greta stared at Aileen then the envelope, finally opening it. She gasped.

"Rudi. It's from my brother, Rudi."

The brother in question joined the German Merchant Marine on leaving home long before Greta went to Canada.. He left Hamburg on a cargo vessel, sailed to the United States, and signed on with another German ship in Savannah. In Honolulu he disembarked to spend his teenage years island-hopping in the Pacific on a small freighter owned by a cranky old Australian.

With the death of his aged captain and mentor, he tried his luck in Australia. Success eluded him at the Noondamurra Pool diggings. A passage to Cape Town followed. Within a month he set off for Johannesburg and worked as a mining supervisor for Cecil Rhodes' Gold Mines of South Africa. Officially an Uitlander he did not become involved in the movement which pressed for voting rights for foreigners in the Transvaal. He believed the Boers had grounds for not granting suffrage. The more he heard the more he was convinced of the validity of the Boers' position.

One morning, after a heavy night's drinking, and suffering the subsequent hangover, he recognised his own mortality. The feeling of loss and loneliness prompted the desire to know whether he were alone and how his family was faring. He wrote to his original address in Germany. Weeks later he received a letter from the Pfarrer of his local parish in Darmstadt informing him his family were no longer alive except for his sister, last heard of in Canada. The minister offered to use his connections in trying to locate her. Six weeks elapsed and he learned she was there but her precise location uncertain. He guessed she might be with the relatives there and he wrote. The vitriolic reply told of their efforts to find his sister, who they accused of theft, and the trail ended in Dawson City.

Undeterred he wrote to the Mayor of Dawson and learned she was now in England. He felt he had gone as far as he could go.

Then, after showing would-be investors in the Star mine around and joining them for lunch, he talked with two of them, who were fellow Germans, from Frankfurt. He mentioned the difficulty of trying, unsuccessfully, to locate his sister. One visitor mentioned the Salvation Army which he knew had recently introduced a service whereby they would attempt to locate lost loved ones.

Rudi went to the Salvation Army canteen in Johannesburg and found them helpful. Yes, they did try to find missing relatives and required only he write a letter to the lost family member and they would attempt to deliver it. He was dubious but did not let it show. He wrote the letter and put it in the hands of the servants of God.

"Do you believe the war coming will be a terrible one?"

"All wars are terrible."

"Yes, I know. Sorry, I am not being clear. So, erstens, England is going to fight the Boers and there will be casualties of both, killed and wounded? Yes?"

"Why yes unfortunately."

"What about the wounded."

"Why, what brought this on?"

"Rudi's letter. From yesterday."

At Aileen's questioning look Greta continued,

"He is going to fight. He believes in the Boer's right to their own country. So, he is going to be a soldier for them." She was apprehensive as she was not sure what Aileen's reaction would be.

"Does your brother have a special affection for the Boers?"

"I honestly don't know. He has been in Johannesburg some time. I do not know what his reasons are other than what this letter says. You know over the years I have had little to do with my family. I have not given to them much consideration. We were close when I was small and, even when he was in gymnasium, high school, he was my best friend. Then life happened. And then we were not so close. But this letter, his intentions, the idea of the war and his suffering hurt bring all my emotions to turmoil."

Aileen rose, and moving to the sofa sat down, putting her arm around Greta's shoulders.

"When I'm troubled or worked up about something, I act optimistically to improve the situation. Something positive. So, let's see what'll fix your worries. Do you want to go to Johannesburg to convince him to change his mind?"

Greta looked at Aileen to see if she were jesting.

"No, I don't believe so because I don't feel I would have much effect on what he does. No, I was considering something else, but I need answers."

"Such as?"

"Be patient with me, Aileen. I am thinking nurses. Do nurses do what they do for everyone?" Greta turned to face Aileen. "Do they tend to the wounded fighters from both sides?"

"I would say yes. Why?"

"I want to help make the effects of this war not so horrible for everyone. Yes, I want to take part but not on anyone's side but just help everyone."

During the ensuing days she did not mention the war or her fears but her prolonged silences were a giveaway to Aileen that her partner had not relinquished her desire to become involved. Then, at breakfast one morning Greta sat back from the table and clasping her hands in her lap, said,

"Aileen, I would like an ambulance."

Aileen looked bemused but stopped eating and devoted her attention to the other woman.

"This would be for the war then?"

"Yes. When I say like an ambulance, I mean pay for one and give it to the soldiers. The ones who are going to Africa."

39

"It would not be cheap, Greta."

"You mean maybe I do not have money enough?"

Aileen laughed softly. "No, of course not. We'd be able to make a large donation touching none of our investments."

"We? You mean you will help?"

Aileen, rose from the table and walking around kissed the other woman on the crown of her head.

"We are partners. Nicht wahr?" she mimicked Greta's accent who good-naturedly attempted to slap the other woman's bottom.

Aileen made some general inquiries about how to donate. In talking to the minister's wife, she learned of Princess Christian's patronage of an organisation created to promote the training of nurses for the Army. A letter to this organisation could provide more useable detail. Would Aileen like her to pursue the matter to get the address and such like? Aileen gratefully agreed. Greta waited anxiously for news. Then a day short of two weeks the reverend's wife called on them at Llety-cariad.

Jenny brought in a tray with tea and scones for the three ladies in the drawing room. Tea poured and a moment or two of village gossip shared, the clergy man's wife produced an envelope from her bag. Aileen took out the letter.

Greta fidgeted impatiently as Aileen read silently. As she did so the visitor explained,

"I asked my husband how one would go about contributing to the funding of the Princess's charity. He offered to contact the Deputy Constable of Caernarfon Castle, an acquaintance and colleague in the good works for the County. That letter," she took a sip of tea before continuing, "contains the relevant points of contact to make a donation."

She cleared her throat and with a touch of embarrassment said, "The Reverend and I may have done you a disservice and convoluted the issue."

"Whatever do you mean?" Greta asked

"The people mentioned there are senior officials. We may have implied the donation might be substantial. I apologise."

"No need, my dear, it will be," Aileen said and shared a smile with her partner.

Aileen had penned a letter to the Private Secretary of Her Royal Highness. Eight days later she received his reply. She could hardly wait for Greta to return from Llangollen to share its contents. Placing the decanter of Amontillado and glasses on the drawing room small table she waited for the sounds of her friend's return. Aileen patted the seat beside her on the sofa as she came into the room.

"This is the reply to the letter I sent to the Princess's Private Secretary. He thanks us both for the impending donation and tells us how it should be made."

"Good. But I suspect there is more?"

"There is," Aileen could hardly contain her excitement. "We're invited to meet with the Princess!" She laughed at the other's look of delighted surprise.

"I know," said Aileen, "me too. The Princess has a busy working schedule, but we are invited, along with other donors to attend a Gala concert at the Royal Albert Hall where we will be introduced to Her Highness." Aileen then poured two measures of sherry and, glasses in hand, they talked about the preparations to be made.

"Brauchen wir Knicks zu machen?" shouted Greta as the notion struck her and she sat bolt upright.

"We must curtsy. But for all the other aspects of the protocol, I'm sure we'll be taken in hand well before we are allowed into the royal presence." The time flew as they prepared for their visit to London. Not least were the arrangements for fittings and tailoring of their choices of evening wear.

They would stay in London for three days reserving rooms at Brown's Hotel. The event was a recital by Clara Butt of whom they knew little and had heard even less of the contralto's work

Their hansom cab came to a halt at the front of the Royal Albert Hall. A man in powdered wig and livery met them at the entrance and asked for their names which he checked against his list. After welcoming them and asking they follow him up the carpeted stairs to the bar on the upper balcony floor he passed them to a distinguished elderly gentleman in tails. He introduced himself as the senior equerry to the Princess. Taking them to one side he described the protocols for the arrival of Her Royal Highness. They then moved nervously to join the guests already briefed. Within minutes the equerry called on everyone to form a line and he positioned them in order of precedence to await the arrival of the founder and patron of the Princess Christian Army Nursing Service.

The Princess stopped to speak to each guest for a moment or two but seemed especially pleased to speak with Aileen and Greta. She expressed her appreciation of their donation but seemed more interested in their volunteering to serve in South Africa. The women accepted her interest was genuine as she tasked the equerry to make the arrangements for their induction at the Royal Victoria Hospital at Netley and arrange passage to Cape Town.

Aileen and Greta took their seats for the performance which they enjoyed immensely but the meeting with Her Royal Highness crowned the evening.

Six days later they received their paperwork and set to work packing and instructing Jenny in her additional responsibilities as housekeeper in their absence.

CHAPTER SEVEN
An Affair

Fergal Boyle renewed his ties with the Brotherhood. His hatred of the English, which lay dormant or smouldered wanly during his time in the western Dominion, re-ignited. It flared during discussions of the worsening situation in South Africa. The more extreme members of the Brotherhood and most other Irish Nationalists saw the breakdown of relations between the Boer States and their arch nemesis as an opportunity to strike back at the evil Empire. Fergal's intent, sparked by a wish to impress Maud and his own ill-will toward perfidious Albion, was to travel to the Southern hemisphere and contribute to the impending conflagration.

His actions did not go unnoticed by British Intelligence at the Castle in Dublin. A memo passed from the Special Branch of the Irish Constabulary in the city detailed the disposition of specific members of the various nationalist organisations considered likely to become "problems." Boyle's developing closeness to Maud Gonne caused him to be 'flagged' due to her vociferous anti-Imperialist outpourings, considered damaging, because of her prominence in Irish society. She and all associated with her were Persons of Interest.

His purchase of passage to Cape Town was 'suspicious' and possibly harmful to British interests. An informant, a chambermaid in Miss Gonne's hotel, provided the information Fergal Boyle had contacted one Solomon Gillingham and intended to meet with him on his arrival in Johannesburg. Gillingham, living in Pretoria, operated a large and lucrative enterprise there. As a rich but unscrupulous businessman, with strong Irish sympathies, and consequently no love of the British, he was a prominent member of a powerful group with close connections to the Boer hierarchy. When he visited London, he unofficially represented Boer interests, specifically those of President Kruger. The organization promoted the ideology of armed resistance to minimise and harm British influence and interests in South Africa. The group's radical convictions conveniently merged with those of the independently minded Irish.

In the weeks following their first meeting Fergal called on Maud Gonne and soon the friendship between the two developed rapidly into a close and physical relationship.

With the first onslaught of his lovemaking, fierce and demanding, she lost consciousness momentarily. His wiry naked body with its hard, well-defined muscularity engulfed her very being. There was no slow, enticing foreplay. Within moments of her coming into his room he pulled her to him. While he held her tight with his left arm his other hand was tugging, pulling, ripping at her clothing. His lips crushed hers. He threw her on his bed then was atop of her body.

The parting of her thighs was violent with not one iota of gentleness. She smothered a scream which swiftly lapsed into a moan of wanton lust. His erection, larger than any her body had known, entered her and the pounding of his hips was savage. When they finished, and he rolled off, she lay breathless, satisfied and fulfilled. More so than at any other time. She was also glad it was what she envisioned, and the expectation, as she climbed the stairs with him, evoked the enabling moistness.

In the passing of one short month, filled with assignations the physical attraction blossomed into even more intense lovemaking then, just as swiftly, waned. Their shared detestation of the British however flourished and they remained friends if not lovers.

Fergal was the father of the child she was expecting. His departure to Africa was imminent. He could leave for Africa at a moment's notice. And his relief when the moment came was palpable.

CHAPTER EIGHT
Comrades in Arms

As the train pulled out of Paddington, Craven checked his watch. His appointment with General Buller was in the afternoon. The General agreed to see him not in his office at headquarters in Aldershot but had invited him to the family estate, Downes House, near Crediton, Devon. Although not close, and despite the clear disparity in rank, the General Officer Commanding Aldershot District did not hesitate in agreeing to see Craven. The younger man had served as a subaltern in Africa as Orderly to Colonel Evelyn Wood, commander of the 4th column. Buller also served, as a lieutenant colonel commanding mounted troops under his orders.

A burly man, wearing a heavy coat with shoulder capes and carrying a whip, greeted Craven at Crediton Station as he stepped down from the train. The man touched the brim of his hat with the handle of the crop and inquired if he were the General's guest. He took Craven's portmanteau with his free hand and both men left the station to walk to a dog cart waiting at the exit.

General Buller warmly greeted Craven on the steps of his home. The visitor could not help but note the thickened waist of his host, since he had last seen him. There had been no change however in the military bearing of the older man. Though junior in commissioned rank, Craven was the son of an earl and this distinction helped to outweigh any perceived disadvantage in standing. Both men were of a similar build, although the younger man was taller than the sixty-year-old officer. Buller's butler instructed a footman to take his bag while the General led him into the library.

"Whiskey? Scotch, or Irish, perhaps?" asked Buller. On hearing Craven's reply the butler poured two measures of Lochnagar Royal. The general led the way to the armchairs on either side of the fireplace and after taking their places the two raised their glasses silently toasting each other.

"So, how have you been?"

"Fine, sir. And you?"

"No complaints. We dine at eight. We always dress." General looked expectantly at Craven but when the younger man was quiet, continued.

"You mentioned Canada in your letter?" As he took an occasional sip Craven superficially described his time in the Yukon.

"I didn't see the part of the dominion you served in. Manitoba? Red River, wasn't it, sir?"

"Hurrumph! Wasn't a long stay, but longer than I would have liked. Subaltern in the 60th. Under Wolseley for the Red River expedition.

Marvellous soldier. The whole affair was arduous, what with over 1,000 of us having to transport our food and weaponry including cannon over hundreds of miles of wilderness. There were portages galore, and roads, demned corduroy roads, to be constructed. And while all that was being done, we endured life in the bush for over two months, in summer heat and the inevitable plagues of blackflies and mosquitoes. Still, enough of my blathering. I assume you want to be involved in the coming South African brouhaha?"

Craven spoke of wanting to do something worthwhile, preferably in his postponed career as a soldier. The General looked at him closely.

"What has prompted this? Your father must be getting on and I assume you would be needed to take over his not insubstantial enterprises?"

"Yes sir, but not immediately. My reading of the current situation regarding Africa is the Army will play a part sooner than most people expect and I want to be part of it."

The General nodded at the reply.

"I know you to be of a serious bent, Nicholas, and you are not the fella who believes in vainglorious exploits. Your experience and common sense must tell you any punitive action we take will not be easy. Or quick?"

"Realistically, sir, it never is. I know little of the political background or any of the underlying elements, although I believe it safe to assume the

50

basis lies in unfinished business. Majuba? Embarrassment over the failure of the Jameson raid?"

"It goes deeper, Nicholas. Milner, the chappie running things out in the Cape, despite being a bureaucrat, would appear to be agitating for a military solution to the quandary President Kruger's actions are causing. Milner is playing his desire low key but to me it is obvious he is going to prod Joe into action."

"Surely Mr. Chamberlain is above all that?"

Buller smothered a guffaw, then leaned forward.

"We're Empire building, purely for economic gain, in the same way we got our hands on the diamond pipe. The development of the gold mines, and their undoubted untapped lodes, in the Boer republics, is causing the Government to regret releasing both those states. Obviously, for public consumption, the cause célèbre is the justice, or lack thereof, for the Uitlanders." The General did not need to explain the term because no other subject hogged the headlines as much in recent days.

"You mentioned the catastrophe of Majuba? Others seem to have forgotten the Boers who spanked us then are the same people who are now one of the world's richest nations with the wherewithal to purchase modern weapons in bulk."

The General pulled on his cigar.

"They're not short of compliant suppliers. Mauser and Creusot are tripping over themselves to give Oom Paul what he wants. We both have experience of what the Boers are capable of militarily and anyone who thinks they are clodhopping farmers is distinctly misguided. Unfortunately, it includes Lansdowne and most of his staff." The conversation died as both men sat in thought.

"D'ye remember old Piet Uys and his sons?"

Craven drew on his cigar and nodded. "How could anyone forget the only Boers to support us against the Zulu?"

"He told me one of our failings was to stand and fight." At the sight of Craven's obvious surprise, he continued, "He said we should fight from the prone position. Lying flat instead of standing. Mobility and field intelligence, that's what's also needed. Mounted infantry will win this war, be it theirs or ours, and good local knowledge. We fight on two feet but the Boers, if war breaks out, will fight on six. Mobility will be the key."

The General had no other guests for dinner, but the two men joined Lady Audrey, the General's wife of seventeen years. The meal was a banquet although constrained to seven courses. As the second footman cleared the dishes from the first course of Mrs. Beeton's cucumber soup, not one of Craven's favourites, the General nodded to the butler to pour the wine for the fish course.

"How soon could you be ready to leave?" At Craven's questioning look the General put down his knife and fork and sat back in his chair

"It's no longer supposition. You are looking at the Commander-in-Chief, British Forces South Africa." Craven offered his congratulations as Buller nodded his appreciation.

"In answer to your question, sir, I'd need a maximum of fourteen days for equipment, weapons, uniforms, what with fittings now khaki is de rigueur. But, while the Samuel Brothers are completing them, I can meantime get my personal affairs, bank and what have you, in order while I'm in town."

The general nodded then both turned their attention to the dover sole. Conversation was minimal with only Lady Audrey asking her husband one or two desultory questions about how he spent his day while she visited the vicar and his wife. When he was taking a portion of the pheasant mandarin and placing it on his plate before returning the spoons to the serving plate the General pointed to the birds and said,

"Shot these beggars meself ten days—" before breaking off to remove a pellet from his mouth. The butler was there immediately with an extended white gloved open hand.

"I'll speak to Barlow, sir. She'll be mortified!"

The General nodded curtly.

Angels on Horseback, a savoury dish to finish, followed the veal escallops, and Gooseberry Fool. Shortly afterwards Lady Audrey excused herself and bade her husband good night tactfully reminding him of an early start next day, and left them to their port, brandy, cigars, and coffee.

"Nicholas, I can get you there but unfortunately I can't get you an independent command. No problem with being on my immediate staff? I'm going to need someone I can trust to liase with some of the crusts I'm going to be saddled with. Between us, I am not happy my nominated selections have all been rejected by Lord Lansdowne. I might need you in action even before we depart for Africa. Remains to be seen."

"I would be honoured to serve in whatever capacity you choose sir."

"Excellent."

They engaged in small talk, while each had a second snifter of *Frapin* and smoked their cigars.

"We spoke briefly of old Uys earlier. We held each other, as individuals, in high regard." Craven leaned forward with his glass held out so the General could pour. "Never a warm friendship, mind you. Couldn't be. Too much bile and bitterness for actual friendship between the two nations. But respect for each other? Without doubt."

Craven remembered how Uys, his four sons, and the other forty or so burghers in their commando had refused all offers of rations or kit from Colonel Wood and appeared positively hostile at the mention of financial recompense for their services.

"We're here as equals to fight a common enemy. Not hired help," said the taciturn old Boer. The experience, fieldcraft, and knowledge of the Zulus probable reactions they brought to those engagements in 1879 were invaluable. There was no doubt the debacle of the Painted Mountain could have been much worse, with more lives being lost over and above those sacrificed. Craven sighed

"Didn't really want this command, d'ye know?" Buller broke the long reverie in an undertone. It was as though he was musing, and Craven was not there.

"Told little Lansdowne and Wolseley because I'd never held an independent command before. I'd much prefer going out there in a supernumerary position; second in command would've been fine. Wolseley wanted it, could have had it for me, but no; he was considered too old at sixty-six and was rejected. So, am I not too old at sixty?" The question was rhetorical, decided Craven and he did not respond. Apparently, he was not expected to comment as

Buller seemed to shrink farther back into his own contemplation.

They retired relatively early as the General was to meet with the Marquis of Lansdowne, the Secretary for War and Wolseley for further discussions on the deployment of the designated units for South Africa. He and Craven would travel up to Town together.

The General glanced at Graven and saw him look at his watch.

"Don't worry. We'll catch it. When a carriage is booked for me the Stationmaster always holds the train if I'm not already there." His brusqueness had returned with the cool morning air.

Minutes later they arrived at Crediton. Buller opened the door and strode off toward the station steps with his guest following and the coach man in their wake with Craven's valise under his arm and their briefcases in each hand.

The train arrived as they reached the platform where the Stationmaster saluted the General's arrival. Buller acknowledged him by touching the brim of his top hat.

"Sudan. One of my soldiers," he said, stepping to one side to let Craven open the carriage door. Once seated, by Buller's posture and demeanour, it was plain there would be no talking, convivial or otherwise.

As Craven took in the countryside, punctuated by brief glimpses of villages, the General closed his eyes and thought of the previous evening's shared memories. He lapsed from consciousness and slid into a shallow doze then deepening but disturbed sleep. Slowly, but inexorably, the mountain, its heights shrouded by mist, loomed above him. Hlobane. The Painted Mountain.

The haze cleared. He was on the plateau with its miles of plain, interspersed with rocky outcrops and patches of thick bush. A rapidly rising sense of premonition took his breath, followed by the ominous dread, pushing to the forefront. "God no! he thought. Not now!" He tried to remain calm and restrain the panic. It would overwhelm him if allowed. The others cleared the lip and leading their horses closed up behind to join him.

He could taste the iron of the blood flooding his mouth. He tried to unclench his fists. He could barely trust himself to speak. He half-turned, and over his shoulder, attempted to give the order. He tried but couldn't. He couldn't breathe. He tried to get air. He couldn't. He strained to shout the command. From a distance he heard his own muffled voice. He tried again, but it was a whisper. He strained but only a faint echo emerged. The others appeared unconcerned and obviously could not hear him. Standing in the stirrups and he tried to wave his sword arm above his head. It flopped uselessly by his side. He heard the growing roar which increased and rose to a crescendo pounding his ears. The Zulus were coming in waves at an incredible pace across the plateau. He strained every sinew and forced the words to come out. This time with success he gruffly called out the instruction for all to mount.

"Sir! General! Wake up." Buller struggled against the grip on his arm but stopped as consciousness and the present returned. He shook the restraining arm free.

"You were dreaming, sir and called out."

"Hmm. Must have been those kidneys. Or the sausage," he muttered as he turned away to stare out at the passing rural landscape.

CHAPTER NINE
The War Office

"What time will he be here?" asked Lord Lansdowne turning from the window. General Wolseley, sitting to the right of the mahogany desk, lowered his newspaper to look at his hunter.

"In twenty minutes. Eleven o'clock," he replied, shaking the paper to show his annoyance before resuming the obituary column of The Times. Lansdowne went back to his chair behind the desk. He pretended to review one of his files and they ignored one another.

Henry Charles Keith Petty-Fitzmaurice, 5th Marquess of Lansdowne served as the Governor-General of Canada and Viceroy of India but was now Secretary of State for War which ensured him of a place in the cabinet. Physically he was a little man.

He is small in every way thought Wolseley. The two men were icily polite toward each other but in private Wolseley could be scathing in his remarks about Lansdowne. Lansdowne, not known for impetuosity, angered the soldier by his ennui toward all things military and his lack of urgency in implementing policy. The present source of vexation was the fractious question of military preparedness and action, considering the present hostility of the Boers. He was not indecisive but was deliberately slow to act. This contrived hesitation was an irritant to the soldier.

At sixty-six, Field Marshall Lord Wolseley was a figure of renown and one of the most influential and admired British generals. After a series of successes in Canada, West Africa, and Egypt, he served in Burma, where a large bullet from a jingal severely damaged his thigh. He lost the sight of an eye in the Crimean War. After taking part in the punitive measures against the mutineers of the Indian Rebellion, he soldiered in the Opium Wars in China. The Red River expedition in Canada succeeded under his leadership and organisational skills. He commanded military raids and attacks throughout Africa—including the 9th Ashanti War. As recently as '84 he served as a member of the unsuccessful expedition against Mahdist Sudan which arrived too late to save Gordon of Khartoum. Despite the outcome the failure did not blight Wolseley's career and he was now the Commander-in-Chief of the Forces. In the hierarchy, he ranked marginally below his political master Lansdowne but in their day-to-day dealings with each other it was barely noticeable.

Both had little time for Buller.

Prior to his assuming his General Officer Commanding duties in Aldershot, Sir Redvers went to Ireland to revitalise the police and curtail the violence of the boycotters and gangs against the landlords. Buller approached his duties from a new direction believing much of the dissatisfaction was caused by heavy-handed actions prompted by the landlords. He made it difficult for peremptory evictions to be implemented without due process. Bailiffs were frequently denied police support when they executed unlawful expulsions. There were obvious financial implications from this policy for the landlords and it was not popular with most, especially those landowners with holdings there. Lansdowne's were extensive and the jewel in his crown was Dereen, a beautiful but costly home, in County Kerry and a drain on his resources. Therefore, his loss was greater than most and it followed he harboured no love for Buller or his actions.

When the Duke of Cambridge was compelled to retire Lord Roseberry offered the position of Commander-in-Chief of the Army to Buller. He turned down the proposal. Buller possessed failings but also virtues and one was recognition of his own limitations. As reason for his rejection of the post he gave his opinion Wolseley was the better man. His mentor and old commander was not an acceptable candidate to the Liberal Government. They disliked his intellectual arrogance and open sabre-rattling imperialism. Under pressure Buller provisionally accepted the promotion. A sudden shock election was lost by Roseberry's Liberals, and the appointment was rescinded. Wolseley was anointed as Commander-in-Chief of the Army.

Buller, overjoyed, declared his pleasure at the news of Wolseley's assignment. His congratulation was profuse and eloquent. Wolseley in this stage of his life, was paranoically dubious and suspected the role Buller played in what he thought were machinations. It had not been a fair selection process by the vacating Government.

Despite Buller having given sterling support to each of the older soldier's prior military endeavours Wolseley was now unashamedly negative in talk of his protégé. Previously admitting the younger General's contributions were superlative, he now frequently expressed his dislike of the other man in no uncertain terms. Wolseley, to the end, refused to believe Buller did not connive to be promoted and never forgave him.

So, Lansdowne and Wolseley shared a common animosity toward Buller. His speaking without forethought on matters in the purview of both did not go unnoticed. Buller's easy access to the Queen, who did not favour Wolseley, and whom Buller once served as an aide de campe, was the cause of rancour. Despite the mutual feeling of ill-well toward Buller this did not stop Wolseley from feeling proprietary toward his former protégé. He responded irately when Lansdowne said,

"I can't help feeling uneasy about Buller and South Africa. He's not quite right I feel. Something lacking."

Wolseley's voice rose shrilly, "Lacking? What would you know? Let me tell you a younger Redvers was the only man of all those on the Red River expedition who could carry a one-hundred-pound barrel of pork on his back. He could mend a boat and have her back in the water, crew and stores loaded, quicker than others could even make a start. His ability in guiding the boats through the rapids on the river excelled even those of the Canadian voyageurs. And his organisational skills are second to none."

"Where were those skills down on Salisbury Plain against old buffer Connaught? Lost every battle?"

"Deference, Lansdowne, deference. But then you wouldn't know."

Lansdowne shook his head, gave a loud sigh of disbelief but said nothing. Wolseley stared balefully through his one good eye then returned to his paper.

The Secretary for War remained convinced Buller lacked a *je ne sais quoi*. Awareness that the General had made disparaging remarks about him to Lord Salisbury did nothing to encourage a liking for Buller. The persistent stating of his view more soldiers were needed in the Cape Colony revealed if he weren't frightened of the Boers, he was very much in awe of their fighting spirit.

Their barely hidden ill-will and antagonism toward each other did not stop them agreeing to nominate Buller to lead the Army in South Africa.

Or because of it.

Despite the chilly wind he decided to walk to Cumberland House. In front of the station, Buller rearranged his scarf and firmly tugged his top hat down. The exercise would refresh, and the stiff breeze would clear the remnants of sleep. He watched as Craven's hackney cab turned the corner then he set off briskly toward Hyde Park.

He suffered no false expectations about the forthcoming meeting. He would accept whatever directions he received but reiterate his demand for more troops. He was realistic enough to accept probably none would become available, but nevertheless he would ask.

CHAPTER TEN
Nursing

At Southampton Station they found a porter who tucked both portmanteaus under his arms and picked up their cases. Aileen told him they were going to the hospital at Netley. He asked, "The Royal Vic?" At their blank looks he elaborated good-naturedly, with a smile at their puzzlement. "The Royal Queen Victoria? On Spike Island?"

"Yes, if it is the military hospital?"

"'Tis indeed" he grinned. "Nurses?"

"Not yet, but soon we hope," Greta returned with a shy smile.

"Right. We'll need a cab. Follow me please, ladies."

He strode off towards the exit and on reaching the stand whistled for the first in line to pull forward. He grinned up at the driver.

"Spike Island for the ladies, Henry," and he hefted the baggage up to the roof where the driver leaned forward and secured the pieces in place. The porter stepped forward, pulled down the steps and assisted them to climb in. When they were both seated, he lifted the shield and put it in place to cover their legs and protect them from splashes while the cab was in motion. Aileen handed him his tip and he touched the brim of his cap in thanks with a courteous "Ladies."

The driver opened the small trapdoor to confirm,

"Reception at the hospital? Fine, get yourselves comfortable and we'll be there in a jiffy." They heard "Walk On," as the trap door clicked shut.

When the cab entered the approach road the Royal Victoria Hospital came into view. A sharp, brisk wind blew inland from the sea. An expanse of the nearby Southampton Water reflected the late afternoon sun against the myriad of windows in the long expanse of hospital. At least a quarter of a mile long the building was inordinately beautiful in its lines.

"My! Look at it, Greta," Aileen said

"It is enormous. And grand!"

The cab turned and halted at the end of the West Wing. The driver passed the luggage down assuring the two passengers he would carry their luggage into the reception area. It was to be the last time someone else would do any menial lifting on their behalf.

On entering, their first surprise was the unpleasant smell permeating the air. They introduced themselves to the sergeant in uniform behind a desk facing the door. After recording their details and time of arrival he stood and called for an Orderly from a group sitting in a small room next to the entrance. A young soldier wearing a grubby grey collarless shirt answered "Sarge" and came to join them.

"Show these ladies to Hut 34, Griffin." The young man repeated what they soon recognised to be the obligatory response of 'Sarge' then stood by looking expectantly at them both. Nonplussed Aileen and Greta waited for him to step forward and assist with the luggage. He didn't but turned to the door indicating they should follow. They picked up their bags and walked behind as he left reception. He marched around the front and to the rear of the building where they could see a cluster of outbuildings. After a long walk to the end of the last row they walked between the rows to an isolated wooden construction. He opened the door, stepped back and with a cursory "Here yese are then," set off back to Reception.

A young woman came from the other end of the room to greet them.

"Hello. I'm Irene. Let me show where you'll be sleeping. When you've unpacked, I'll tell you what you can expect in the next few weeks."

Two rows of beds lined the room. Only four appeared occupied. Irene said,

"Take any one. Pick two together if you wish. This is mine and those three belong to the first intake who are on the wards now. To use the Army vernacular, I'm the Barrack Room Orderly today." At their questioning looks she explained what her duties entailed. "Everyone has to do it. You'll both get your turn as it changes daily."

All the beds had an accompanying locker and a small night stand on which stood a water jug and bowl. At the end of the bed, squared off, were two blankets, two sheets and an uncovered pillow. They unpacked as Irene described what they could expect each day.

"We rise at five. Breakfast is at six. Then after you meet the West Wing Matron you'll go on the wards and be "Nurses"." She grinned. "Everything we are to learn begins with an introductory 'Pay attention and watch this.' It really is basic. Right, now for the duties of Orderly."

The new arrivals sat on their beds and began their first day of instruction.

Early next morning Greta shook Aileen awake and they dressed in the uniforms they had purchased in London. The girls who worked the day before were up and about as they got ready. Nodding towards the others, Greta said,

"They must have worked late. I did not hear them come in."

"It was after ten," said Aileen quietly.

As a group the other occupants came toward them. A petite dark-haired woman said brightly "Good morning. My name is Annie, and these …" she turned to the group, and each gave a smile and said her name.

"Aileen"

"Greta"

"Welcome then to your first day of your new life. Let's take you to the dining room. It'll be opening soon." Together they left the building and were soon chatting without inhibition on their way to breakfast.

After the meal Martha, one of the trainee nurses who seemed to have warmed to Greta in particular, took them to the matron's office.

"Matron is a devotee of Miss Flora Nightingale. It is best to look apprehensive when you are to be seen by her. This way she will believe you already intimidated and not come on too strongly. It can be dire." She smiled, "But, fortunately, not fatal."

"Good luck," she whispered as they entered the ante office.

A caped sister behind an immense desk told them curtly to take a seat on chairs back out in the corridor and await the Matron's return from rounds. Forty-five minutes later, through a door appearing miles away at the end of the long corridor, Matron entered escorted by two sisters.

"Stand!" barked the shorter of the two. Both young women got to their feet. "You are to stand in the Matron's presence. Always."

The Matron stared at them for moments then walked past to her office accompanied by the taller of her escort. The other, after a scowl at both, turned on her heel and set off down the long corridor. Fifteen minutes later the keeper of the gate ushered them into the Matron's presence. In front of a mahogany desk twice the size of the vast one in the outer room she subjected them once more to the steely gaze.

In a surprisingly soft voice she said,

"Tell me about yourselves and why you want to serve."

"We want to contribute to the common goal," said Aileen.

"And you?" the Matron asked nodding at Greta who repeated word for word what Aileen had just said.

"You will be sorely tested here in the short time we have you. I'll be interested to hear your response then. Discipline, self-discipline will be required. An adherence to the tenets of hygiene will be needed. And hard work. There will be long hours. Backbreaking, long and unremitting labour. Attention to detail at all times, in everything you do."

She reached for a file in one of her trays, glanced at it before she continued.

"Your contribution to the Princess Christian's charity will not earn any favours here. Your turnout, in such rumpled aprons and headdress, is unforgivable. You will learn a pristine appearance garners respect. Sister Walton, the laundry, two days."

Perplexed both remained motionless. Sister Walton touched each on the arm and said they should follow. The rest of the day and the next two in the washhouse, made their ascent of the treacherous slopes of the Chilcoot Pass pleasant in comparison.

The hot vapours from the lye in the vats, pungent acrid and burning, teared their eyes. Their lungs hurt. Their throats were scraped raw with every shuddering breath. The kerchiefs they wore were dismally ineffectual. To pull the soaked sheets from the scalding water required herculean effort and even Greta who had experienced backbreaking work on the farm in far off Canada found it hard to return to the laundry for their second day.

They experienced respect for the local women who worked there permanently. And gratitude, when one asked for "help" in hanging out the sheets on the myriad of washing lines in the fresh air and sunshine outside.

On their third day, relieved to join the others on the ward, they made beds, rolled bandages and refilled water jugs. They enjoyed the shared experience of treating the patients. The days passed in applying ointments, changing dressings, learning to staunch the flow of blood, and stitching cuts. They were present at operations, assisting the surgeons with amputations, removal of gallstones and appendixes, gaining a rudimentary knowledge of administering inhalant anaesthetics, chloroform and ether, and other more intensive training. The skills learned fired a sense of accomplishment and inspired the confidence that would be needed in the coming war.

Aileen felt a flare of annoyance at her failure to notice sooner the changes in Greta's mood. She knew she had not been attentive to her friend, attributing the oversight to the communal tiredness affecting them all. But there would be no excuse in not broaching the subject now, on their one day free of the wards.

Greta found it difficult to explain to Aileen.

"I have been having many doubts after reading my brother's letters. He writes of wonderful things now we are in touch. We are closer as brother and sister because of our letters."

"Then how can it be a cause for sadness, Greta? Because you are unhappy and worried too, it seems."

"I have a decision to make because of what he says. I believe the things he writes. He asks nothing of me. He tells me of his convictions and why he fights for the Boers. Do you know the Boers left their homes to start anew because they could not live under the Empire's rules? Or that we already made war on them once when we wanted to take away their sovereignty? Then they kept their independence. But now they have diamond mines and gold mines we want to take it away from them again. Their freedom."

Aileen remained silent.

"He believes so much in their right to be free he says he will die for it." A tear rolled down her cheek. "He cannot understand why I will be nurse for the enemy. No, say nothing Aileen. Please. You know I do not see us as enemies. Someone who wants to help wounded or sick need not take sides. We are not going for the same reasons our soldiers are. They are going into harm's way, but we go to ease any hurt or injuries they suffer. I know Aileen, and it hurts me now, but I have to do the same for my brother. I want him to understand he is not my enemy and that I am a nurse for all. But it is difficult to express that in a letter." Now the tears were flowing freely. Aileen moved from her bed and sat beside Greta so she could comfort her.

"I understand. Greta, I will always understand. Du bist meine Schwester. You are my sister."

CHAPTER ELEVEN
The Prize

The first record of the presence of Europeans, in what became South Africa, was of Portuguese navigator Bartholomeus Dias and his crew. They rounded the Cape of Storms in the early fifteenth century. Then in 1497 Vasco da Gama went ashore on Christmas Day and named the land 'Terra do Natal', Portuguese for 'Land of The Birth.'

In the years following, the Cape of Storms became the more optimistic Cape of Good Hope and saw Portuguese, British and Dutch expeditions, all claiming possession of parts of the coast on the Atlantic side of the headland. The Dutch efforts were long-lived and more substantial. Jan van Riebeek brought one hundred men and four women. He founded the colony at Table Bay. Dutch Calvinists, ex-mercenaries from Germany and a few Huguenot refugees soon populated the Colony under the aegis of the Dutch East India company. As a way station, it provided fresh supplies and drinking water for trade vessels plying to and from Holland and its territories in the Orient. Most of the settlers were Dutch and their language developed as the Colony's lingua franca.

Great Britain, during its wars with Napoleonic France, asked by Prince of Orange to hold safe his overseas territories, did so. It also recognized the colony's strategic importance. The colony could serve as a re-supply depot. The outpost became a naval base en route to Britain's own possessions in the Far East. It was a haven for its warships in the southern hemisphere.

The outpost was not as attractive to would-be settlers as were other lands of the Empire, such as Canada, Australia, and New Zealand. It was not a destination of choice for British emigrants. Most inhabitants were Dutch. A determined group of these would not accept Ordinance Number 50, decreeing the discontinuation of slavery in all lands under British jurisdiction. The grant of equal status to all races was an anathema. A further regulation proved difficult to accept. The Dutch speakers hated the proclamation that English would be the only language of the Cape Colony. It outlawed the use of the Dutch language in all aspects, prohibiting the use of their Bible, church services and school lessons in Dutch, and denied the Dutch speakers their culture. Five thousand colonists left to establish independent new settlements. They were the voortrekkers or pioneers. They trekked northwards from Cape Colony, crossing the Orange and Vaal rivers, and set up two fledgling Afrikaner states. The British Government reluctantly accepted the existence of these independent Boer nations for the next sixty years.

British merchants settled Natal, administered by the Cape Colony. The province later became a separate state. The number of inhabitants rose when an influx of more Cape residents arrived, both British and Boers, who at first lived together without enmity. Within a few years, however, problems arose from the inability of elements of both communities to co-exist.

A second wave of Boers arrived establishing the Natalia Republic and took over the administration. Poor relations, between these Boers and the neighbouring Zulus, led to strife. Forces of the Governor of the Cape Colony then occupied the port of Durban. The Voortrekkers migrated again. A powerful complement of Boers did remain in the State when it became a British colony with its own administration. The numbers of the once powerful Boer community haemorrhaged and a steady flow of settlers from Britain increased the English base. However, the increasing tensions between the original inhabitants of the land, the Zulus, and the white settlers erupted into the Anglo Zulu war. The British won, after a crushing initial defeat, and this resulted in the Zulu kingdom's annexation. This doubled the size of the state of Natal.

In the late eighteen-fifties the Boers declared the Transvaal an independent republic, but Britain soon annexed the state. Resistance fermented and in 1880 a rebellion erupted. The blaze ignited when a Boer named Piet Bezuidenhout refused to pay an unjust and inflated tax. Government officials seized his wagon which they attempted to auction off. A hundred-armed Boers interrupted the proceedings and reclaimed the confiscated property. The group fought back against government troops who tried to conduct a punitive action.

The Transvaal declared independence from the United Kingdom, igniting the first of the Anglo Boer wars. After initial skirmishing, the situation worsened, when an ambush at Bronkhorstspruit by the Boers destroyed a British Army convoy. The Boers then lay siege to all the army garrisons in the Transvaal. They would repeat this tactic a decade later.

Although the engagements were limited in scale the Boers were the more competent participants. With no standing army, when danger threatened, all the men in a district formed up into Commandos. They elected their officers. There was no recognisable uniform, and everyone dressed as he pleased, in dark-grey, or earth tone farming clothes, such as faded yellow corduroy jackets and trousers. Each militiaman supplied his own weapon and horse. The Boers who made up the Commandos, were farmers who had spent their working lives on horseback. However, the term 'farmers' was a misnomer and many of the British pursuing this war thought they were taking on untrained and unskilled combatants. Their very existence on the wide-open veld of Africa ensured the Boers adeptness at fighting natives and defending their homes. They developed a special expertise while hunting. The standard of their shooting was high. Their weaponry, in the First Boer War, was single-shot breech-loading rifles such as the Westley Richards, the Martini-Henry, or the Snider-Enfield. A minority had repeaters such as the Winchester or the Swiss Vetterli. It was rare a Boer fired from a standing position; he favoured the prone position and preferred to fire from cover. At gatherings they often had shooting matches where the targets, such as hens' eggs, rested on posts over one hundred yards away. The Boers were naturals as mounted infantry. Born to saddle and gun they were skilled in field craft and hardened by experience. They would use every scrap of cover to decimate the ranks of the British with accurate and destructive fire. Their prime attribute, which the British paid an exorbitant price to experience, was "invisibility."

Despite the frequent attacks and losses the Army suffered, few British soldiers had seen a Boer in the initial stages of the conflagration. Launched as surprise ambushes, with a devasting rate and level of fire power the attacks ceased before there was time for retaliation. Attacking only when their Commandos were superior in number to the opposing force they would strike then mount up, having hidden their horses in "dead" ground and vanish.

British army infantry units fought in serried ranks They wore toy soldier uniforms, red jackets, dark blue trousers with red piping on the side, white pith helmets and pipe clayed equipment. Highland regiments wore the kilt. This presented a vivid contrast to the African landscape. Standard infantry weapon was the Martini-Henry single-shot breech-loading rifle with a long-bladed bayonet. The Boers did not use the bayonet, which was a deadly British tool in close quarter combat. They hated its use, as they did lances. Their extensive experience fighting against indigenous African tribes, fostered mobility, camouflage, marksmanship and initiative. The British adhered to traditional military credo of command, discipline, formation, and synchronised firepower. The British soldier was not a marksman. Target practice was rare and accurate individual fire was not a prerequisite. Units firing volleys on command, in full-on frontal formation, at hordes of massed warriors, with no firearms, had defeated every foe for years. However, two humiliating and bloody defeats would be inflicted on the British. The deciding factor was the unexpected number of British deaths and casualties on the "Hill of Doves", or Majuba Hill, resulting in a negotiated peace. The Transvaal achieved the status of a Republic once more

In the early 1880's the discovery of gold at Witwatersrand and the subsequent gold rush caused many settlers in Natal to stream to the goldfields and brought many from other countries into Africa through the port of Durban. The thousands of gold seekers, mostly British, became known as Uitlanders or foreigners by the

Boers, and their demands for equality and the vote, created suspicion.

Egos and duplicity of two Britons played a role in bringing in bringing conflict closer. Both were Imperialists, working in tandem, to poison the climate. James Milner, Governor of Cape Colony, muddied the political waters trying to achieve his aim of a unified South Africa under the Union Jack. Cecil Rhodes, ambitious, ruthless and rich had sponsored an abortive attempt at resurrection several years earlier with The Jameson Raid. The incursion into the Transvaal was to be the trigger that ignited armed revolt against Boer rule by the foreigners, Uitlanders, who worked in the mines. It failed miserably and instead wrecked any possibility of trust between Great Britain and the Transvaal. The Boers were not without guile and deception. President Paul Kruger was a wily and obdurate old politician who in the past had fought against the British and Zulus for autonomy and sovereignty for a nation of Boers. Kruger was also an expansionist but forward thinking and used wealth, created by the gold discovered in the Transvaal, to purchase artillery, from Creusot and Krupps, and magazine loading rifles from Mauser A.G. Tons of ammunition for both were bought, while negotiations for peace were taking place. After diplomatic bargaining ended in disarray and British troops remained on the Transvaal border President Kruger issued an ultimatum. The British ignored the demand. The Boers then declared war and invading forces rode into the Natal. They laid siege to the towns of Ladysmith, Kimberley, and Mafeking in the Cape Colony.

The stage is set, the tragedy that is the second Anglo-Boer War is about to begin and the curtain rises.

CHAPTER TWELVE
Departure

Craven opened the door of his room to one of the club's servants who handed him a calling card.

"The gentleman is downstairs in the coffee room, sir."

"Thank you."

He read the card from General Buller's young ADC. Craven had expected him and putting on a jacket went downstairs. The young officer stood as Craven walked over.

"Morning, sir. The General's compliments. He tasked me to deliver the details of the departure."

"Thank you, Algy," said Craven taking the envelope from the equerry, "Were there any specifics apart from the information in here?"

"I don't believe so, sir, I believe it's all in there. Good morning Major."

"G'bye, Lieutenant Trotter," smiled the older man.

Craven sank into an armchair and opened the envelope. The instructions were brief and to the point. He was to depart from Waterloo Station on the twelve minutes past two train. There would be several dignitaries present and the General would introduce him to General Wolseley. It reminded him to ensure his baggage was available in Southampton for loading on the RMS Dunottar at Quay XX.

On the afternoon of his departure the Commander-in-Chief of the British armies in the field against the Boers, Sir Redvers Buller, arrived at Waterloo Station. The Duke of Cambridge and Lord Wolseley, the past and present Commanders-in-Chief of the Army, were there, with the Prince of Wales, and Lord Lansdowne to bid him goodbye. The farewells were brief. No one had to disguise the nature of their feelings toward one another with no reporters in close attendance.

At the docks in Southampton many of the hundreds there to see him off failed to recognise the burly figure in mufti as he made his way through the crowd to mount the gangway of the RMS Dunottar Castle. When the multitude did recognise him the air resounded with robust choruses of 'Rule Britannia' and 'God Save the Queen'.

The ship's captain greeted the General's party and escorted them to the stateroom on the upper deck. Buller's luggage was already onboard and had been unpacked by his batman. A table, prepared with a glistening white table cloth, ice buckets, magnums of champagne and a myriad of flutes stood in the centre of the room attended to by Beacon. The number of visitors added to those travelling meant the group spilled over into the passageway. At a nod from the

General, Craven left the cabin and moved out into the passageway to host the echelons of the lesser visitors, while Buller concerned himself with his VIPs. Craven was chatting to one of Buller's cousins when he heard feminine chatter and saw a group of nurses being assigned their cabins by the supervising sister at the far end of the gangway. He returned his attention to the conversation and thought no more about it.

Aileen laid her case on a bed bolted in place then laughed aloud at the recollection of their accommodation on the journey to Canada. Greta looked at her in askance then laughed with her friend when she explained.

"So, beds not bunks this time and no question of the top occupant being seasick over the lower occupant." They both continued to laugh remembering Greta's first ever words to Aileen. They unpacked their suitcases and hung their next-day uniforms against the bulwark. They brushed and redid their hair in preparation for yet another lecture, 'Behaviour of Single Ladies at Sea' from the supervising sister, and then made their way back on deck.

Fifteen hundred soldiers were still embarking and trudging up the two gangways with their shouldered equipment. There were some good-natured catcalls and banter as they spotted the nurses leaning on the rails above their heads.

The nurses watched with interest as the horses were swung aboard on the under-belly-sling. It was easy to see from the extended whites of the horses' eyes they were not enamoured of the process. Finally, embarkation of personnel and loading of stores, equipment and animals was complete. The quay had emptied except for small disparate groups of single-minded farewell wishers. Orders were given to cast-off and quay staff freed the ropes from the stanchions and the Royal Mail ship Dunottar Castle left port.

As the ship made its way into the open sea the wind velocity increased driving thick black storm clouds across the sky which added to the lowering darkness of the coming night. The first blaze of lightning illuminating the shrinking coastline followed by the deafening crack of thunder was not an auspicious sign. Craven lit his cigar in the sheltered hatchway and decided to stay there protected from the buffeting wind. He knew, when he read between the lines of Buller's brief speech in farewell to his admirers, there would be little time on the voyage to enjoy leisure hours. They would be scarce and far between.

News the war had broken out in earnest came while in harbour at Madeira reloading with coal. Craven had accompanied the General ashore and collected a sheaf of telegrams waiting for the new Commander-in-Chief. Buller leafed through them and selected one from General White in Ladysmith.

"Why in God's name is he in Ladysmith? That's about as far north in the Natal as he could go! The Orange Free State and the Transvaal border three sides of the province there! A trap waiting to be sprung." He read on. "It's in earnest now, the Boers have arrived in strength and are converging on Dundee and Ladysmith. Oh, the Devil take him. He's got my chief-in-staff designate, Hunter, and says he needs him to stay. Bugger!"

More followed when, on a day out at sea after refuelling, a small cargo ship came in sight. The group working for Buller, in devising and reviewing plans for every eventuality, had been permitted a thirty-minute breather on deck. Craven was with the group when Buller called him over. Buller passed his binoculars to Craven and said,

"Look at her. There appears to be a communication of some sort on her side." Craven read out the message,

"Boers defeated. Three battles. Penn Symons killed."

"Not an encouraging start." The news though not wholly disquieting did not help to dispel Buller's sense of gloom. His unusual pessimism was triggered by his evaluation of the enemy in the face of all the optimism in other quarters. Despite his advice to the contrary, White's forces were now dangerously too far advanced into the northern apex of Natal and would be in difficulty in the event of a large-scale invasion by the Boers. If the invaders swept round the British forces Durban would be theirs for the taking.

Worries such as these led to behaviour many of his fellow travellers felt unsociable. His reserve and aversion to conversation caused embarrassment. Craven, as a member of Buller's inner circle, knew what prompted this reluctance to fraternise. Abruptness often masked Buller's inherent shyness and the more obvious justification of not disclosing any of his intentions. Purely to get a reaction from his chief, Craven semi-jocularly suggested it looked as though it might be all over before they arrived in Cape Town. The General did not smile but responded,

" I dare say there will be enough left to give us a fight outside Pretoria."

CHAPTER THIRTEEN
Cape Town

On two occasions in the ensuing days, Major Craven caught sight of the nurses' group as they were leaving the open deck and returning to their quarters. On the second occasion, a nurse, who turned and briefly held his gaze, looked remarkably familiar but from the fleeting glance he couldn't recall where they might have met. Then one morning while stripping and cleaning the Winchester he had used to deadly effect in Canada, the answer came to him. *Looks amazingly like the German girl Greta from 'The Valkyrie' but what's the chances of meeting her here?*

Greta sat on her bed staring at the opposite bulkhead. *It's not possible. Is it?*

"Penny for them Greta?"

Greta, disturbed from her daydream, looked at Aileen blankly before replying ,"You'll think I'm silly, but I have just seen someone from Dawson."

"A Canadian on the ship?"

"No, do you remember the Englishman your friend sent to help when Conway threatened us?"

"Belinda Mulroney's friend?"

"Ja, him."

"It's a bit unlikely , isn't it?"

"I guess. And this one has an eye patch the other didn't. He's an officer."

"Hm. Let's get ready for the bandaging and applying dressings refresher." She checked her brooch time piece pinned to her uniform. "We've got eight minutes."

The night before they docked in Cape Town Aileen found she couldn't sleep. Greta was snoring gently and lay motionless under her blankets which still kept the hospital box shape. She was a light sleeper and Aileen tried not to waken her as she rose and dressed. The interior of the cabin, though cooler than its daytime temperature, was still uncomfortably warm. There was a specific reason Aileen could not sleep and it was not the humidity. The thought of the days ahead when they would treat human bodies ravaged by war was intimidating, especially during a wakeful night. It was several minutes after midnight when she slipped out of the cabin and felt the cooler but bearable sea breeze on her face.

She thought she must have been looking toward Africa's coast for at least ten minutes before she caught the whiff of cigar smoke. To her right, roughly fifty yards away, was the silhouette of a soldier also leaning on the rail. The cigar glowed like a fire fly as he drew on it. He appeared to see her presence for the first time and made his way toward her.

This is Greta's hero. Or at least who she thinks it is...

"Do you mind if I share your rail?" He smiled widely revealing even white teeth. At her nod he asked,

"Does this bother you?" showing his cigar. Again, she was silent but shook her head.

He offered a hand, "Craven. Nicholas. Major. Currently of General Buller's staff"

"MacLean. Aileen. Sister. Currently of Princess Christian's Nursing Corps." She mimicked his delivery deadpan before they both broke into laughter.

"Has it been decided where you will serve, Sister?"

"No, too early for individual assignment. My friend and I will probably go to a base hospital temporarily and won't be assigned until the actual battle plan goes into effect."

Craven nodded. He smoked as they watched the coastline, both silent. Aileen broke the stillness as she said,

"Greta, my friend, thought you might be someone we knew in Canada."

Craven halted the movement of his cigar to his mouth. "Dawson?"

Both smiled at each other like old friends when she nodded.

Next day in the late evening, after a day of further lectures on propriety for single ladies for

Aileen, and the study of the General plans for the major, they again stood together at the rail. The dark shape of Robben Island, which was once a whaling station but named after the grey seal whose colonies inhabited its shores, floated past. He told her it became a destination for convicts, but was now home, albeit a barren one, for lepers. It was Aileen's first sight of the continent providing the unforgettable backdrop to influence the rest of her life. Together they followed the faint contours of South Africa as they took on shape and became a huge silhouette in the moonlight.

The rock face of Table Mountain was crowned with a wisp of garlanded cloud emphasizing the height of the dark cliffs still shrouded in shadow. To Aileen, in all its dark majesty it was an awesome sight but to Craven it was a grim harbinger, with its severely harsh outline of bare sandstone. It was coffin-like with its two pallbearer buttresses: Devil's Mountain on the left and the scarred visage of the Lion's Head drawing forth hideous memories of another mountain in Africa.

The Dunottar Castle negotiated its way smoothly into harbour. A multitude of vessels, converted liners and transports, lay at anchor waiting to be called forward to dock or to have their cargoes unloaded onto flat bottomed lighters. The tiny windows of the houses, low and flat, in the belt of land between the shore and the lower slopes and miniaturised against the hulk of the mountain, became alive as here and there lights twinkled.

"Do you know where you will serve? Which hospital?" he broke the silence.

"I don't know where we will eventually work but we are to go to Wjnberg first. I'm told it is vast."

He looked serious.

"It's huge. Most of it tents. You can't see it from here, but it is beyond those suburbs and on the other side of the mountain." He pointed out into darkness.

She smiled then checked her brooch watch.

"I have to go now, Major. I have to wake my friend then get ready to disembark."

"Please call me Nicholas or remember me as Nicholas," he said in a serious tone.

"Thank you, Nicholas, I will." she said turning to look up at him. The sight of her face and her clear gaze framed by her glorious auburn hair would form a vision recurring many times in the coming weeks. He bent to kiss her cheek but, with a slight motion of her head, her lips met his. Neither pulled away and she was compliant in his hold. The sudden sound of a nearby hatch harshly clanging against the bulwark and locking into place broke them apart. The emerging crew member touched his forehead, quickly looked away and hurried along the ship's side

She touched his cheek, held his gaze for a moment then walked toward the open passageway. In the hatchway she stopped, faced him and they shared one last long look before she stepped into the ship's gloomy interior. He turned to lean on the rail and again looked toward the city, as the first heavy drops of rain fell.

Later the staff were assembled on deck where they learned of the disaster of Nicholson's Nek when General White's report was read by an A.D.C. A sombre mood pervaded the group, and no one found the words to speak.

CHAPTER FOURTEEN
Sir Arthur Milner

Craven knocked then waited. Buller's "Come in" muffled by the cabin door, did not reveal his mood. The major entered to find the General in a stiff fronted shirt, black tie nestled under his ample chin, fastening his cufflinks. Nodding to a side table as he faced the mirror to adjust the set of his tie, Buller said,

"Coffee? In fact stay for breakfast. They've brought far more than I can eat."

Craven voiced his thanks and helped himself to a plate.

"Not looking forward to this meeting. Not my kind of animal. The High Commissioner I mean. Cold fish. Without doubt suited to be a politician or a diplomat or whatever."

He expected no answer and they finished breakfast in silence. Craven helped the General with his jacket and passed him his cane.

A crowd of spectators waited to cheer as the General descended the gangplank. Minutes later he climbed into an open top landau for the ceremonial drive waved on by a rapturous throng. The coach passed along the lined streets of Cape Town to Government House where he was to meet with the individual who was both Governor and High Commissioner. This was the man who, in his duplicitous stoking of crisis in South Africa, would bear a large share of blame for the coming conflagration.

Buller stepped down onto to the gravelled driveway, studying Sir Arthur Milner as he walked toward the diplomat waiting on the steps of Government House. They shook hands cordially which to the waiting reporters reflected a warmth which did not exist between the two men. In his small spartan book-lined study Milner invited Buller to sit and took one the stuffed chairs opposite. He asked "Brandy?" as he raised the solitary decanter. Buller murmured his thanks as he took the snifter from Sir Arthur.

"Voyage satisfactory, Sir Redvers?" Milner asked pronouncing it as "Reevers," having read the research notes from his secretary.

"Yes. Very pleasant, but I believe I have a mare's nest waiting for me here?"

"Hmm. I'd like to say no… tell me, what have you heard?"

"Nothing heartening." Buller growled and the anger he felt but had held in check surfaced. He took a breath and said with stony calm,

"The God-awful delay in the movement of the reinforcements I requested, the…"

"They are at sea Sir Redvers."

"Where they are no use to anyone," Buller ploughed over the High Commissioner's response.

"I tasked Penn-Symons and White with two objectives, one to defend Natal and two to hold the way open for my forces. Despite all my warnings and orders to the contrary, Penn-Symons, well outside the boundaries I set for him gets his hair well and truly mussed at Talana. Blow me if White doesn't obey either, chances his arm and takes a hiding at Nicholson's Nek and Lombard's Kop, then holes up in Ladysmith."

"If I may, Sir Redvers I am concerned about your present plans and not those errors made in the past. My primary concern is the safety of the Cape. Natal is not a major concern for me as most of its settlers are British, and whether or not the Boers occupy they can't hold it. Unlike the Cape Colony which is virtually all Dutch. Ripe for resurrection. Any successes by the Boers, and they have nothing but so far, could very well precipitate an unmanageable crisis here."

"Point. I will assign sufficient forces to provide security against such an eventuality despite having to split my remaining forces to lift the sieges on all three towns." Buller was referring to Kimberley in the Northern Cape Colony, Mafeking, also in the Cape Colony but even further north near the border with the Transvaal and, beyond the Tugela in Natal, Ladysmith. All caused drastic alteration to Buller's original plans.

"One advantage is divided the Boer forces are weakened, and better still, their mobility, their strongest strategical and tactical strength, curtailed. They still remain a formidable foe, however."

He paused but Milner, looking at him in pointed appraisal, interjected, "What you say there, General, is akin to what the previous commander British Forces felt about the Boers and hastened his resignation."

"His forced resignation. Commissioner, my sympathies are with General Butler. I make no apology. Any right-thinking man would want to pursue a peaceful solution. But make no mistake my opinions of the enemy's strengths do not stem from weakness but result from clinical analysis and experience, with and against, our former citizens." The last point was to emphasize Buller was no stranger to combat in South Africa.

Two hours later the visit ended. Buller was not persuaded his impression of Milner as puppet master manipulating situations and individuals had changed. Milner felt no doubt that Buller had sympathies no general engaged in war should hold for his enemy. Both were convinced the future lay in their hands.

"I can tell you Nicholas, I'm in the tightest corner I have ever been. They denied my selections of officers. My advice goes unheeded. Orders I give are ignored. I am starved of troops to do the job, and every plan I make is subject to political interference here or at the War Office. I feel like a man who has slept-in then has to do everything on the run to catch up."

Craven knew Buller was venting to diffuse his frustration and nodded.

"With what I've got I must raise all the sieges simultaneously as opposed to meeting and trouncing the enemy in the field. This will prove a marvel of improvisation. I will command the relief force for Ladysmith myself and . . ." He became more animated as he devised and planned the alternative strategy. He was also more optimistic.

Buller did not announce his departure to Pietermaritzburg and left Cape Town without informing Milner. He would spend ten days in the town concentrating on the logistical aspect of his advance to Ladysmith. He paid particular attention to medical supplies and equipment for his field hospitals. Some sixth sense told him that there would be great need for medical support.

CHAPTER FIFTEEN
Secondment

Craven did not slow Remus as they trotted through the picket but nodded as the two sentries stepped back from the path of his horse. General orders prohibited saluting officers to protect them from Boer snipers. The younger of the two sentries, still to assimilate the new practice, stopped his slope arms in mid motion as the Major passed. He reined Remus in at the Headquarters tent in the middle of the encampment. The tent sides were rolled up and fastened. The duty sergeant and a runner were seated at the trestle table. He leaned down from the saddle and called in to the NCO.

"The General rode out about forty minutes ago, sir." The NCO stood at the Major's stirrup and pointed to the crest of the largest of the two kopjes. "He requested you join him, on your return."

"Thank you, Sergeant." As the NCO stepped away Craven nudged his mount and pulled the reins, turning around and heading towards the hill. He dismounted as he reached the base of the hill and walked alongside his steed up the incline avoiding the rocky outcrops. On reaching the level ground at the top he mounted and rode towards the other crest.

The mounted figure of General Buller did not turn or acknowledge his approach. His aide, a young fresh-faced subaltern, who stood yards away, also remained silent. Craven edged forward but a little to the rear of the General. The senior officer continued to stare out at the veld. The quiet clink of Remus's bridle and bit as he pulled on then chomped mouthfuls of coolatai and the creak of leather passed unnoticed. Still motionless, Buller said,

"This land has tarnished our hard-earned reputation for invincibility and damaged our leaders' esteem in which we have held them over the years. It will continue to do so," the older man said sotto voce before addressing him,

"How far are we with our preparations?"

"Completed, sir."

"Including the medical support? Supplies?"

"There are some requirements still to be filled but they have been expedited. Transport is up to the mark. The previous issues with the food supplies have been corrected. Your emphasis on the availability of medical material has been effective, sir."

"Fine work, Nicholas. Do you think your deputy can manage without you? Good. I have another task for you which will require some expertise. I want you to go see Lord Methuen in the Cape. What I've seen here has convinced me that on the ground intelligence is scant. There's no doubt that trying to catch up is going to be hell. The Boers will concentrate of killing the scouts. I want to emphasise the importance I attach to this but be tactful. He can be prickly. I will be sending him an observation balloon up the line but, more importantly, I need you there. Eyes and ears, you know. When can you handover the quartermaster department?

"Day after tomorrow?"

"Fine. I've already signed your orders and a letter of introduction to his Lordship. And Nicholas you are improperly dressed. As of this moment you have the rank of full colonel. Congratulations, my boy.

"Thank you, sir." He turned and giving a slight pull on the reins, headed Remus down the rocky slope.

CHAPTER SIXTEEN
1879

Neither Craven nor Remus were happy during the voyage from Durban to Cape Town. While still in harbour the sky lowered as it filled with dense black mounds heavy with rain. The storm erupted ninety minutes after putting to sea and was so extreme the Captain warned his passengers a return to port was not out of the question. However, the course remained in a southerly direction.

He bought a half bottle of Irish from the purser and retired for the night. Despite two large measures and his head on the pillow sleep would not come. His thoughts drifted back in time to his first stay in Africa when he was little more than a youth with downy cheeks. Maturity would come quickly during that short but bitter Anglo Zulu war. He stared, into the dark at the deck above his head, and the visions, hazy at first then more definitively, filled the space. His eyes felt heavy and his breathing deepened. In sleep the throng of apparitions from the past grew and in the form of his younger self he joined them to relive that part of his youth.

As an immature freshly minted subaltern, with less than three month's service, he was euphoric when his posting order materialised. Nominated, as were men of his class, because of family connections rather than meritorious selection, he was to proceed by sea to South Africa to replace an aide of Lord Chelmsford's who had died of pneumonia. There followed a hectic fourteen days of checking the requirements for uniform, equipment and the "good-to-have items" that made life in the field bearable. Three visits to Herbert Johnson provided all the required uniforms. The military outfitter met the orders for his personal accoutrements within a week. He hurriedly wrote the standard letters to his bank and parents but did not take his leave entitlement to say farewell in person.

He embarked from Southampton with two recently recruited and trained groups of reserves for the 24th of Foot. He had little doubt he would see action. The rumour mill's main theme forecast an invasion of the Zulu kingdom of Cetshwayo.

He arrived in Durban to the news he was no longer required to join Lord Chelmsford's immediate staff but was to join Colonel Wood's 4th column of the British invasion force.

On his first day as a member of No 4 Column, while eating the midday meal with the other junior officers, he first learned of Buller. He had been a major at the beginning of the Anglo-Zulu War. Now, a lieutenant-colonel, he was in command of the Frontier Light Horse. From the conversation Craven learned the colonel had prior service with Chelmsford in the 9th Cape Frontier War. He frequently proved he was ideal to command the independently minded colonials. Well- respected for his personal courage, strength and powers of leadership, together with his skills on recce patrols Buller was successful in bringing Uhumu, half-brother of Cetshwayo, and his tribe of seven hundred defecting Zulus, to Kambula.

Craven often saw the colonel in the company of an old Boer with whom he appeared at ease. The civilian was the leader of the forty strong contingent of Boers serving in Wood's column. With his four sons he motivated the burghers, the only Boers who agreed to fight alongside the British against the Zulus. Each generation of the Uys family had battled the Zulus in ferocious clashes suffering significant loss. Their hatred of the "kaffir" was implacable.

Though not sanctioned by London the General Officer Commanding Lord Chelmsford in South Africa crossed into Zululand with a force consisting of five columns with differing routes of march. Each one, however, with the object of converging on Cetshwayo, in his capital of Ulundi and 'bringing him to heel'. Cetshwayo, however, pre-empted the planned attack by sending his impis to greet the invaders and delivered the crushing defeat of Isandlwana by using their renowned, and effective, "zimpondo zankomo" ('horns of the buffalo') battle formation.

A range of factors contributed to this defeat not least Chelmsford leaving a third of his force at Isandlwana in a poorly selected and weak defensive position. He rode off with the remaining two thirds of the column to 'find the Zulu.' He ignored two messages brought to him which warned of the imminent threat to his men in base. He held the arrogant belief the British soldier could defeat any unclothed spear-carrying native. He pressed on with his search for the Zulu horde. The news of the destruction of more than half of No 3 column and the annihilation of Colonel Durnford's Natal Native Horse astounded the world, soldier and civilian alike. Eight hundred and fifty-eight British and four hundred and seventy-one native troops, massacred and gutted, covered the hillside. Cetawayo's impis had blunted the major thrust of the invasion.

On the coast but heading inland en route to join the main column against Cetshwayo Colonel Pearson's column barely repulsed an attack by a regiment of four thousand Zulus. He halted his march to Ulundi and prepared defensive positions at Eshowe to hold out against a protracted siege.

The original purpose of Wood's column was to counter any surprise attacks on Natal by the Zulus and to harry their allies to prevent their joining the main Zulu impis. The most important of these supporters lived on the plateaus of a mountainous area to the north-west of Ulundi and to the east of Kambula. Rising from the plains, these mountains were some distance from the capital Ulundi. The chief of AbaQualusi had qualified autonomy from Cetawayo, allowing him to use his fighting men to defend their homes, rather than operating as an element of the main Zulu Army. Chelmsford wanted to prevent these outlying Zulu forces from interfering with the thrust of his No. 3 Column and hindering its progress toward Isandlwana and onwards to Cetshwayo's capital Ulundi.

Wood advanced to the north-east and ordered a defensive wagon circle to be formed at Tinta's Kraal, nineteen miles south east of a series of the flat-topped mountains, home to the AbaQualusi. A nek, or ridge, linked each of the three heights and formed a massif stretching for fifteen miles in a north-easterly direction. During fortification at Tinta's Kraal a roving patrol was engaged by an AbaQualusi group of a thousand from Zunguin. The British broke off the action and returned to the main force.

At dawn, the next day the British attacked the AbaQualusi on Zunguin, but the natives withdrew to Hlobane, where later four thousand drilled in formations and performed military exercises. A further attack on the tribe was called off when the shocking news of Isandlwana reached Wood's No 4 column.

Comprised of eight companies of light infantry, artillery and cavalry, civilian irregulars and supply wagons, two thousand infantry and two hundred mounted troops, the column would be the sole viable British force. Wood and his men had the daunting prospect of facing the not inconsiderable horde of exultant Zula warriors. It seemed at first unlikely there would be any reinforcements soon, but unexpectedly Lord Chelmsford transferred three mounted units comprising of the Edendale Troop, the Natal Native Horse and the 1st Squadron of Mounted Infantry to his command. Wood with alacrity moved his column from Tinta's Kraal north-westwards to Kambula, due west of Zunguin, a more suitable position for fortification.

Throughout February 1879 he prepared a strong fortification at Kambula. He received further unexpected reinforcements in the shape of a contingent of mounted Transvaal Rangers, a group of German settlers and five companies from the 80th Regiment of Foot, the South Staffordshire Regiment. Further orders from Lord Chelmsford required him to draw off part of the Zulu strength threatening the British relief attempt of Pearson's beleaguered column in Eshowe. Based on other intelligence, Wood knew an impi or regiment of Zulu was preparing to depart Ulundi to attack Kambula. He decided to pre-empt such an assault by harassing the AbaQualusi, and driving off their livestock, on Hlobane mountain. His prime objection was to lure approaching impi into a premature attack on his reinforced base. He knew the attackers would have to pass along the southern flank of Hlobane to reach the fortified Kambula. Wood knew the AbaQualusi were not his only opponents in the area. They were joined by a band of renegade amaSwazi, led by Mbelini kaMswati. Most amaSwazi were loyal to the British, but Mbelini, with a disputed claim to the Swazi chiefdom, broke with them and allied himself with Cetshwayo. Mbelini and about eight hundred of his followers surprised a company-sized detachment from the 80th (Staffordshire Volunteer) Regiment encamped along the Ntombi River and killed seventy-nine men. Afterward, Mbelini withdrew, taking with him the weapons, ammunition and supplies he found in the British supply wagons, to join the abaQualusi on Hlobane.

THE BATTLE OF HLOBANE

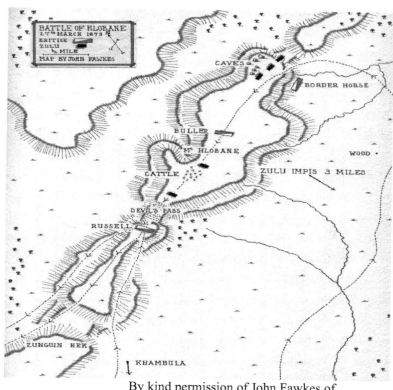

By kind permission of John Fawkes of
https://www.britishbattles.com/

CHAPTER SEVENTEEN
Hlobane 1879

Colonel Wood, accompanied by his escort, made a reconnaissance, with a long spy glass and from a safe distance, of the AbaQualusi mountain home and its environs. The Painted Mountain formed by two plateaux, the smaller, at the eastern end rose to the higher and larger one which connected to a ridge which ran south-westwards toward Zunguin. At this end of the plateau the ground fell away steeply, bisected by a narrow, boulder-strewn defile of giant steps, each four feet or more in height. This egress from the western plateau of Hlobane to reach the nek below was known as the Devil's Pass. The AbaQualusi had corralled their herd at the western end above the Pass. Nearby were fourteen hundred abaQualusi and Mbelini's amaSwazi.

An attack would not be straightforward as the Colonel's reconnaissance showed. Steep cliffs or krantzes formed natural barriers around the mountain and were predominant on the south-facing side. It would be possible, however, for a dismounted force, leading their mounts, to ascend to the higher slopes, and onto the plateau from the north-eastern end.

At that part of Hlobane a ridge, Ityenka Nek, linked the two mountains. The western end of the link ended at the base of the cliff wall of the

Painted Mountain. A workable way up the rock face existed in the shape of a narrow path twisting its way to the plateau. At the higher levels was a warren of caves overlooking the path. This track could also be a way off the mountain after the action.

Minutes after midnight Buller described the plan of the forthcoming action to his officers and senior NCO's gathered in the HQ tent. Next to him stood Piet Uys with two of his sons. Redvers towered above those present with exception of the fresh-faced subaltern who stood at the back of the group. Colonel Wood agreed to Craven's request to be included with Buller's attack group. Both thought it would be invaluable as an induction to active service.

Buller's voice was louder than normal to combat the rattle of the rain kettle-drumming on the canvas above their heads. He described the ascent of the incline at the eastern end of the lower plateau emphasising the difficulty to be expected for their mounts from the rocky nature of the terrain. All the foot soldiers were African because implied was the fact no white soldier, with equipment, could outrun their native opponent.

". . .the force to support our action will be Major Russell and his men at the other end of the plateau. Are there questions? No? So, we are all clear on our aim and how it is to be accomplished? Good. Then, gentlemen disperse and ready your men. You have thirty minutes."

Hours before daylight the mounted column with the Irregulars in the rear wound its way out of Kambula which soon disappeared behind them in the darkness and the teeming summer rain.

Craven wiped the rain from his face with a soaked bandana. The darkness was punctuated by the periodic flashes, followed by the booming thunder, that illuminated their line of march. His mood lifted as the day lightened, the clouds breaking and dispersing toward the east and the summer rain gave way to early sunshine. The horsemen reached the eastern base of the lower of the two plateaus at four a.m. The storm unleashed rain on the horsemen and auxiliaries. Buller ordered the advance to the higher level. Led by their African guide, the way forward, over traitorous rocks, slick with the nocturnal rainfall, dictated they should all dismount. They led their horses. Many fell, including Buller and Craven, some more than once. The horses struggled to maintain their footing.

The mist was lifting as they climbed the final slope before the plateau. The emptiness surprised them as they expected a response to their presence. Then the first shot came from defensive positions among the rocks and caves. Mbelini's amaSwazi were armed with British Martini-Henry rifles. Two officers and two troopers of the Frontier Light Horse (FLH) were killed in the first volley. The party pushed forward through the defences and reached the top. The Zulu Irregulars were soon rounding up the cattle and shepherding them across the plateau. Clusters of abaQualusi declined to engage and stayed out of range. The probability of the column descending from the plateau at the western end without great loss was high.

"At this rate," thought the young Craven, "we'll be back in Kambula and I'll have seen nothing."

They reached the western lip of the upper plateau. Buller looked down the mountain as Craven halted his mount alongside.

"Men on foot might get down. The horses might, with difficulty, but I'll wager the cattle won't."

"Sir," Craven said in agreement.

"We'll gather up the herd and go back to where we came up." Others of the group joined them including the Frontier Light Horse's commanding officer Captain Barton. Buller remained silent for a moment longer, taking another look down at the rocky descent, then turned back to address the captain.

"Take as many of your men as you see fit, Captain Barton and get back to the other end where we lost Otto, George Williams and your two troopers. See they are buried. When you've completed the burial detail locate Colonel Weatherley, tell him to return to Kambula then go with him."

Captain Barton touched the brim of his hat and beckoning to the men of his group wheeled his horse and galloped off toward the eastern end. The main party waited as the Irregulars pulled in the strays. Buller was facing Craven when he started and pointed over the other's shoulder,

"Good God," he said pointing to the south-east. Craven turned and for the first time in his life saw an army en masse. Five or less miles away on the plain a black multitude of tightly packed ant-like figures was oozing its way toward them. Even on foot, at the speed they were travelling, the Zulus would reach the Itenyeki before they could.

"Tell the Irregulars to abandon the cattle," he ordered Craven. "Trooper, ride as fast as you can and tell Captain Barton to ignore my previous instructions and ride north immediately. Go!" he shouted.

Unfortunately for Buller and his men the advancing horde were also seen by the abaQualusi who, enervated by the sight, were now eager to engage. They attacked as their numbers increased with reinforcements of their own from the north.

As the natives on the plateau moved to attack, and the impi reached the slope behind his group, there was no choice for Buller but to order the descent onto the plain to avoid slaughter by the baying swarm of abaQualusi. The rocky, uneven draw called the Devil's Pass was his only option.

"Get the Irregulars down and off this bloody mountain," he roared at Craven. The African foot soldiers scrambled down but many were stabbed and clubbed to death by the warriors swarming up the gully and its sides to meet them. Buller with a small group brought up the rear and attempted to hold off the attackers.

Craven felt the fear coursing through his body, but it was exhilarating. He held his ground on the edge of the plateau as the last man in the rear guard. He was about to descend into the whirling mass of screaming Zulus when a solitary horseman broke through the ranks of approaching warriors and pulled up alongside Craven.

"Come on, we can do this together," Craven waved a hand at the grotesque swarm of heaving bodies in the ravine below and then beckoned to the other man.

"Not today," said the trooper placing his mouth around the muzzle of his carbine and pulling the trigger.

"Damn," shouted Craven then tugged at the reins of his horse to descend. The animal would not budge. Immovable, with its forelegs braced and the whites of its frenzied eyes growing even larger as the terrified and tortured screams of its fellows below filled the air. The unfortunate horses below were blinded, maimed and crippled by the stabbing and chopping of the induna. Craven checked the load in his pistol then shot his mount through the ear. As he turned to flee, he saw four men of the Frontier Light Horse trying to reach the gully. They were rapidly overtaken by a mob of natives, dragged from the saddle, swiftly disembowelled, and hurled from the cliff top to the rocks below. This happened in a flash and the pack surged onwards.

Craven leapt with a roar into the melee below. Slashing and shooting he was a whirlwind of blade and welters of blood as he thrust himself ever downwards toward the plain. At one point he was swerving away from one spear point when another assegai raked across his chest and tore through his tunic. He shot the first spear's owner in the face, then holding on to the entangled shaft as the other native tried to pull it free with both hands, cleft the man's skull with a downward cut.

There was a moment's respite. Through the ever present sweat he saw his commanding officer pushing, pulling troopers down the steep slope, lifting fallen men while all the time shouting encouragement to fight their way through. Inspired, Craven fought his way towards two of his brother officers and formed with them a trio of bodies facing outwards to defend the less fortunate. Eventually, the surviving members reached the plain below where the fighting continued without let-up.

Craven wiped blood and sweat from his eyes. He saw Piet Uys standing close by then the next moment he was running toward a group of abaQualusi who were closing in on a man trying to quieten his horse. Craven realised the man was one of Uys sons. Uys warned his son and they thought they were clear when a Zulu leaped onto to the elder man's back hacking him to death. Craven shot the warrior and after making sure there was no life in the old man escaped with the two Uys boys. He learned later Piet Uys's father was killed in a similar battle against the Zulus and died with Piet's brother whom he had tried to save.

The descent was a rout, vicious and unrelenting, by the savage onslaught of assegais and knobkerries. The survivors were not yet clear. Buller gave the order to his broken and disorganised force to make for Kambula. The men far outnumbered the remaining horses, and the retreat entailed the mounts having to carry two men. They were followed right up to the defensive bulwarks of home by skirmishing parties of the Zulu impi.

Buller also, in the frantic race to get to Kambula, stopped and returned to make three forays to rescue members of his force who lost their mounts and were fleeing on foot. It was difficult because of the ferocious and persistent actions of the enemy. Then with two other officers, after reaching Kambula, he rode back to pick up stragglers.

The other half of the expedition led by Colonel Wood, with his escort, together with his Zulus who were mounted and eight mounted infantrymen, followed in the footsteps of the first party, to the lower reaches of the mountain. There they encountered Colonel Weatherley's Border Horse, who had been the vanguard of Buller's force, but had lost contact on the ascent in the torrential downpour and darkness. Wood ordered them to tackle the enemy lodged in the caves and behind the boulders strewn over the area above them. They were to break through and join Buller whose party was still within sight at the lip of the plateau. The first group's ascent up the mountain was resulting in heavy fire from the abaQualusi defenders and its continuance could still be heard. Colonel Weatherley's reluctant response to the commander's order incensed Wood who made no concession as to any logic embodied in the other's concern.

In what was described later as "a fit of pique" Wood turned to the mountain and led his party forward. Within yards they came under the intensive fire from the riflemen above. Five of Wood's escort broke away and rushed forward to storm the AbaQualusi defences but two were brought down at once in the hail of bullets. Wood's horse was shot from under him. One of the dead had been close to Wood who dismissed all thought of the ongoing skirmish and ordered the immediate burial of the deceased. The bodies were moved further down the hill and the native troops dug out makeshift graves in the rocky ground using their assegais as spades. This was done with great difficulty, but Wood was not satisfied until he could see his friends would not be interred with their legs doubled up. He sent one soldier to retrieve his bible from the saddle bag of his dead horse and then read the service over the graves. When it was finished, Colonel Wood abandoned his intention to join up with Buller and instead led his party back down the foothills and along the southern base of the mountain to join up with Russell at the western end of Hlobane.

Meanwhile, Weatherley and the Border Horse fought their way upwards and reached the plateau. The unit was volunteers and not regular soldiers. The Colonel's son, a fifteen-year-old sub-lieutenant was at his side. The ground under foot was treacherous and far from ideal for mounted men. They made their way along the northern side of Hlobane seeking a way off the mountain but encountered steep krantzes or cliffs. They crossed the plateau and encountered Barton and an element of the FLH accompanying him. They set off together to descend the eastern end of Hlobane only to be met by the leading elements of Cetawayo's Zulus. The slopes were a heaving multitude of frenzied warriors who formed a solid wall without break.

The riders veered away and attempted to reach the saddle of open land forming Ityenka Nek but were forestalled by the abaQualusi who appeared from nowhere and were swarming around them. There was nothing for it but to charge in desperation at the black wall of assegais, shields, and knobkerries. To no avail. The abaQualusi held firm and only twelve horsemen broke through led by Barton and his colonel. Despite having broken through the frenzied cordon the Colonel, realising his son Rupert had not emerged, galloped back. He found his son with grave wounds but free from the mêlée. He reached the boy, dismounted, and heaved him onto his horse as the oncoming abaQualusi spearmen reached them. As they held each other close they were slashed and hacked to death by the plumed warriors.

Captain Barton and his men reached open country, but it was not a blessing. They were confronted by mounted Zulu skirmishers from the umCijo ibutho or regiment who massacred two thirds of Barton's group within minutes. Barton and his horse suffered countless spear wounds but broke free. He tried to head to Kambula. Other survivors lost their mounts to the savagery of the long-bladed spears of the black shielded umCijo warriors and on foot they had no chance of escape. Barton recognised a fellow officer and pulled him up behind him on his horse. The over-burdened beast stumbled onwards for miles before the swift of foot Zulus reached them when the poor beast could do no more. The two men left the horse and tried to escape on foot, but the officer Barton rescued was overtaken and stabbed again and again until he sank to his knees and died.

A Zulu leader reached Barton and told him to surrender. King Cetawayo had given instructions to all his commanders that where possible, officers were to be taken alive. Barton was about to surrender when another Zulu charged up and shot him. Deprived of his prisoner the first Zulu in petulance hacked the gravely wounded Barton to death.

When the weary, beaten remnants of the group reached Kambula, the ensuing roll call revealed the extent of the loss suffered. The revelations by the survivors of the fates of the missing members amplified the tragedy of Hlobane. The toll of dead British, military and militia, Boer, and African levies, was high, and the result was an indisputable victory for the abaQualusi and Cetawayo's indefatigable izinDuna and their warriors. The massif would be named anew by the victors. In Zulu folklore, the mountain was where they "washed" their spears.

The Stabbing Mountain.

CHAPTER EIGHTEEN
Johannesburg

On arrival in the Transvaal Fergal was briefed on the intricacies of the prevailing political climate. By interacting with the large Irish community among the miners in Johannesburg, he could contribute in a meaningful way to the proposed British downfall. With the financial backing of Gillingham's group he established himself as an assayer, while initiating and building an association to promote friendship. Its social aims were a fraud. It was the framework of a force with a more warlike purpose. By dint of arduous work and by visiting many of the mines in the area Fergal soon recruited over two hundred volunteers, not all Irish, but all fervently committed to joining the Boers to fight on the field of battle against their common enemy.

Solomon Gillingham was fundamental to the success of Boyle's enterprise. He arranged for Fergal to meet with government of the Transvaal.

The meeting took place on the veranda of the President's house in Pretoria. Paul Kruger and two members of his Volksraad cabinet were present and sitting on a bench against the house wall. Near to the group Oom Paul's wife, Gezina, or to intimates Sannie, was knitting.

After the introductions and at a nod from Kruger Fergal sat down in a rattan chair. Gillingham took a seat slightly behind him. The President stared at both for a long time. He ordered coffee. When it arrived, the black retainer served the President, who then indicated everyone with a wave of his hand.

One of the men, alongside the President fidgeted and this must have prompted Oom Paul to speak.

"So, gentlemen, you have a proposal for us," he said in accented English.

"I do, sir," replied Fergal. "You know the people of my land also wish to be free of English domination. There are many of us, here in your land, who would welcome the opportunity to join you in your struggle against tyranny, which is the same poisonous abomination plaguing our land."

"You are presupposing a war? We are negotiating to avoid a war, Mr. Boyle." said the President with a frown."

"You are. Yes. But who are you negotiating with? The English? Perfidious Albion?"

Kruger held his gaze.

"If war does come you would fight alongside us?"

"We would. Mr. Gillingham has agreed to provide us with mounts, weapons and horses."

"How many men?"

"Given time I could promise five hundred. I have two hundred at this moment. I am sure I would be able to get more from overseas."

"Unnecessary. No, unnecessary. The English have ten thousand soldiers. They are spread thin. We have enough. And more Uitlanders zijn nicht nodig." He turned to his companions with a questioning shrug for agreement. Both nodded vigorously.

Kruger continued. "We will supply you weapons and ammunition. And your horse. In the field we will provide food." As an afterthought he asked, "And in return for these services?"

"Nothing, Mr. President, only outfitting and keep."

"You shall have citizenship of the Transvaal."

One of the men, who Fergal learnt later was Wolmarans, spoke for the first time,

"It will be time enough after the war."

"No. All volunteers will be burghers on the first day of war. They will make sacrifices. They will be citizens."

Now the President of the Transvaal had accepted the offer Fergal Boyle worked with a new zeal. He circulated a manifesto to his followers; a call to arms to join the Boers in their struggle against the British. He was once again called to the residence of the president where he was made a burgher of the Transvaal and a Justice of the Peace. Gillingham explained after the brief ceremony the magisterial rank had been conferred to enable him to swear in others to the cause. That evening he prepared and sent out flyers to all the mines advertising a meeting to be held in two days' time and calling for support.

Fergal sighted Gillingham at the back of the audience and motioned him to join them on the platform. The crowd was unduly quiet for a gathering of Irishmen, who had been drinking at the make-shift bar prior to the call to the main marquee. The onlookers consisted of expatriates working in Johannesburg, Pretoria, and other mines in the Transvaal. The atmosphere was vibrant with a sense of expectancy.

Gillingham pushed through and after shaking hands took the vacant chair next to Fergal.

"Just come from the Volksraad. The Government have accepted our help. Officially. They have also agreed to provide all equipment and supplies so I can stand down."

Fergal nodded then looked at his watch.

"It's time." He pushed back his chair and stood.

"Welcome my Brothers-in-Arms. Yes, you heard right, my brothers-in-arms. The talking here at this meeting will be short. The time for talking is over. As from this moment our

125

organisation is officially the Irish Transvaal Brigade!" A roar of jubilation erupted from the gathering and many turned to their neighbour and hugged.

On the platform Gillingham and Fergal waited for the hubbub to die down but as it went on both tried to gain the crowd's attention once more by trying to shout above the noise. They failed. It was then Fergal brought forth the flag and signalled Gillingham should take one end and as he did, Fergal pulled out his end. Both held the stretched flag in raised hands. As individuals in the audience saw the standard, they brought the sight to the attention of their neighbours. A section of the Irish American volunteers on seeing it started a measured chant. Within seconds the disorganised tumult of noise from the others grew into a swelling of "Fenians, Fenians." Fergal called one of the nearest men to come forward, indicating he should take his place holding the flag. He then moved to the front of the stage, bible in hand. The noise abated.

"This beautiful banner you see will be the flag of our Irish Brigade. The Irish Transvaal League back home have donated it. Behind this standard we will go into battle." He then held aloft the bible Gillingham had provided when he had suggested earlier the meeting would be the ideal opportunity to swear in volunteers.

"We will go forth together with our hosts and allies the Boer Nations of Transvaal and Free State and do battle against the English. You will

126

Robert Davidson

all become citizens of the Transvaal when you take the oath of allegiance. Come forward one at a time."

The ceremony lasted late into the night.

Fergal Boyle was the first choice to lead the newly formed Brigade, but he declined. His reason was logical. He had had no military training. He willingly accepted the post of second in command, confident of his administrative abilities. The refusal of the role of commander presented no problem because Gillingham knew of an American, an ex-cavalryman who could lead the Brigade.

John Blake had been in South Africa for four years. A competent horseman he had passed through West Point and served for sixteen years in the Fighting Sixth, a cavalry regiment, reaching the rank of 2nd Lieutenant. He accepted the rank of Colonel, commanding The Transvaal Irish with Major Boyle as his second in command. Together, with the other officers selected to staff the Brigade, they were invested with their commissions by President Kruger on the steps of his house.

Three days later the Brigade marched in formation to the railway station. The flag of the gallant but failed Connaught rising of 1867, took pride of place at its head. After a tumultuous send-off by the Boer community, the Brigade entrained, with horses, on their way to join Piet Joubert's command. There was a brief stay at Sandspruit, where they spent two nights under field conditions on the veld, a first for the city dwellers among them, before continuing to Volkrust.

CHAPTER NINETEEN
Frere

On the north bound platform at Durban Railway station they became flotsam on a sea of khaki. They were buffeted and pushed but understood it was not the fault of the individual men. The alacrity with which the soldiers answered to the various calls to assemble, stand down and fall-in again, did not allow for courtesy. Most of the rank and file, who nudged, pushed, and jostled, attempted apologies as they swung their packs, dangerously close, onto their backs. With each hand holding a piece of luggage, and their arms pinioned by the crush, they could not ward off the accidental blows. Aileen winced and cut off a shout of pain as a rifle butt cracked against her shin. A moment later she was helpless to assist when Greta's cape caught up on a cavalry sergeant's sabre scabbard as he tried to hold it aloft for his company to rally round. A sergeant major roared for his men to make their way to the end of the platform for yet another roll call. Despite fifty or sixty khaki clad infantry men leaving, the crowd did not diminish. The space they vacated was rapidly filled by more soldiers.

They were relieved and thankful when a young officer pushed through and taking Greta's arm, guided them both to a waiting room full of officers. He quickly cleared room for them to sit down. Greta noted it was two junior officers who made way and the more senior studiously ignored their presence. After a time both women were regretting their decision as the cigar and cigarette smoke proved almost unbearable. The train's whistle started a flow of movement and they tried to stand but their knight-errant of earlier made it clear they should remained seated.

"Don't worry," he called. "We'll get you seats when you board."

When the waiting room emptied two other subalterns who stayed behind, took their baggage and together they made their way towards the front of the train. True to his word, all three bullied two of their already seated companions to stand and give up their seats. The first young soldier to look out for them remained standing, with his back to the carriage window, and offered his opened cigarette case.

"We don't, thank you," Aileen smiled but Greta did not refuse when one of the others proffered a small metal cup and unscrewed the lid from his pocket flask. While he was pouring introductions were made.

"So, you are nurses, ladies. Bound for the hospital at Frere? The Field Hospital?"

"We are not sure where we will finish, but we were told to get off in Pietermaritzburg. Apparently, there are more people assembling there."

130

"It's likely you'll be going to Frere fairly quickly. The General has his headquarters there now." At the women's blank look, he offered "General Buller?"

The third one, obviously older than his companions, who had not yet spoken, said grimly, "If you're nurses for No 4 Stationary Field Hospital you're going to Frere, as we are." Aileen nodded as he spoke.

"Stay on the train."

Greta looked askance at Aileen who thought for a moment then agreed, "We'll go through to Frere. Will there be a battle soon?"

"You'll be in action very soon." He turned to stare out of the window. "Probably the day after we are."

The train slowed as it pulled into Frere. When it shuddered to a halt one officer threw the door open and helped Greta and Aileen to alight. The other two shouted a hurried farewell and stepped down smartly to join their units while the first stayed and handed down their bags. As he descended, he said goodbye. Then, surprising both the women by the quickness of the action, he impulsively kissed each on the cheek, and with a smile and a wave he ran off after the others.

The platform of packed earth was strewn with crates, boxes, and sacks. There were saddles, kitbags, and ammunition containers in disordered array watched over by soldiers in various stages of working dress. At one end of the platform a company of infantry sat with crossed legs in lines of three. To their front were rifles, stacked, muzzles up, in clusters, like sheaves of wheat. At the other limit cavalry troopers were leading their horses down wooden ramps from the train. The air was still, and the heat had not yet risen to the daily high. Both women felt uncomfortably warm despite wearing lightweight clothes. They made their way to the waiting room looking for a water faucet only to find the floor carpeted wall to wall with sleeping soldiers.

The outside of the station was bespread with boxes of supplies. Ammunition crates, sacks of flour, iron water tanks, kegs and wooden barrels formed bastions ten or fifteen feet in height. The outer limit was defined by a rickety wooden fence. Beyond the fence stood four buildings, three trees and the stationmaster's house. It had been looted and what had once been a garden now lay in trampled ruin.

Further out the surface of the plain had been ripped and torn by the incessant passage of the guncarriages and limbers, transport waggons and troops. Movement caused great clouds of dry powdered dust. The gusting winds swept in high spiral columns of sand, invading clothes, eyes, nose, and mouth.

A voice behind them called out and they turned to see an officer with a millboard.

132

"Are there any more in your party? More nurses? We expected there to be four of you. What? No? Alright then. The transport for the hospital can leave when you are ready." He was marching away when Aileen called to ask,

"The transport for the hospital? Where is it, please?"

Without breaking stride he called over his shoulder, "End of platform. Train's end!"

The sun's heat was stifling as they made their way, with their luggage, through the piles of stores to the end of the train. They sweated profusely. As they weaved between the mounts the warm distinctive odour of manure filled their nostrils. The sight greeting them did not resemble the cab rank of a London station. There was a sorry looking elderly mule between the shafts of a ramshackle scotch cart loaded with sacks of mealies. No driver was in sight. As they looked around, the beast suddenly heehawed loudly. The noise woke a small black man who had been asleep between the sacks. With alacrity he jumped down, snatched at their bags, threw them on top of the load then motioned for them to climb up on the driver's bench. Equally spritely he jumped back up and cracked a long sjambok above the mule's head. The animal looked around with disinterest, turned back then leaned its weight on the traces. With a jerk the wagon rolled forward. The jolting and bumping revealed there were no springs to lessen the shaking. Soon their cart joined the end of a convoy of wagons stretching out of sight before them. Their driver looked sideways and gave them a devilish grin before pulling on the reins to begin the long stretch of overtake. To their left towering above them each of the high wagons, drawn by at least sixteen oxen inspanned by yokes, were reminiscent of antediluvian monsters. Huge clouds of dust rose as thousands of hooves and wheels churned the dry surface of the veld then hung in the air. Aileen and Greta covered their faces with handkerchiefs, but it was scant relief. The clamour was pervasive and inescapable. The rattle and cracks as the steel-rimmed wheels crunched over rocks, the screams and shrieks of the drivers as they cracked their whips, the creak of axles taking the duress of the rough terrain created a wild, strident cacophony. But it hardly mattered. At long last, they were on the finishing lap to their new workplace. They were unable to reach the head of the wagon train before reaching the camp, but a rising breeze cleared away the dust clouds. Their first sight of the encampment in the distance, as they rolled down the slope to the plain, was of a myriad of conical white tents rising from the ground as thousands of hands worked canvas and pegs. Row after endless row of identical bivouacs appeared simultaneously to fill the space stretching to the horizon. As they drew closer, they could make out bustling figures to-and-froing in the avenues between the acres of canvas. At the perimeter to the camp the first of the wagons in the column waited to move into an unloading space. Here there were a hundred or more bearers, swarming over the wagons to unload them. Their cart at last pulled up in front of a marquee. They climbed down and the driver handed down their bags as an NCO approached.

"You'll be for the hospital, right?"

"Yes corporal," answered Aileen knowing the rank, remembering the helpful young Mountie and his chevrons at the Canadian border.

"They've been expecting you. I'll take you to the duty M.O. Hang on a mo, ladies." He shouted to someone in the marquee and two soldiers appeared. At a nod from the corporal they picked up the cases and set off down the lines of tents.

"It's not too far, ladies, the hospital is near the centre."

Moments later they introduced themselves to the duty M.O. who mentioned he was a surgeon before handing them over to an Orderly who showed them to their new home.

In the tent, despite their fatigue, they looked at each other, then simultaneously broke out in gales of laughter. They came together still laughing and hugged each other. The laughter was a mixture of relief; in having accomplished the long journey from faraway England, anticipation of the days ahead and an element of excitement of the unknown.

There were two metal beds with springs erected in their tent which they later learned were from a donation of eight hundred to the Army from a merchant in Durban. After filling their palliasses with straw and making their beds they prepared their working dress for the following day. The next few hours were taken up by collecting bedding from the QM stores, towels, metal plates and other paraphernalia. On the way back to their "quarters" they were surprised at the sound of a train nearby. The railway line from Durban to Ladysmith was only a half mile away from the camp.

They were disconcerted at how quickly night fell bringing a breeze pleasantly cooling at first but as the darkness deepened it brought a penetrating chill. Soon, cheery campfires lit the night, and voices of men singing with an accompanying harmonica or concertina, in one of the outlying lines, made the vastness of the land less intimidating. The huge searchlight on a neighbouring kopje, sending messages to the besieged Ladysmith was awesome at first but the regularity with which it beamed through the night soon made it commonplace. The black of night, however, brought with it relief. It blotted out the dusty lanes between the tents, the ugly haphazard heaps of stores, and to a degree, the dread of the coming battle.

As they lay in bed for their first night under canvas, they were unable to get to sleep right away though physically tired.

"Isn't it an enormous difference from what you would expect, Aileen? Everything is not what it was in England and yet everyone appears

136

capable and yes, warrior-like. Have you noticed the soldiers, even the officers, do not look like they did in Southampton when they wore pressed khaki uniforms, shiny buttons and boots? Here all the clothes look as though they have been slept in, soaked, dried on the wearer more than once, bleached by sun and all the colour of earth, brown and dull. No one shaves and they do look so unkempt. What do you think Aileen?"

An even steady breathing was her only reply as her friend had slid into sleep.

It was still dark when they woke to the sound of a camp of thirty thousand soldiers coming back to life for a new day. The rousing of the sleeping soldiery by the shouts of the orderlies, interspersed by a raucous curse as a soldier tripped over an unseen guy rope, added to the noise. Hoarse calls, the clatter of tin basins as the multitude fetched water from the barrels to conduct its morning ablution rounded off the morning symphony.

"Do you remember how we get to the M.R.S?" Aileen asked.

"Yes, I remember what the Doctor said," Greta replied, "to get to the Medical Reception Station. Just follow me. If we keep the mountains on our left it will be no problem."

Like a theatrical backdrop the ridge of the Drakensberg peaks formed a wolf's teeth horizon against the sky. The range, barren and stark, became less forbidding as the morning rays created a slow change of colour from forbidding battleship grey to pale misty ocean blue. They hurried and soon saw the flag with the red cross hanging limply in the still air. Near the base of the flagpole there were two nurses talking to a tall grey-haired man in a white coat. As the two approached the group's conversation stopped and all three turned and smiled. Both new arrivals were surprised to see the shorter of the nurses was their nemesis from Netley who chastised them on their first day. However, her open smile and outstretched hand of welcome reassured them.

The officer, the hospital's commanding officer, was courteous and not overbearing in his remarks to them. He gave them a brief description of what would be expected and handed them over to Senior Nurse McCaul. This time she was open and friendly and treated them as colleagues. The two established sisters suggested they go to the medical tent where they would brief them on the schedules and practices to be followed. They watched their more experienced fellow nurses deal with the morning sick parade, parrying the banter and jocular remarks of the soldiers, while they changed dressings and administered medicine. Evidently there was a more human side to Sister McCaul. When the bulk of the sick had been treated and while the tent emptied, the other nurse, Helen Metford, told them what to expect and what would be expected of them when the next action took place. There was still no sign of when a major engagement would occur, but theory and rumour were rife. Helen was well versed in military tactics as she had a brother serving in the Gordons and described the probable form of General Buller's plan of battle. The days following were nigh idyllic. After a morning's work dealing with the daily roster of sick and its element of malingers, the afternoons were mostly free of tasks. The nurses wrote letters home to friends. They did their own laundry before they found out that service staff would wash, starch, and press their aprons for a small remuneration. They went for walks on the nearby kopje but were always accompanied by an armed soldier.

Both were working on the ward when an orderly came and said Sister MacLean was to report to the HQ tent. When asked for what reason he apologised and said he did not know but Matron and the Senior Medical Officer were there. Apprehensive, Aileen promised to come straight back to let Greta know what was happening.

When Aileen returned Greta saw immediately that everything was not well. Aileen's eyes were full of tears, but she was trying to smile.

"I've been reassigned to Wynberg, Greta. There was no choice. It was either you or me and I thought I'd better go."

Greta stared at her friend. She tried to speak but the words would not come. They hugged silently before they broke. Greta went to request permission from the Senior Sister so that she could help Aileen with her packing. In the privacy of the tent they hugged again both with tear filled eyes. Aileen pulled away saying, "It won't be for long and we have got to be realistic. We are here to go where we are needed." Greta nodded but had no words.

She watched the train until it was out of sight. Greta had a premonition and a strong sense of foreboding Her world was darker from that moment.

THE BATTLE OF TALANA HILL

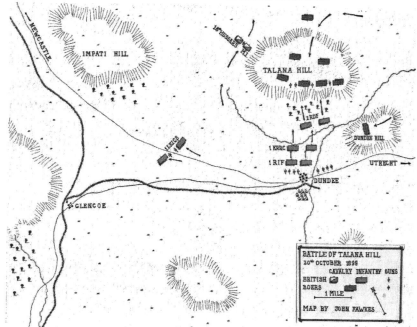

By Kind Permission of John Fawkes of
https://www.britishbattles.com

CHAPTER TWENTY
Talana Hill

The Irish Brigade received orders to move out. Horses were saddled and supply wagons in-spanned for the incursion of Natal. British Natal. The contingent was part of five Boer Commandos of twelve thousand armed men converging on Ladysmith. They completed the march to Newcastle in less time than expected by dint of hard riding.

In sight of the town the volunteers saw the Union Jack lowered and the Vierkleur of their adopted country raised. In town, Colonel Blake and Major Boyle met with Commandant Trichardt of the Staats Artillerie, an organisation which was to play a large part in future actions of the Irish Brigade. The next town on the plan of attack was Dundee.

On the evening before the advance Commandant Trichardt sent for Colonel Blake. One item discussed was the Artillery's commander's request for the Irish Brigade to provide security and protection for the Boer Artillery. Their first action would be to protect the guns and gunners in the next assault. Blake agreed. On his return he briefed Fergal. The major was to select forty members of the Brigade to join the Staats Artillerie and their cannon in the forthcoming attack.

The Irish Brigade took part in the first major combat of the invasion which began shortly after midnight. It was bitterly cold. Fergal's group left in the early hours, escorting the Boers' guns and their crews, in heavy torrential rain. Their objective was the occupation of Talana Hill which overlooked the town of Dundee. The Boer's forward scouts had returned during the late hours of the previous night with the intelligence that the high ground, Talana Hill, Dundee Hill to the east of Dundee and the larger Mount Impati to the north west, were not invested by the British. All had clear fields of fire on the town below. The top of Talana was more accessible than its neighbour Dundee and ideal for siting the guns. General Lukas Meyer, the Commando commander, found the scouts' information surprising, but did not doubt the reliability of his patrol. He knew the Impati was in the path of General Erasmus' advance and knew he would place his artillery there. The specific remit of the Irish volunteers was the three Krupp guns providing artillery support for their commando.

Fergal and his mounted group, many of whom had never ridden before, and now suffered the aches and stiffness of the beginner, followed close behind the last limber. They were part of a six-mile-long convoy of covered wagons, pulled by oxen, and of horsemen, on the first leg of their journey to Ladysmith.

143

The gun limbers within the convoy peeled off and headed towards the long sloping ascent of Talana Hill. Fifteen hundred members of the two Commandos under General Meyers followed. The flat top of the kopje was ideal to site the cannon close to the reverse slope. The Irish commandos unloaded and placed the shells next to each gun. Left and right but forward of the guns the volunteers lay along the crest. Lying flat each could see the veiled shape of Dundee far below through a slowly lifting mist. Closer to the Boer lines could be seen the lines of "Khakis," in full combat equipment, drilling as though on a square in Aldershot.

The area around the Krupps guns was alive with quiet but efficient activity as they were unlimbered, and the animals outspanned and led away. The gunners took up their positions. The men of the Artillerie were young, the majority in their late teens and the rest in their early twenties. They were the only Boer participants who wore uniform, dark blue jackets and white trousers.

Dawn morphed into daylight with not a ray piercing the murkiness as they waited in silence, and some trepidation, for the next phase. The weather was dismal, damp and as the fog continued to thin, the mining town, on a low-lying ridge, became clearer. Fergal could now see the surrounding hills. There was one other hill, Dundee Hill and to the north, with a thick collar of mist, Mount Impati, loured over the town. The mountain, the source of fresh water for Dundee, was named "Leader" by the Zulus because of its predominant position.

He turned his gaze along the line of Boers on the edge of the escarpment then down among the rocky outcrops of the forward slope where they had pockets of riflemen in shallow trenches. They were of all ages, grey bearded elders, young rosy cheeked boys, youths with the first shade of virility darkening their cheeks and chins. All wore bandoliers with pouches to hold the clips of ammunition which fed their Mausers. Fergal took in the assorted range of headgear, mostly wide brimmed, but with the occasional flat cap and even a grey bowler. There were no official uniforms but the general choice, corduroy, and a wide range of homespun, together with the ubiquitous waistcoat, represented conformity.

He could not hide his wide strained yawns. Nervousness the like of which he had never experienced oozed up threatening to take over his body and swamp the last vestiges of control. He coughed and cleared his throat to master the fear threatening to hold dominance. One of the Brigade said quietly, "It won't be long now. It's always worst before it starts." Fergal recognized the voice of Plummer who had served with their enemy in India as a Connaught Ranger. Fergal could not think of a suitable reply but nodded.

The sudden crash of the first Boer gun shattered his eardrums as its shell whirred and screamed along the valley through the morning air. Fergal did not see the shell strike. There was no explosion. He watched the flight of each one as the two other 75mm Krupp field guns came into play. There was a singular lack of eruptions in the target area. Noticeable was the lack of response from the British.

Some hours later the Boers saw the first of the British soldiers forming line. Fergal gave his full attention to the panorama below. He saw a series of stone walls and a wood lying between them and the British. Two of the walls ran across the foot of Talana, connected by a third, joining both at right angles. These walls could provide protection for the attackers, and he sensed they would play a part in the coming action. The copse of eucalyptus trees provided yet another possible cover for the oncoming attackers. A stream ran across the plain, but Fergal knew the water posed no hindrance for the infantry.

Trichardt had told Fergal the Boer's guns could fire greater distances than those of the British. This gave him some comfort until the British horse-drawn limbers hurtled past the edge of the blue gum trees. In seconds, the artillerymen below had dismounted and rapidly deployed within three thousand yards of the foot of Talana. Less than a minute later they loaded and fired their first salvo. The result was ineffective. The defenders saw the eruptions far down the slopes of Talana and cheered derisively. Their tangible relief was short lived as the gunners limbered up and moved three hundred yards closer. The first shell from the second location landed just to the rear of the second Boer gun. Fergal momentarily lost consciousness as something heavy struck his neck and shoulders. He struggled to bring his eyes into focus. The object was weighty inhibiting the movement of his upper body. He tried to roll sideways. It clung to him and he couldn't sit up. The weight shifted and as he struggled awkwardly to his knees the head, shoulder and arm of a mutilated gunner fell away. He gagged and swallowed heavily. The accuracy of the batteries below was deadly; the incoming shells causing havoc as they indiscriminately shredded metal and flesh. The screams of agony, shrill and high pitched, blending with the strident clamour of explosions following each salvo, added to the terror. Within moments, two guns had been destroyed and their crews pulverized. The gun commander quickly withdrew with the remaining gun and the remnants of his crews.

The riflemen were ordered to stand fast.

"Here come the khakis!" said the young Boer next to Fergal, with a smile. He was beardless and Fergal put his age at sixteen. He was to find later Trichardt's boy was thirteen. The British deployed and began their advance over the open grassland remaining in extended line. They appeared to be out of range, and knowing with certainty he would miss, he still could not resist. Fergal took a savage delight in firing his first ever shot at the line. As they rushed forward and disappeared into the copse the rapid and heavy fire from the Mausers, over the reduced range, chopped at the tree trunks. Each fusillade ripped off huge splinters of bark and wood to fly through a thick confetti of minced leaves. The copse was providing scant cover for the soldiers and many dropped into lying positions. The staccato rattle of rapid fire from the rifle next to him amazed Fergal and he realized most of the Boers, young and old, were expert handlers of their weapons.

A muffled exclamation from the teenager caused him to look over to see the boy indicating the wood below with his rifle muzzle. He quickly returned to his firing position and, with the other marksmen, poured fire into a small group of soldiers. One, obviously a high-ranking officer was standing in clear view, shouting and chivvying his soldiers to advance, deliberately ignoring the volleys of shots fired at him. His endeavours were cut short when a bullet found its mark. He stiffened, throwing one arm up into the air, but remained upright. He turned and retired to the rear. Fergal felt an inordinate flash of admiration for the wounded officer which disappeared when he spotted the Orderly holding a red pennant. It might as well have been a sign which said, "Shoot me." Madness.

In the wood the rear ranks came forward and pressed on those already there forcing the advance to start again. The defenders on the hill saw the first sortie from the woods come out in single file. The soldiers made for the protective connecting wall. Rifle fire from over the top of the wall and from chinks in its construction had its effect on the Boers. Fergal heard the whoop of hurt as someone was wounded or killed. At that moment Fergal became aware, conscious of his circumstances, of the high risk of death or severe injury by a bullet. *Or a traitor's rope if those bastards below catch me!*

The sudden flurry of movement drew Fergal from his thoughts of harm, as an officer below leaped over the wall and twenty men followed to charge the hill. The British were now within four hundred yards of the summit and coming hard. In one's and two's, the Boers retired and made their way to their horses at the bottom of the hill. Fergal determined to stay, gratified at seeing all his Irish still firing. The Mauser bullets dropped many of the approaching soldiers, but the gaps filled immediately by others moving up.

"Ons vertrek. Vinnig. Kom ons gaan." The words came from the crouching youngster tugging on his arm. Fergal didn't understand the words, but the message was clear. He turned to run, and noticed for the first time, the English had fixed bayonets. He screamed at his men to break off contact. The English had only yards to climb before they were among the riflemen. It was over, thought Fergal.

A British shell landed and exploded with devastating effect among the attacking soldiers and was followed by two more. The leading

149

ranks were decimated and those behind did not press on but turned and ran back to escape slaughter by their own guns. The intervention by the British artillery was heaven-sent for Fergal and the other members of the Irish Brigade. He shouted and swore, and his men pulled back. He continued shouting "Move! Get to the horses!" In his haste his leading foot thudded into the side of a man lying face down. He tripped and staggered before realizing it was one of his men. Dead.

The remaining members of the group took off at a run; closely grouped, weapons at the trail and in good order. They reached and mounted their horses as the British reached the undefended top of Talana Hill. With shouts of scorn at the khaki clad soldiers above they wheeled their mounts and galloped off to join their column.

Fergal was mortified when he reported to Colonel Blake. The American asked,

"Can you account for your men? All of your men?" He couldn't. Blake was coldly cynical. He lectured Fergal on the duties of a commander. He belaboured keeping track, of knowing the whereabouts, and the condition of his men. Always. Aware the colonel was right did nothing to relieve Fergal's discomfort. He did not know if any of the missing men, whom he assumed were dead, were wounded. If alive, they were now prisoners.

Later in the afternoon, in the late sunshine, Fergal sat a short distance from the colonel and the other officers whom Blake was regaling with tales of derring-do during his cavalry days in the West.

Fergal was determined to learn by heart the names of his soldiers. He remembered a ploy from Haddington Hall used by old Mr. Tennant. The butler used it with various outdoor staff, often temporary, and the many suppliers who brought their wares to the house. He would ask the individual, "What's your name again?" If given a surname or a first name he would reply, "I know. It was your first (or second) name which has escaped me." Invariably it worked and the full name of the person was elicited without causing offence or appearing highhanded. The main thing was to remember the names together with the faces. He turned his full attention to the register of names representing the Brigade's roll call. Before long he was engrossed.

"'Allo, Irishman. You are well?" Fergal raised his head to see Commandant Trichardt's son standing before him with two steaming mugs in his hands. He offered one to Fergal.

"Koffie. Werkelijk koffie."

"Thank you." He took a sip and tasted real coffee, the first since Johannesburg. Both sat in the wagon's shadow. Conversation was difficult at first, but they were making headway when the Commandant appeared and sat beside them. After a brief spell, in answer to Fergal's question about the boy's marksmanship, earlier in the day, his father answered on his behalf.

"Our burghers have had no specific military training apart from frequent shooting competitions. The way we live, however, ensures we can defend ourselves. Every male from an early age knows about hunting game where shooting is an essential survival skill. You don't train your young men to shoot?"

"No. I'm afraid we don't. Your son showed great courage today." The boy smiled and looked at his father who nodded briefly.

"Ja, good." Trichardt reached over and ruffled the boy's hair. He went on,

"He has to be able to hit moving targets, estimate distance, know the strength and direction of the wind and not forget to adjust his sights. Equally important is to be invisible until it is too late for your prey."

Fergal nodded. Trichardt looked past him. Fergal realised he was looking at his horse which was hobbled but quietly eating grass.

"We never hobble our horses. We have trained them to wait in place. There is no problem when we need to leave quickly, and we don't lose the use of good men by having them look after the horses while the others fight. Also, my young friend, make sure he has water and food, even before you have satisfied your own needs. He will be your saviour."

He took out and filled his pipe. He offered the pouch to Fergal who politely refused. After he had lit up and smoked silently for a moment or two Trichardt continued.

"Skill with horses. Long hours in the saddle. Important in the days to come."

In the subsequent pause Fergal commented,

"I noticed our shells did not seem to do much damage today,"

"Bad intelligence," Trichardt said curtly. "It was a mistake. It should not happen again. The ground was too soft for many of them. But na ja!" he shrugged. "Next time will be better."

The Artillerie Commandant did not divulge another weakness of the shells in comparison to those of the British. The British used air burst shells delivering shrapnel which were more reliable against infantry and cavalry in open country, precisely what the Boers needed. Unfortunately, because of British blockades, the error could no longer be rectified.

BATTLE OF LADYSMITH

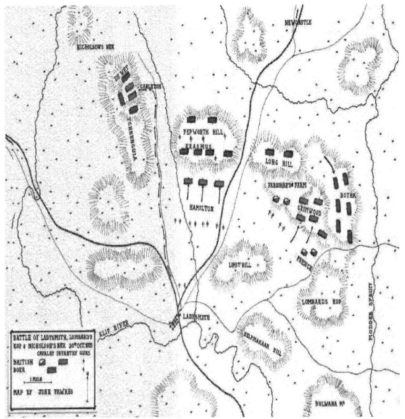

By Kind Permission of John Fawkes of
https://www.britishbattles.com

CHAPTER TWENTY-ONE
Battle of Ladysmith
Fergal

I was up early on the morning we left for Ladysmith. It was still dark when I was pulling on my boots. The African night had been colder than one would expect, and I had not slept well. We had had a pretty boisterous night, it being the first opportunity we had to celebrate our baptism of fire at Dundee and we had a wake for the boys we lost. The atmosphere between myself and Blake has not improved, and I find his arrogance annoying. However, if he has forgotten the first choice for command of our Brigade was Fergal Boyle himself, who graciously deferred to Colonel His Almighty Blake, thanks to his sixteen years to become a lieutenant, the lowliest of commissioned ranks, in the United States Seventh Cavalry, then I have not.

We assembled after breakfast and mounted up to set out for Ladysmith. Word had filtered down General Joubert might be in no hurry to reach the port Durban, which we all presume is our objective. I found it strange we did not pursue the English when they limped back to their base, but the General decided otherwise. So it was an unhurried advance toward to Ladysmith.

Once again Commandant Trichardt requested our help in the movement of the guns and the transport of the shells. Besides our prime purpose of guarding the passage of the armaments there was a certain amount of physical labour, but it was a relief for us all to get off the ball aching saddles and work off the stiffness. Our objective was the heights overlooking Ladysmith. We were discovering the English had a clear aversion to occupying any high ground which would give them an advantage in defence. We had all the high ground, which worked decidedly to our benefit at Dundee, and intelligence gathered confirmed Pepworth Hill had not been invested so we would just walk in.

Not long after our deployment a foraging party of our lads located and took possession of a large quantity of dynamite. Many of the boys who had worked the mines around Johannesburg had more than a passing notion of the use of bang. This skill and the dynamite were to come together to prove a boon in our forays into the realm of bridge demolition much later in our service to the Boers.

Next morning, well before five, I spilled a mug of hot coffee all over my lap, when the English fired their first shell giving notice of their intent to clear us off the hill. Weapons were taken up and we quickly stood to at our allotted positions. I felt a flash of pride, and had the proverbial goose pimples on my neck, at the sight of the Brigade flag fluttering in the breeze. I made a mental note to give a well done to Fenton for thinking to raise it. Unfortunately, it was not to be as Sean was destined never to leave the crest of Pepworth Hill.

My earlier thought about the advantage of high ground has modified as result of McCready pointing out the English have not hidden the fact they have measured the yardage to specific points on this kopje, from the bottom to the top of its slopes. The evidence is clear, and one cannot miss the daubs of coloured paint on some of the outcrops. Having discovered them, I confess it was not until after the battle we thought we could have eliminated or hidden them, with mud or rocks or whatever. We didn't and we suffered.

Our Long Tom and two of the Creusots took centre stage while the Kermelo Commando were to the left of the cannon and our Brigade to the right. We were, I should say, about five miles from Ladysmith. Proud to be in a such a prominent position for the coming battle, I had to admit to a queasy butterfly sensation again. We were all in lying position, except the gunners of course, and it gave a feeling of protection. Until the English barrage. The rain of shells far exceeded the barrage at Dundee which, in our ignorance, we thought was the worst ever experienced.

A new hell dawned on the heights of Ladysmith. The English gunners threw a mélange of projectiles at our position. It was of variable calibre and they were decidedly using all their guns in an attempt to annihilate us. There were grape shot, cannister, time concussion,

157

explosive shells and the yellow lyddite destroyers.

Colonel Blake was one of the early casualties, being hit in the arm with a pellet, some forty minutes after the saturation bombardment started. I assumed command of the Brigade, the whole brigade this time, when he left the field of battle. There was a lull but not a silence because each of us had problems hearing because of the ringing in our ears. The English appeared to be in no hurry to follow up the barrage with an infantry attack. The reason soon became clear.

Two monsters entered the fray in the shape of two naval guns from a warship in Durban. Their initial shots obliterated one of our guns and six young members of its crew. Two difficulties arose for us. The effect of the English guns was to drive virtually all of our people from the summit and the supply of shells for our Long Tom was quickly dwindling. Resupply was called for. The crews of our big guns had remained in action and of course our Brigade remained in situ prepared to defend them. At the request of Commandant Trichardt calling for volunteers to carry forward more shells for the guns more than a dozen of our lads jumped up to volunteer. Our shells were put to effective use decimating a nascent infantry attack as its men were forming up. The remnants of the battalions were scattered to the wind as the cavalry panicked and rode helter-skelter, over their fleeing infantry comrades across the plain.

Despite our grievous losses which thinned the ranks of the Brigade, the English were broken, and the field was ours. Unhappily, yet once again, General Joubert would not allow our chasing the fleeing English. Trichardt was most generous and spoke to many of the Irish volunteers thanking them for their contribution

CHAPTER TWENTY-TWO
Hospital Train

The train donated by the Princess Christian, designed and equipped for the sole purpose of transporting wounded soldiers, was in constant use. Named in her honour every wagon had a huge Red Cross emblem painted on each side.

The number of dead and wounded from the battles in the north of the province had dismayed and appalled all echelons of the Army. The shock was greater since all had been convinced of an easy victory with minimal losses. Now, the burden of the aftermath fell to the medical arm of the service. Defeats and dubious victories alike had created a dreadful harvest. The dead posed no quandary but the wounded from Talana, Erlandslaagte, Ladysmith in Natal and Belmont and Graspan in the Cape were to be of great concern.

Aileen was co-opted and appreciated the diversion. Helping and being occupied might take her mind off the suddenness of the change of station.

"Nurse MacLean?" She looked up from the soldier's dressing she was replacing, then having completed tying the final knot, stood upright. His white coat revealed he was a doctor and from his grey hair and bearing she assumed he was the Senior Medical Officer (SMO) of the train.

160

"Yes, sir."

"I'm sorry your change of duty station has been so sudden. It is unfortunate but we welcome your extra hands at least as far as Cape Town. We're glad to have you with us. Have you met Senior Sister Carstairs? She is Scottish too." He seemed hurried and she knew it would be a taxing journey before they reached the Cape.

"Yes I have, thank you." He nodded, then caught sight of two nurses, one of whom had beckoned, at the sliding door of the next carriage. He strode quickly toward them. They spoke and he bent to examine the soldier at his feet, straightened, and inclined his head. The nurse knelt and covered the warrior's head and shoulders. Filled with the shattered bodies from the decimated companies, the engine growled into life and with clanks and screeches started to roll on its way south.

As the Princess Royal steamed across the Veld, the nurses worked ceaselessly to attend and care for the wounded. They helped the patients drink, changed dressings, straightened blankets, and constantly assured and quietened the ones whose pain was unbearable. They administered laudanum to the worse cases. In the small hours two orderlies carried in a huge tea urn and slabs of buttered bread. A third carried in a tray of bowls with the ubiquitous tins of condensed milk. The nurses and the orderlies served tea and bread to those of the wounded who could eat. It was quickly completed because of the one hundred and twenty casualties only thirty could manage to sit up. The bread was cut up and soaked with tea and milk and the protracted process of spoon feeding the wounded began.

Four more would die before the train pulled into Wjnberg Station. On arrival the waiting bearers swiftly loaded the stretchers onto the transport for No. 1 Base General Hospital (BGH) Wynberg, Cape Town. It finished without the loss of more lives.

Aileen and the other nurses climbed wearily back on the train to make it ready for its next journey. She welcomed the work which made her ignore the aching muscles and mind-numbing fatigue. Darkness fell before the work ended. She emptied the last bucket of effluence into the wheeled tank manned by an African helper and burnt the soiled bandages twenty or so yards from the railway line. With the other nurses she stepped up on to the coach for the hospital and sat back wearily on the bench. She awoke to a sister colleague gently shaking her and saying,

" We're here." Together they walked to the nurses' quarters. A female servant told them the Superintendent of Nurses had arranged for hot water and towels to be available for her nurses to bathe. Aileen enjoyed the luxury of the body length zinc bath and warm, sudsy water which held her fatigue at bay She did not allow herself to dawdle as the others also waited to bathe.

162

On the beds assigned to them were uniforms and pristine starched aprons. The servant was sitting on one of the end beds and said she would take them to the dining room for supper. The food was indifferent, but they ate every morsel. The large cups of coffee were an unexpected delight. At the end of the meal tiredness flooded every part of Aileen's body and she caught herself nodding on two occasions before she excused herself.

Tired as she was, she paused in her walk to admire the starry cloudless sky and the dark mass of Table Mountain in the distance. It took only a matter of moments to undress and slide between the crisp linen sheets. As she said her prayers, a routine Greta had persuaded her to adopt, she thought of her friend and hoped she would be back in Chieveley soon and they would be together again.

No 1 General Hospital at Wjnberg Barracks was bigger than anything Aileen had seen before. Netley was large but it did not have nearly the number of patients who were under treatment as Wjnberg. There were over a thousand beds. And all were occupied. In addition, there were another nine hospitals for soldiers in Cape Town, mostly under canvas. As the nurses, previously serving on the hospital trains, had been "stood down" while the trains were not ferrying the injured from the field hospitals, they were given gainful employment in the network of Cape Town hospitals. Aileen was included and was assigned as a junior theatre nurse. The hospital operating department was equipped with the most modern equipment available, much of it possible by generous donations from benefactors.

The operating theatres were well appointed in spacious rooms or under canvas with duckboard floors. There were X-ray machines which saved the unfortunate Tommy greater discomfort and pain, discovery by early detection of bullets or shrapnel without the need for radical investigative 'cutting' surgery. Aileen found she could tolerate the copious flows of blood or the sight of gaping wounds, often with internal organs clearly visible, but the loss of a patient on the table was hard for her to bear.

The hours were long, but they were made bearable by the number of successful operations she witnessed. The stoic dignity, and in numerous cases, the good nature of the wounded soldier could be moving to the point of tears. It was hard to contain emotion at the pitiful sight of a convoy of wounded. Two to three hundred or more stretcher cases, shot through thigh, foot, or spine, would arrive at any one time. Jolted over rough veld in ambulances, ox carts and wagons the men then endured the lengthy train journey. Each stage would be borne with dogged acceptance of the pain. The dedication of everyone, surgeons, sisters, and orderlies, working on regardless of time or hunger until all had received treatment, tugged at her emotions.

164

With few suffering from disease most cases were surgical. Operations would continue all day, long after the arrival of a fresh convoy. X-ray machines hummed constantly. The operating table was never empty.

Three days elapsed. The flow of men dwindled then stopped. Everyone knew it would a short respite. Ladysmith, Mafeking and Kimberley remained under siege.

They were at lunch when a helper came to tell them of the invitation to afternoon tea with the Superintendent. Cap firmly in place over her folded braids and her cape brushed and free of lint, Aileen set off with her colleagues for the small cottage partially hidden by a grove of sagewood. In the still air was a smell of its sweetly scented blossom.

The Superintendent greeted them all warmly, leading them to the dining room where a table, complete with napkins, was laid with cups, bread and butter, scones, and slices of seedcake. They sat while she busied herself with teapot and boiling kettle. Aileen looked around the room with interest. She could not help but compare, without jealousy, their tented temporary home at Chieveley and the homely comfort of this room.

As she poured, their host chose Aileen to tell about herself. She deliberately kept the theme impersonal. The nagging suspicion there was a motive, yet to be revealed, behind this invitation, would not abate. When the sandwiches had disappeared, the cake eaten, the plates empty, and second cups finished so did the small talk. Her unease was justified. The Superintendent put down her cup, clasped her hands in her lap and leaned forward.

"There is no uncomplicated way to say this, so I'll just be direct, ladies. You will not be going back to... Frere, or was it Chieveley?" She looked at Aileen who made no response. The others as a group stiffened.

"I am afraid not one of you will. We are desperately short of nurses to support the drive to relieve Kimberley. Enteric fever seems to be stalking the cadre of our qualified nurses in the war zones. You are to travel on the hospital train and join the field hospital at De Aar. You will stand down from all other duties and prepare yourselves ready to entrain on Monday morning. Early."

The nurses spent two days at the hospital warehouse selecting items and packing the wicker hampers with bandages, slings, field dressings, and packs of sterile pads, poultice mixtures, powders, disinfectants, and sundry supplies. Sunday was free. They washed and mended their clothing and packed the rudimentary comfortable clothes they possessed. Aileen had nothing to pack.

The four nurses ate breakfast before collecting their baggage from the entrance hall to get on the coach for the railway station. They reported to the Railway Transport Officer (RTO) who directed them to the waiting room. He would call for them when the train had been loaded. The train's primary cargo was stores and supplies for De Aar with few passengers. Subdued and untalkative they whiled away what was to be a prolonged period. Two read while the third knitted. Aileen was lost in thought. And depression. Will I ever get back to Chieveley and Greta? Her rumination was broken when Daisy said, "It's always the same with the Army. Hurry up and wait." The others laughed without mirth.

Soldiers in shirtsleeves, many capless, moved the equipment and material to the edge of the platform in preparation for its move onto the train. Finally the engine wheezed into place, and the sides of the cargo sections were lowered. The platform cleared completely in several hectic minutes. The RTO fussily directed the nurses to their assigned seats. Although the carriages were not armoured the engine was draped with a heavy web of anchor rope in lieu of additional steel plating. Minutes later, accompanied by a whistle blast plus several indecipherable shouts, the train pulled out.

Once the environs of Cape Town fell behind the gradual climb to the uplands and the initial leg to De Aar began. The train headed northwards. Between Cape Town and Worcester, the line was bordered by well-watered fields of vines and mealies but there were also many acres of sad neglect. North of Worcester the women felt the train shudder then begin the steeper ascent of the Hex River Mountains foothills. Viewed through the train window as it drew close the range appeared to bar the way. However, the swinging motion of the train following the meandering track through the valleys and gaps showed the mass would be circumnavigated and not climbed. The engine and its carriages undulated through the loops and up the spirals. The sudden onset of darkness as the train entered the first of many tunnels shook the nurses and caused some nervous giggles. The gradients increased and the erratic swerves rattling over bridges and on the lips of breath-taking ravines made them grab and hold each other.

Then, without warning, the train broke through onto the Karoo. Night descended. The cloudless sky and full moon emphasized the uniformity, in symmetry but not in size, of the rugged kopjes studding the vast expanse of veld. Seen closely the sides of the hills were thick with rocky outcrops like ugly burrs. The level ground was owned by the short stubby scrub whose patches seemed thick and impenetrable. The moonlit landscape was a theatrical backdrop illustrating an alien planet.

The train slowed though did not stop at Beaufort West, whose skyline boasted of no architectural gems, but pressed on toward De Aar.

CHAPTER TWENTY-THREE
The Tigers

Baron Methuen, General Officer Commanding the 1st Division tasked by Buller to relieve Kimberley, read the telegraph from his superior. It was several minutes before he looked up and said sourly to his deputy,

"It's all I needed at this stage. Here, deal with this."

His deputy read the message then asked,

"Will you be seeing him when he arrives?"

The pale blue eyes held his gaze

"I said deal with this. And no, I do not intend to meet with messenger- boy colonels. Give him no cause for complaint but farm him out to one of the colonial units."

The second in command had gone back to reading the signal when Methuen said,

"As soon as we have rolled up the Boers and are in Kimberley any significance this visit may have had will be overtaken by events."

On the third day Cape Town came into view and shortly thereafter Craven and Remus were the first to disembark due to the letter of authorisation from General Buller. Remus was winched ashore as soon as the ship's hawsers were secured. The disgruntled and indignant charger was skittish as they walked to the arranged horse box but soon quieted when he found the hay.

There was a brief respite at Cape Town main rail station. Craven walked the stallion up the ramp to board the train north to De Aar. There were no horse boxes as such and they had to share an open top flatbed. It was armoured with heavy metal sides with rifle slits. Besides the riflemen it was equipped with a Maxim machine gun and two gunners. The nearest soldier kept a wary eye on the colonel's horse as it fidgeted uneasily when the train pulled out but Craven soon settled him. After several hours of travelling Remus voided his bladder and evacuated his bowels. The pungent smell of ammonia followed the deluge of several gallons which had the rifleman hopping from one foot to the other trying to keep his feet dry while, in mock anger, shouting expletives at his comrades who were hooting with laughter.

There had been mild euphoria in Cape Town at the news of the victories claimed by Methuen on his march to relieve Kimberley. Among the men on the flatbed mixed reactions were evident. The heavy casualties were the subject of bitter witticisms and crude humour. The butt of most ribaldry was the General Officer Commanding (GOC) himself, to which Craven turned a deaf ear. What might have been considered mutinous in other armies Craven knew to be the safety valve of expression, which was endemic, and essential, among the lower ranks. If Tommy Atkins was grousing, then he was in relatively good spirits. Ominous was when he was not.

Belmont and Graspan were old news. Modder River had taken place with severe losses and, according to Methuen's despatches, Kimberley remained a distant goal.

While the train continued its journey north, Craven ate a thick dried beef sandwich passed from the front of the train and preparations were continuing at the 1st Division for the forthcoming onslaught at Magersfontein. African collaborators had brought news of the Boer general, Koos de la Rey, who had re-joined General De Cronje. He had been temporarily away from the front attending the burial of his son, killed at Modder River, where he himself had been wounded. This news, treated as trivia by the British, was to have dramatic consequences.

Craven rested, the reins loosely held in his hand, and studied the camp. Thirty or so tents, deep brown unlike the white of the regular Army's bivouacs, were strategically placed amongst the mimosas on the western side of the farmhouse. There was little activity in the camp although a group seated around the table in front of the house drew his eye. He was aware earlier his presence was known to the camp as he had caught the signal to base by an outlying picket who had deliberately revealed himself by standing whilst sending the visual warning to the camp.

The men in the camp were excellent horsemen and renowned good shots. and although they had occasionally been called the *Night Cats*, because of their frequent use of the night, as cover for their movements, their C.O. called them his "*catch-'em-alive-o's*". The bulk of the Army knew them as *The Tigers* because of the distinctive hatband they all wore.

He touched Remus' sides with his heels and his mount moved forward. As he drew closer, he saw the group were playing cards. One of the players stood then left the table and advanced toward him.

"Colonel Craven?"

"Yes, Colonel," he said as he dismounted. He offered an outstretched hand with a smile. Colonel Rimington was not as tall as Craven, few were, but he was not a small man. His face was deeply tanned.

"Welcome. Let's get you settled then you can meet the officers at dinner. Fine looking English charger. Came with you I take it." he nodded at Craven's mount.

"Yes, he did. Travelled surprisingly well and acclimatised quickly."

"Not a thoroughbred, though, eh?

"Yes, again. He comes from a family of mixed heavy draught horse and Arabian. We breed them on our estate for large riders like me."

As they approached the group another player stood and welcomed the newcomer while the others either smiled or nodded or both. Rimington gave him a friendly wave indicating he should join him and the new arrival.

"I'll leave you with Captain Marsh," said Rimington, "I'll get back to the table." He smiled conspiratorially and whispered in a staged sotto voce, "I think I'll rummy with one more card." The others at the game laughed mockingly

"Let me show you where to water your animal and we'll tether him with the others. Name's Marsh. Phillip."

"Craven."

"Colonel Craven?"

"Yes. But I'm here on the forbearance of Colonel Rimington so I won't have any regular standing. Name's Nicholas and no, I don't mind it being shortened." Both men chuckled.

"Fair do's, Nick."

Marsh watched as Craven removed his rifle from the scabbard while Remus lowered his head to drink.

"It is a Winchester?"

"It is. Used one in Canada to good effect and thought it would be suitable to use in the light of my deficiencies."

"And is it?"

"I had to get used to it but with one eye it is better than anything else I had access to."

Marsh frowned. "And how are you for distance with the . . ." he nodded to Craven's patch.

"Surprisingly not too shabby. Provided I hold it steady and point in the right direction, whoever is with me is reasonable safe." He kept a straight face. "And I can frighten whoever or whatever is in the general frontal direction."

"Should work. In our business we mostly just need to keep the other side's heads down as we move to cover."

Craven grinned.

"I can live with that"

The meal over and the metal plates dry rubbed with sand and rinsed in the pool in the shade of the mimosas everyone sat round the fire. Phillip did not join them as he was officer of the watch and was visiting the sentries. Craven sat with the others for their post prandial smoke. There were some pipes but most of the officers smoked cheroots.

As the general conversation went to and fro the arrival of a horseman caused a lull and they watched for a few seconds in silence as the rider dismounted and gave a message satchel to Rimington. He had a few moments in low key talk with the messenger, dismissed him then ducked into his tent. The fireside banter and chat renewed.

More wood had just been placed on the fire when Rimington came to join the group. He made his way to where the new addition to the Tigers was sitting. The guide on Craven's right vacated his folding chair so the Colonel could sit next to him. The CO refused the offer of a cheroot

"Not that I don't smoke old chap but I'm rationing myself to a cigar a day and I smoked one during cards when I thought I was winning." Those close by who heard this laughed and Craven instinctively joined in. .

"So, Nick, what do you know about us?"

"I know you are a Light Horse unit of guides and scouts. You are known as the Tigers because of the hat bands you sport. There are times when you operate in an active role when you engage in armed reconnaissance. And much to the disgust of Tommy Atkins who gets a shilling a day for his services, your men receive ten shillings a day and all your rations."

Rimington remained expressionless.

"Yes. That's the universal view of who we are. Let me give you our version. We number, when at full strength one hundred and fifty, but rarely operate as a cohesive battle group. Our value to the Army is the unit is made up of locals.

We will have on hand one or more, at any time, who know the specific area of operation by having lived there. So, we function as guides or scouts more often than not. There's forty of the Guides out at present. They all speak Taal, the Boers' language, and most know an African dialect or two. All can be called upon to function as interpreters.

So, we operate in the field of intelligence on many occasions although it's been disappointing as much of what we give in the way of information is rarely acted on by the staff. Hopefully, that will change. We try to avoid actual contact with the enemy unless we are required to bring some live ones back for interrogation. We are lightly armed considering, carbines and pistols only. As you can see, we don't wear uniform as such. Mobility is our friend and, of course, fieldcraft."

He waited for Craven to comment but the colonel only nodded.

"Here is a pugaree for your hat." He handed Craven the hatband which distinguished them from all others.

"Thank you, Colonel." Craven looked at the band of leopard skin for a moment or two before putting it aside as Rimington spoke again.

"We are riding out tomorrow in troop size force. We reported to headquarters the Westerlo Commando were gearing up to move out from their present location and our assessment was they would move closer to the railway with the intention of attacking the rail link to the Cape. HQ have tasked us with confirming our original finding and if it is a fact, we are to interfere with the smooth transfer of the Westerlo commando. Phillip, pick the riders and put them on notice. Assembly at zero four hours. He stood.

"Good night, gentlemen."

Craven woke with a start and supported on his right elbow looked out of the tent to past the nearby silhouetted trees over the silver veld. Above a distant ridge The Milky Way, clear and luminescent flowed across the night sky. He looked at his watch just as Phillip Marsh ducked under the tent flap.

"Morning, Nick. Came to wake you and to stand by in case there was anything you needed. I guess you'll well stocked with ammo for your sidearm and carbine?"

"Yes. thank you."

"When you've got your boots on, come with me for the packed rations and get your water bottle filled. We're great believers in boiled water here. Don't forget your bedroll." They emerged from the tent into a cool sparse mist hanging over the camp.

"Hello old lad, good night's sleep?" Remus snorted and gave a robust push with his head against his master's chest as Craven maneuvered him into position to throw on the blanket and saddle. Craven walked him to the assembly area where the group was gathering. After a few brief words from Colonel Rimington, Captain Marsh took over. As the early morning light lit the western sky the Tigers moved out to reconnoitre the Modder River landscape and beyond.

Marsh's troop rode mainly in silence with ten or fifteen yards between each member. Craven noted they avoided all skylines and kept the pace to a relatively moderate tempo, so the advanced outriders were never out of sight although hundreds of yards away. Just before noon they reached a slow-moving stream where they halted. In parties of four they watered their mounts while the rest of the troop maintained an all-round watch from the shade of a small copse of thorn trees.

CHAPTER TWENTY-FOUR
Prisoners of War

The journey was uneventful. Until fifteen miles from De Aar.

The train slowed violently, and the women were thrown forward then forcibly back in their seats. The screech of tortured metal, as the wheels of engine and wagons locked, then lost continuous contact with the rails, assaulted their eardrums. The Princess Royal shuddered to a halt. Rushing to the windows, two to each side, they strained to see up ahead. Aileen saw a section of rail had been torn up and cast ten or fifteen yards from the main line. A fusillade of shots erupted and hammered into the sides of the carriages the length of train. The women threw themselves to the floor. The sound of rifles, more immediate and closer, as the soldiers on the train returned the fire was intimidating. Then, abruptly there was an eerie silence which was broken by a whistling, ever-increasing scream and followed by a massive explosion rocking each and every carriage. Eardrums ringing, their hands flew to cover their ears. They were not aware the quiet had returned. Moments later they heard a shout and saw a rider with a white flag.

"Who is commander of this train," he called.

"I am," a voice replied, which sounded as though it came from the next carriage. "I am Major Cunningham, Durham Light Infantry."

"Good. Please listen." His voice sounded gruff. "We are asking you to surrender to avoid any bloodshed. We have proved, as you can see," he continued, pointing to the remnants of the guards van where the twisted metal chassis hung drunkenly on one rail. "that we have the precise range. If you do not surrender, we will reduce all of this," he waved a dismissive hand, "to matchwood." He did not address the presence of the passengers.

He waited patiently and the women surmised a hurried discussion was taking place in the next carriage.

"We surrender." The reply was subdued. "Please give me some minutes to tell everyone to leave the train."

"Of course," the rider said. He turned in the saddle and waved vigorously with the flag. Other riders appeared in the mid distance and rode toward the train. The commander of the train and his adjutant moved down the corridor ordering the passengers to leave the train on the opposite side and reminding them to take their baggage.

The nurses helped each other to step down from the train and formed a forlorn group on the veld. Minutes later with the soldiers and train crew they were taken prisoner by mounted Boers who had crossed the rail and rounded them up. They were driven, as sheep, but not roughly, to stand at a distance from the train.

The train blocked much of their view of the other side, but they heard, rather than saw, the

180

oxen and wagons. For ninety minutes the contents of the train, medical supplies, ammunitions, and foodstuffs were loaded onto the waiting carts. They heard the exhortations of the drivers together with the crack of whips as the carts left with the pillaged stores. Twenty minutes passed.

One of the Boers rode toward them and commanded the party to lie face down on the ground. They did as bidden. The women puzzled over the reason. The answer was swift in coming. It slammed into the train, followed by four more shells. With great accuracy, they demolished every carriage. Shards of panelling and assorted segments of the doomed train hurtled through the air. Falling debris struck three of the soldiers but did not cause injury.

Herded by the mounted outriders the group set off across the lines toward a rock covered kopje two miles distant from the railway. No one knew how far they would have to walk, and all were despondent. Aileen had her own theory that they were being taken towards the gun that had obliterated the train. There they would find other Boers waiting for the return of the attackers. After two hours of walking, they did not, thankfully, have to climb the hill but were directed around its base to the reverse side. Her theory proved correct as not only was the 75mm cannon there but three more covered wagons and thirty or so Boers. The women were lifted roughly into the back of one of the wagons. From the open rear they watched the rest of the prisoners jostled into a column before the order rang out to march.

Seated in the rear of the wagon next to the tailboard Aileen saw the rolling clouds build into a dark bank of impending storm. The air cooled as she watched the wall of rain form in the distance. It moved threateningly across the veld and the downpour created low waves of grey dust appearing to bounce in advance of the deluge. Within minutes it had reached the wagon and the four women had to crawl over the bales and boxes further into the interior of the cart to avoid the drenching downpour. The storm rattled viciously on the canvas above their heads then, as rapidly as it had come, it lifted allowing the weak rays of evening sun to break through. One hour later they heard the command to halt. The wagons formed a four-sided laager before the oxen were outspanned and turned loose to graze.

Darkness had fallen when they smelled first the smoke then the enticing aroma of meat roasting. There were sounds of laughter and what appeared to be banter in Afrikaans from the Boers gathered round the fire in the centre of the circled wagons. Out of the gloom two women appeared and beckoned them to get down. The nurses awkwardly clambered over the tailgate as the Boer women looked on. With gestures they signalled the English women should sit against the wheels. As they did so two more came out of the darkness with metal plates with meat and bread. There was noticeably no cutlery, but there was one tin cup, filled with hot coffee they realised they should share.

While the other Boer women returned to their menfolk one stayed behind as the English women ate their meal. She gathered in the plates and tin mug and disappeared into the darkness on the outer side of the wagon then called, "Kom! Kom." Aileen rose and helped the nearest nurse to her feet. Together they rounded the wagon where they could only just make out the silhouette of the Boer. From the actions of hiking up her skirt and bending her knees then gesturing at the four others it became clear they should take the opportunity to relieve themselves. After a moment of hesitation Aileen walked off five or six yards, turned her back on the group and lifted the hem of her dress. She heard the others follow suit.

Back at the rear of the covered cart the Boer matron watched as they climbed in before she walked off. She returned moments later with two rugs, a blanket, and a British Army greatcoat. She hefted the bundle over the tailgate, nodded then returned to other Boers gathered round the central fire. The night the four spent in the wagon was the coldest night any of them had experienced.

Dawn had been a relief to them as they found it impossible to sleep but did not feel up to conversing. Unwashed, and unfed, they had remained in the wagon as the column set off. Low lying mist hung in the air. After an hour of travel, shaken and bruised as the wheels trundled over rocks and large stones, the sun appeared and quickly burnt off the damp haze. Aileen felt her spirits lift although she knew of no logical reason why she should feel positive.

"What do you think will happen?" asked Dilys uneasily. She was clearly apprehensive about the immediate future. There was a silence then Aileen spoke.

"They'll put us to work. Hopefully, it will be doing what we were trained to do."

"Do you really think so, Aileen!?" asked Christy, a small woman from Arbroath.

"It is the most logical thing for them to do. They must have wounded, as we do." The silence returned but the improvement in spirit was clear.

The wagon they were in left the main column as it entered Westerlo. Minutes later they heard the hand brake applied and the wooden chocks locked onto the steel rims. A bearded man lowered the tail gate and waved, indicating they should leave the wagon. They found it much easier than before to climb down. He pointed the sjambok at the small mound of baggage they recognised as their cases. Then he completed the series of actions by indicating the elongated low building and the tents behind it. They had no difficulty in understanding when the Boer spoke.

"The Commandant comes. You stay here." They stood beside their luggage in front of what they recognised as a cottage hospital for the best part of an hour then it started to rain. At first a light drizzle of rain it quickly became heavier. A huge intimidating bearded figure, wearing a faded corduroy suit and a wide brimmed hat strode towards them. Without stopping, he said as he went past, "I'm Commandant Rutgers. Come. Ladies. Please, come with me."

They picked up their luggage and followed him through the low door of the building. As their eyes became accustomed to the gloom, they saw the rows of beds, all occupied, along each side of the hall. Aileen eyes picked out a blackboard standing forlorn in the far corner. Beside the doorway at the end of the room she made out two elderly women, silently watching them with sour expressions. The Commandant called out to one. She made a brief comment to the other woman then limped across the floor.

"Mevrouw Brunijnx. These ladies are to be your new helpers," he said in English. There then followed several minutes of Afrikaans which evidently did not please the old woman who turned abruptly and after a disdainful frown at the English women, re-joined her companion.

The Commandant turned his attention to the nurses.

"Na ja. She is not happy. Her two sons died three weeks ago at the same battle. But she is in charge of this hospital. We have no doctor all the time. But one visits. She will give you work. You will find not all will like you here. My men here were wounded by your Lancers and some were bayonetted. Of course, there are shot commandos but not as many. They will be in your care as you work under Mevrouw Brunijnx. Have you questions?"

"When is the doctor coming?" asked Aileen.

"Sometime today. Maybe tomorrow," was the reply. "Now you go to work."

It was not long before the nurses found their patients were a taciturn breed of man. Their humour was earthy and uncouth, but their stoicism and endurance was exceptional. Their attitude to Aileen and the other nurses contained no malice but neither were they overly respectful. The English women were to discover the male Boer considered all women, regardless of their ability to administer care, as subordinate creatures. The attitude of the Boer women was infinitely more extreme.

Most of them had travelled many miles to see their menfolk and did not as the nurses previously thought all travel in the field with the Boer Commandos. A few showed gratitude to Aileen and her colleagues, especially those with kinfolk among the more seriously wounded. The majority were disparaging and scornful. They would be openly critical. The care and attention the English nurses gave their menfolk did not win anyone over. They would only reluctantly move out of the way when beds were being made, bedpans emptied, or dressings changed. Assistance was never offered.

Their first week of work in the Boer hospital was filled with a roster of menial tasks Mevrouw Brunijnx had assigned them. When Aileen found that previously the night soil was emptied on the ground close to the rear of the school, she demanded a spade, through one of the English-speaking patients. She made sure her colleagues buried the contents of the night buckets one hundred yards from the back wall. The pails were then scalded with boiling water before the next use despite the additional effort the women had to expend. The English nurses were tasked to bathe the seriously wounded who, in the absence of bed pans and regular opportunity, evacuated their bowels directly onto to the sheets. Aileen ensured the sheets were changed immediately, and the dirty bed clothes scraped and boiled in the fire fed boiler in an outhouse. Despite her best efforts with the Boer matron she was unable to get bedpans. The nurses also had to work in the hospital kitchen, preparing vegetables and cleaning the pots and pans. The hours were many and arduous. Aileen decided this could not continue and determined to broach the subject with the doctor on his next visit or precipitate a confrontation with the old supervisor. The confrontation erupted before the doctor came.

Each morning, in the dim dawn light the grey silhouette of Mwr Brunijnx would loom above their makeshift sleeping spaces on the packed earth floor and they would be subjected to fierce kicks and shouts to "Wacht Op!" They thought of a simple a plan to avert most of the unnecessary discomfort by tasking whichever one of them woke first, to stay awake and warn the others of the harridan's approach. It worked well on the first morning it was in use. The women were all in their chemises tidying the area when Brunijnx entered silently. On seeing she could not set about them with her boots she screamed at them in choleric fury. She grabbed Aileen by the wrist and attempted to twist her arm. The force of the English woman's response, by reversing the direction of the turn, and causing the Boer woman's elbow to crack, made her yelp. She struggled to get free but the pain in her injured arm negated any strength she could muster. Aileen pulled her close and fixed her with steely stare she had used in the Valkyrie in Dawson City to intimidate any hairy drunken miner. The tears in the old woman's eyes weakened her attempt to stare the English nurse down. Aileen pushed her away and the suddenness of the release caused the woman to topple over. Aileen stood over her briefly then turned away. All four nurses then returned to folding their blankets.

The retaliation was sudden and brutal.

At ten o'clock, when Aileen was bent over a patient, a sudden blow on the back of her head followed by the vicious impact of sticks and broom handles caused her to fall forward over the injured man. Brunijnx and five other women jostled for position to rain blows on the nurse's body. Moments later the three other English nurses joined the fray with clenched fists and hair grabbing hands. Surprisingly, the ferocity of Aileen's colleagues and her own tenacity drove the attackers back just as several of the walking wounded patients intervened and restrained the women on both sides.

Within thirty minutes of the brouhaha the Commando commandant entered the ward and demanded an explanation from Mevrouw Brunijnx who volubly, with much arm waving and pointing towards the English group, gave her side of the story. The Commandant listened, then dismissed the matron and the other assailants. He sternly beckoned Aileen and her colleagues to join him.

"I have heard, as you saw, Mevrouw Brunijnx's version of what happened. What do you have to say?" He waited with cold eyes as Aileen steadily stared back.

"I have nothing to say about the disagreement. But I will tell you without equivocation what you can now expect from us." He struggled to hide his surprise and remained silent.

"First of all, we are not prisoners of war. We are professional nurses and as such our first duty is to the wounded, injured or ill patients of any side. We are there to ease their pain, see to the wounds, to provide comfort and succour. We are not limited to caring for our own wounded; we serve whoever needs us wherever we are. But we will not, I repeat not, quietly stand docile, to be beaten by anyone, male or female, no matter what grief they are suffering. We did not kill her sons but can understand her hurt. We will not, however, allow her to chastise us physically."

"Have you finished?"

"No. You are fortunate any of your patients have survived. It is certainly not down to the care administered prior to our coming here. We will continue to provide help to the best of our ability. But for it to be effective there must be a greater effort to provide more medical supplies, utensils, and equipment, such as bedpans, and there should be a doctor visiting more frequently. Now, I have finished."

"Miss MacLean, I cannot tell you how angry I am. Yes, filled with rage. Your brashness, impudence and lack of knowledge with regard to our circumstances is astounding." he said coldly. "Doubtless, some of what you say is true. I will apologise for Mevrouw Brunijnx, and the actions of her friends, and give an assurance you will suffer no further consequences or ill treatment from her. I have an answer to your criticisms regarding the medical side of your tirade. Fortuitously, for both of us, in a day or two a German ambulance will be operating here. If I can get agreement from their chief, you and your colleagues will be handed over to them."

"But… " Aileen attempted to say.

"There are no buts. Our hospitality was not to your liking. Perhaps, the Deutschers will be more to your taste. Good day." He turned abruptly and strode out of the ward."

The arrival of the German Ambulance was a welcome sight. They had four wagons with twelve well-sprung lighter coaches. These would be a boon in collecting and bringing wounded burghers to hospital. Some of the ambulance coaches were driven by the nurses themselves and it was clear they were proficient horse handlers. Aileen watched from the doorway as one young nurse led her horse from between the shafts of the cart then called to Aileen in English to ask where the stables were. Aileen left the doorway and joined the new arrival to show the way to the stables.

"How did you know to address me in English?" she asked.

"We have been told about you and I didn't think there would be another red-haired person in nurse's uniform," the other laughed. The news did not please Aileen, but the German nurse was in such good spirits it was contagious, and soon Aileen could not help but be in better spirits.

The captured English nurses were soon merged into the framework of the German ambulance. The leading surgeon told them he did not consider them prisoners. He was grateful for any help they could give but if they wished to return to the British lines, he had no objection. Of course, the circumstance must present itself and only when it was opportune could they go. It must cause no problems between the German Ambulance and their Boer hosts.

At the end of the week a small group of Uitlanders arrived at the hospital. They were wounded survivors of an attack by Rimington's Guides. They were on the veld as reconnaissance outriders for General Piet Cronje when they were confronted by the British riders engaged in the same task of intelligence gathering. There was a spirited shoot out and the English being more numerous won the day. It was notable the English mounted soldiers were adopting tactics which had been the preserve of the Boers. Many of the Light Horse companies were made up of colonials living in South Africa before the conflict and who, like many of the Rimington Tigers, spoke Afrikaans and some of the native languages.

There were three German commandos among the injured who were pleased to be in the hands of their compatriots for their care.

Aileen was renewing the dressings of a young Boer who had an uncomfortable night when she sensed the presence of someone behind her. She started.

"I'm sorry, sister, I did not mean to startle you." The bearded Commando supported by a crutch smiled widely. His teeth appeared whiter than white, enhanced by his dark facial hair and tanned skin.

"When I learned you were English nurses, I asked your colleagues for help, but they said it were best I asked for your assistance." His English though heavily accented was excellent and attractively cadenced.

"I wonder if you had perhaps met my sister in your time here in South Africa?"

Aileen stared at him with a strange, enjoyable dawning sense of delight. Could it be possible? Scarcely able to believe what was transparently happening she asked,

"What is your sister's name?"

"Greta Schopenhauer. I am Rudolph Schopenhauer," he said bowing his head.

"To my family and friends, I am Rudi. Please call me Rudi, Sister," he beamed.

Aileen knew her desire to talk was as intense as his, but her professionalism and her dedication dictated she should finish her rounds.

"I hope to finish in the wards mid evening, but I would love to tell you about Greta. We're close friends. Shall we meet say at eight?"

"With pleasure, Sister."

At a little after eight Aileen found Rudi waiting at the makeshift Nurses Quarters, she and the other captives had curtained off at the end of one of the three huge wards. They sat opposite one another at the board trestle table where the nurses had their snatched meals. He had come from the marquee which was the operating theatre but had been cleared for a diversion by the doctors, nurses and walking patients. The German ambulance members had been celebrating an impromptu Abwesende Freunde evening. He brought two minute carved wooden bier steins and a flask of cognac. At Aileen's frown he said, with a mock apology

"Please excuse me but I don't feel I should forego all pleasure in time of war" She couldn't resist smiling.

"You certainly don't possess one iota of Greta's earnestness."

"I lost mine when I left Germany to see the world. Besides, by nature the average native of Darmstadt does not incline toward sobriety. We do love life."

CHAPTER TWENTY-FIVE
Escape

Over the following days, when his visits became more frequent and the visits grew in time shared, Aileen began to feel different in her attitude toward him. At first, he had been an ambulatory patient, who was a pleasure to treat, due to his optimistic outlook and his gentlemanly behaviour. Then a friendship formed, seeded by the fact he was Greta's brother. Later, it was patently obvious he had stronger feelings toward her. She was not sure how she felt about this new development. She was not displeased by the attention; it was just she felt bound not to commit unless she had first let Greta know.

She had canvassed the other nurses about leaving and returning to the British lines. To her surprise they all were indifferent, if not averse, to the suggestion. Two had developed close friendships with members of the local Commando and one felt she could do more good staying with the German ambulance until the end of the war. She believed the Boers would have a greater need for nurses in the coming months when the British Army found its feet and turned up the pressure. Aileen could not gainsay the nurse's belief. However, she desperately wanted to see Greta again and to be among her own people. Then one evening Rudi surprised her with a heaven-sent suggestion.

"Hello Rudi. Whenever did you get those from?" she asked eyeing the loosely bound bouquet of blooms he held.

"I exchanged a packet of tea with one of the burgher's wives. Please don't say you would have preferred the tea?" He laughed.

"No, not at all. In fact come and sit and I'll make some."

"No thank you, Sister Aileen, I have brought something stronger. Schnapps."

"For once Rudi, do you mind if I joined you in a glass."

He must have been expecting something of the sort because he produced two shot glasses from his pocket. They sat together on the bench outside the hospital and sipped the jenever. After the first sip Aileen knew it was not for her, but manners dictated she did not pour the contents of the glass on the ground. Rudi was lost in thought and did not appear to notice her reluctance. For a time they sat in comfortable silence.

"Aileen, do you intend to sit out the war here?"

She turned to him but said nothing.

"I ask because I've reached a conclusion about my life. I've fought in two battles during my service here. My wounds and my nightmare at Belmont and Graspan have brought home to me just how slender one's chances are in an artillery barrage."

196

She nodded quietly and waited for him to go on.

"I came out here to fight against the arrogance of the British Empire and welcomed the opportunity to do so, especially since it suited my ideals. Perhaps, after hundreds of lyddite shells and torn bodies I am not so idealistic anymore." She placed a hand on his and waited patiently for him to continue. She understood it was not easy for him, but she was also conscious of a growing sense of excitement as she hoped the answer was in line with her intentions.

"The news my sister, my little sister, is here in South Africa also has influenced my thinking. I would dearly love to see her again before anything else happens. I will have no problem in resigning, other than the obvious guilt I will have when I do. There are no formal terms of service and they'll let me go, perhaps reluctantly, but with no recriminations." Aileen held her breath for a moment then whispered,

"I'll miss you."

He appeared not to notice as he concentrated on the next part of his explanation.,

"There will be two difficulties as I see it. If I am to see Greta I will be in danger of capture by the British and I've have heard they have prison camps all over the world in some desolate places for us." He lapsed into silence. She waited then asked quietly,

"And the second?"

He turned in his seat and placing his hand gently on her upper arm said.

"I can't leave you here."

As a member of the German Ambulance she was no longer someone of interest to the Boers. The number of fighters had drastically increased in the town and its surrounds. With the rise of activities and the social interaction in the evenings and into the night of the Commandos lodged in Jacobsdal, movement and noise was unavoidable.

The various groups had sentries on guard, but Rudi was confident that anyone coming from the town and going out into veld would be of a lesser interest than one approaching. Over the week he gathered the bedrolls, water bottles, food they would need and picked out the two Basutos they would take. He purloined an extra saddle and adjusted the stirrup leathers for Aileen. He had an extra coat and a slouch hat of indeterminate shape for her to wear.

It was dark and the cold was increasing when Aileen reached the lean-to behind the cottage where a crippled commando had set up a tavern of sorts. The windows to the bar were brightly lit. She heard a concertina and raucous singing, shouting and the occasional crash of upended furniture as she waited in the shadows.

The moon was full and there were wide swathes of shadow between the neighbouring buildings. Despite her highly charged state she was enjoying the music when the lightest touch on her shoulder startled her.

"With me, to the stable, there." Rudi said in a low whisper. "I've got the clothes for you in the stall. Put them on while I get the ponies out."

She put on the coat and found the hat dropped over her eyes. Rudi noticed and taking a handful of hay rolled into a band which he put into the hat. It fitted. They led the horses out, mounted and rode, slouched in their saddles, toward the outskirts and the town's perimeter.

"Halt friends," the call came from an armed youth in a small group of guards. "Which commando?" He sounded bored and almost disinterested.

"Johannesburg" slurred Rudi smothering a realistic hiccup.

"Have a good night and don't fall off," laughed one of the group. The group joined the laughter then lost interest almost immediately, returning to their previous conversation.

Two hours later they halted and stood for several minutes beside the mounts. There was, as they expected, no sign of pursuit. As Aileen raised her hands to mount, Rudi leaned in and kissed her neck. It was their first intimate touch. She turned and as he pulled her close, she raised up on her toes and found his lips with hers. His beard against her skin was abrasive and deliciously rough. She had expected it to be soft as down but the discovery it wasn't did not disappoint. The palms of his large hands were those of one accustomed to manual labour and the strength they possessed was evident when he cupped the back of her head and drew her face closer to his. He exuded raw power and it gave off an aura which was almost tangible. She smiled inwardly as she thought if she had been one to swoon this would be the time. The sensation bordering on ecstasy increased when he lifted her bodily and carried her to the mimosas lining the bank of the stream. They continued to kiss, feverishly and passionately, as they lay on the ground. His hands searched her body and the upsurging, intense emotion she felt was overwhelming. She felt his fingers fumbling with the buttons on the front of the trousers she was wearing. She ignored the apparent difficulty he was experiencing and wallowed in the anticipation. *They're men's trousers. He should have no problem.* She felt the cool night air on her buttocks as he pushed down the trousers and her undergarments and rolled over, so she was astride his supine body. He entered her and she filled with a sense of elation and threw her head back with a muffled scream of the coming fulfilment and — saw the two unattended Basutos trotting off in single file towards home.

It was much later when the recovery of the two ponies and the associated relief allowed them to burst into laughter. Both had the incongruous image of the chase with each naked below the waist calling, mostly ineffectually, to the walkaway ponies.

In the early evening one of the British outriders cantered up and announced two Boers had been seen and would reach then in ten or fifteen minutes. Marsh thought for several moments then ordered his men to assume defensive positions close to the stream with the horses below the level of the bank. The pair might be advance riders for a larger group.

The horsemen appeared to be moving toward the stream and if they did not change direction would reach the water just in front of the waiting group. As they drew closer Craven's attention was drawn to the smaller of the two Boers. There was something different in the posture and seat not quite right, but the thought passed. They halted and dismounted and led their ponies directly to where the hidden Tigers lay watching their approach. The taller of the two spoke to the other Boer and, to the surprise of the waiting soldiers, it was in English. They couldn't hear all the words precisely, but those they did hear were undoubtedly not Taal.

"We don't seem to have been followed, as least not yet. We'll water the horses and make coffee before we head toward the English hospital." said Rudi over his shoulder as he led the way.

"How do you think the soldiers will treat you, Rudi?"

"That might be a problem, but I intend to see Greta whatever I do and if the consequences are capture then I'll take the risk." After a short silence Aileen said,

"I'll tell them you are from the German Ambulance and are bringing me back to the British lines."

"Hm" said Rudi non committedly.

Aileen removed the wide brimmed hat and wiped her brow. As she did so ten or fifteen yards away five Tigers stood up with levelled rifles totally surprising the newcomers.

While Marsh interrogated the two Boers Craven could not take his eyes off the redheaded woman. He knew her. She wasn't a Boer! They had only spoken that night at the rail of the Dunottar Castle and in failing light, but her beauty left an unforgettable impression. Unless she had a doppelganger, this was Greta's partner from the Valkyrie saloon.

"What's your name, Miss?" asked Phillip.

"I am Sister Aileen MacLean. I am trying to return to my duty station at Number Four Field Hospital"

Her words were the decider. *How could I forget her voice?*

"Are you one of the four nurses taken from the hospital train? Where are the other nurses?"

"I am alone. We were together and helped the Boer wounded. Then the German Ambulance arrived in Westerlo and we could work with them. The others did not want to take the risk of travelling on the open veld. However, I felt I could do more back at Frere. My friend here, from the ambulance agreed to help."

Marsh and two of the tigers standing by restrained their smiles. It was obvious why the big German would offer to help. To this point Craven remained silent but then said,

"Can I have a word, Phillip? In private, please."

"Of course." They left the group and walked a few yards away to the trees closely watched by Aileen and Rudi.

"Phillip, strange as it seems, I know the woman."

Marsh grinned openly and said, in obvious disbelief,

"In the biblical sense, you mean."

"I'm serious, Marsh old man, we were in Canada, in Dawson City. If you are in doubt, ask her the name of the saloon she owned. It was called the Valkyrie."

"Colonel," replied Marsh in a serious tone, "your word is good enough for me. But it does create a problem. I can't take them with me on this operation."

"No, I can see that."

"Any thoughts?"

"I could escort them back to our lines?"

Marsh thought for a moment then nodded.

"Miss MacLean you have been vouched for by the Colonel here. He will escort you to our lines at De Aar." Aileen looked at Craven expressionless.

"Herr Schopenhauer your weapon will not be returned to you. You should be aware we are not convinced of your non-combatant status and therefore you will remain in custody. Provided you give us your word you will not commit any hostile act while in the care of Colonel Craven you will not be fettered."

"I have no option. You have my word. From the number in your party I think you form a reconnaissance. If your plan, is to scout out the forces around Westerlo I would warn you of the likelihood of a party of Boers in your path. They will have realised we have escaped and sent out commandos to bring us back. Not for us but the theft of the horses will be like a slap in the face. I suggest you take a roundabout route to the town to avoid contact."

Captain Marsh eyed Rudi reflectively but made no comment.

The Tigers scouting party rode off and Craven turned to Aileen and Rudi,

"We are a few days ride from our lines. We'll remain here until morning. Let's get the horses down the bank to the stream and watered. Then we'll make camp." He suggested Rudi should go first then followed. Once the horses had been tethered Craven suggested Rudi should fetch forage for the animals while he and Aileen made a fire and prepared hot food. Convinced that Rudi could be trusted, he did not intend to stand guard over him.

He knelt beside the wood and twigs Aileen had brought. He placed the longer pieces over the space of the two rocks he would use as an anvil and broke them into sizable shapes. Without a word Aileen cleared a small area below the level of an outcrop and piled an armful of dried grass on which to place the kindling to form a small pyramid. Craven watched, said nothing but mentally approved. He leaned forward to light the fire and noticed she was walking away.

"I need thicker pieces now,"

"Fine I'll keep this going but hurry. It's burning quickly." He busied himself with the fire and did not notice her stealthy look over her shoulder before she ducked down behind a clump of scrub.

She found Rudi returning with a huge armful of veld grass.

"Rudi, we've got to talk."

"Yes, I know." He put down the grass then sat on it. She ignored his gesture to sit with him.

"You understand they are not fools?"

"And I am not either. Do I think I have a chance of fooling them with my Dr Schopenhauer disguise? No, I don't, frankly. But I'm committed now and more than ever I want to see Greta." He paused, then added,

"Before anything else happens."

Together they realised the Colonel had approached and was no more than ten feet away. Both wondered if he had heard anything. They hoped he had not.

"Take the grass back and feed the animals. And if you would, Nurse, come help me find some more useable wood." he snapped.

It was apparent to them both he had heard.

As he led the way across the veld toward the British lines Colonel Craven was lost in abstracted thought. The object of his preoccupation rode behind him, followed by the Boer. Or German. Or whatever. He was not sure of his conflicted feelings toward the nurse. What was plain to him was the animosity he felt toward the mercenary which he reluctantly admitted to himself stemmed from the man's apparent closeness to her. When he first recognised her he experienced differing sensations. One was a pleasing mixture of unexpected happiness and disbelief. *Who would have thought someone who had been in his thoughts since the all too brief, fleeting moment on the Dunnottar Castle would appear on the veld wearing a Boer's mackinaw?* Then this delight was dashed when he saw the bond between the two which he assumed stemmed from sexual relations.

"Blast!" The exclamation exploded into the heat of the day causing Rudi to ride forward quickly and look at him questioningly. Craven flushed.

"It's nothing. Just thought of something distasteful and gave vent." Rudi nodded then dropped back.

Since she had been in captivity Aileen had assiduously boiled any water she intended to drink. She awoke before the two men and started a fire with the aim of first boiling up batches to fill their water bottles and to make the first coffee of the day. Already early morning sun was burning off the light mist hanging waist high above the river bank and the surface of the water. She walked through it down to the edge and filled the pan. On returning to the site she found a glowering Craven adding more brushwood to the blaze. He looked up as she approached and bade her a curt good morning before returning his gaze to the flames. She busied herself making the frugal breakfast by warming the hunks of round bread near the fire and carving thick slices from the salted bacon for each of them. Craven left and made his way to the river to wash followed shortly by a taciturn Rudi. She looked at the backs of the two men and shrugged.

He tore off a piece of bread and chewed stolidly while frowning at Rudi across the flames of the fire. There was no certainty the two were lovers at least so he told himself. The fact that he didn't want to believe it paradoxically made the likelihood a fact in his mind. The envy he had because of the German's closeness to Aileen was not the only reason he did not like the foreigner. His distrust of anyone coming from Boerland under such dubious circumstances was a factor. And yet there seemed to be a link between the two that, though subdued, was nonetheless in place. He wanted to trust Aileen but the head to head conversation between the two had created doubt. He wished he had caught the words of their conspiratorial interlude. He was confident that he was personally in no danger. But just what was the underlying bond?

They ate mostly in silence. When they had finished Craven collected the plates and dry washed them with sand nearby. Aileen watching had the inane thought that he was surprisingly like Rudi. If only he wouldn't sulk. Somehow, she felt the resemblance strangely erotic.

Rudi broke her chain of thought when he said without preamble,

"It might be longer but it's probably best to head west to the Riet then just follow it."

Craven said over his shoulder as he packed the plates into one of his panniers,

"And that would be in which direction?"

"Well, the sun is over there, it is mor—"

"I was being facetious. You're right. It's a good suggestion."

They had not unsaddled the horses the previous night in case they needed to move quickly. To preserve the energy of the animals they dismounted and rested frequently, allowing the mounts to graze on the tussocks of veld grass.

Craven could not help frequently snatching glances at his two companions and seeking signs of intimacy when they halted. His first thought on not seeing any was relief which evaporated immediately when he thought of the conspiratorial conversation back at the river. What did they intend doing?

The first globule of rain struck his hat brim like a large pebble causing him to look skyward and see the low black ceiling of heavy cloud for the first time. He rallied his senses and searched for shelter. Nothing was readily visible. The first wave of lighting sizzled across the open veld followed immediately by the explosive assault of noise on their eardrums.

Rudi was the first to dismount and urge his pony down to the ground where it stayed. He helped Aileen dismount then pushed her horse down so both animals lay parallel with a gap between. Unrolling his waterproof and holding it above his head he shepherded Aileen into the gap where they both hunkered down under the makeshift shelter. With difficulty Craven managed to ground his horse but had to be content by getting as close to the animal's side as he could with his knees up to his chin and water cascading off his hat.

Fergal's mind raced. To do what was asked would mean leaving the Brigade even though he would have the company of the dynamiters. His Wrecking Corps. But no, his place was with the majority of his men for whom he knew he had a greater responsibility.

Botha waited for his reply.

"I am afraid, although I would welcome the diversion, my place is with the Brigade. However, General, I have an excellent leader of men who is also a first-rate blaster. If agreeable to you when would they have to leave?"

"As with every requirement in this war, now but preferably before," said the General with a sour smile.

"Who does he report to when they get there."

"General de Cronje has overall command, but I think any targets selected will be down to General De la Rey."

Fergal left the presence of Botha with his mind in an excited turmoil and on a higher plane. He embraced the esteem his Brigade had achieved and the warmth of the praise from Botha, Trichardt and others was intoxicating. He determined there and then he, with his Brigade and his detachment of blasters, would cement glory into the folklore of the Boer struggle for independence.

". . .and it would be an ideal opportunity to show our hosts just how we are contributing to this war."

Cauley eyed Fergal shrewdly. He knew Fergal was sincere and nodded before asking,

"Will I be able to select the men I want? And who will make the arrangements for us to get there?"

"There'll be no objection to choosing who you want. I'll get with General Botha's administrative fella for passes as well as notifying the other end you'll be coming."

Three wagons with Boer drivers conveyed Cauley, his men, and their baggage together with the all-important boxes of dynamite, cordite, guncotton, and detonators to the rail head in Newcastle. Here they caught the train from Lourenco Marques when it stopped on its way to their destination of Johannesburg. The journey was boring and uncomfortable but the alcohol the men had purchased, in quantity, before boarding the train helped to alleviate the adverse aspects. They stayed for two days in Johannesburg before proceeding southwards. Cauley was angered and frustrated on the second day when he got the news two of the men 'were in the wind' having deserted. Fortunately, they were not part of the core group of experienced blasters. On the evening of the third day they embarked on the train taking them south to join General Cronje's forces. On this lap Cauley required they stay sober and the majority did so simply by falling asleep.

Cauley was called to join General De la Rey in the dining room of the Island Hotel. He walked through the poplar grove and across the well-kept lawn.

The General was apart from several others including De Cronje at another table. His new commander was reading a small pocket-book bible. Cauley removed his hat as the general rose and shook his hand while looking directly in the Irishman's eyes. After asking if he would like a coffee the small talk was cursory and brief.

De la Rey unfolded a map and identified the dispositions of the defending Boers on the banks of the Modder. He then identified the rail bridge across the Modder.

"Time is short. This must go. And quickly."

Cauley was confident he knew all there was to know about demolition. In addition, his blasters respected his leadership and expertise giving him of their best. The Wreckers were lodged in tents behind the hotel but before stowing their personal belongings they found the farrier, who was also in charge of horse allocation, to get their mounts for the operation. They were issued with saddles and bridles from the back of the stores wagon. More difficult was finding the armourer. They found him fishing in the Modder and he was not pleased at being disturbed. He returned with them to the weapons tent and, with poor grace, issued the requisite Mausers and rounds. Each then put away their personal baggage and reassembled near the hotel patio. Cauley selected the six "blasters" who would demolish the bridge and gave orders to mount up in ten minutes. At the appointed time they rode out to reconnoitre the bridge and decide how they would place the charges. The bridge had seven stone piers or columns which supported the girders carrying the rails. Cauley and two of his men walked the length of the bridge while the remainder of the group took up defensive positions and kept watch. At one stage they saw riders in the distance identifiable as British scouts who did not try to come closer after outlying Boer sharpshooters brought down two of their number.

The Brigade members finished their inspection and returned to base. Cauley opened the boxes and spent the next hour preparing the charges. During the hours of darkness, the dynamiters rode out in single file toward the bridge.

With the binoculars and his one good eye Colonel Craven was experiencing difficulty in focusing on the skyline. He braced his elbow against his abdomen. The others watched uneasily. To spare further embarrassment, Aileen asked,

"Might I have a look through them please, Colonel?" She pretended, while she was looking, to be unable to move the adjusting diopter. Craven leaned in close to move her fingers.

"Those are poplar trees around the building," she gave a small murmur of delight. "And lots of tents, too." The pseudo coyness vanished. She stiffened then handed the field glasses to Rudi,

"I think those are Boers."

He looked briefly then handed them to Craven,

"So do I."

The colonel returned the glasses to the case.

"It's probably best we wait for dark then strike out for the railway but on a diagonal line of march. Away from those poplars."

The wait for dusk was interminable. There was no shade other than that provided by their hats and turned-up collars. Craven controlled his fury, with difficulty but anger, at his own incompetence was still palpable. They had veered drastically off track and it was his fault. His jealousy had prompted him to relinquish the position of lead rider. The German and Aileen had been so engrossed in each other. Nothing concerned them. And he had followed, like a mindless troll marinating in his own petty envy. The hours of waiting seemed interminable. They kept a constant watch on the distant tents for movement in their direction. They stayed down but their worry was the horses and the danger some sharp-eyed Boer would glance across the veld, see their movement and ride out to satisfy his curiosity. At long last the sun's oblique rays lengthened the shadows and the long-awaited dusk fell. All three rose and stretched their limbs before mounting and, with Craven leading, set off wordlessly into the night.

Due to the open construction of the bridge Cauley decided to "go heavy" with gelignite. In reply to a question on the time needed to prep the bridge the blaster calculated four hours.

"We'll prep the rails up top then set charges on the girders," he explained to the group.

"I think we better leave the piers. The Orange Staters will want to re-build at some stage and we just want to stop the English getting across quickly any time soon." Cauley called for two men to unload the water tight boxes containing the guncotton slabs while he cut the powder hose into suitable lengths. Givens, his

American assistant, opened the red tin of detonators and prepared the primers. Gathering up the material they went onto the bridge while the others maintained all round defence. The blasters worked efficiently and silently with the occasional low toned instruction or question.

The night was still except for the occasional call of a foraging nocturnal mammal or a flying predator. The clouds had cleared, and the moon invested the veld with a clear blue light causing the scrubs, agitated by a growing berg wind, to wave and ripple in the cool night air. The various outcrops of rock took on dark threatening forms populating an alien planet.

The embankment leading to the bridge came into view. As they closed the distance to the river a bridge's silhouette, black and clear, stood out. Craven suddenly held out his arm to stop the others. He raised a hand and said,

"Listen."

"It's ready," came from Givens as he reached Cauley.

"How long are the fuses?"

"When I light them up, we have about three minutes to clear safe."

"Right, I'll get the others back here and wait until you give the word.

They held their breath as the shapeless mass of shadows separated in places and became human figures. The outlines of the wide brimmed headgear and distinct size and shape of the Basuto ponies clearly identified the riders. Despite the closeness of the newcomers they remained undetected as Cauley had gone back to the bridge to ignite the fuses. All eyes in both groups were on him

The sibilant hiss of the fuses was clearly heard as lines of brilliant, rapidly flickering light gnawed their way to the charges then simultaneously vanished. The following silence was brief, then creation erupted in a roaring, raging, brightly illumined fireball. Back lit by the explosion huge dark fingers of torn girder, slabs of shattered masonry and sleepers with remnants of rail populated the explosion.

Aileen and the two men struggling to control the rearing ponies heard the rush of air above their heads but were forced to ignore it in their efforts to quieten their steeds. A length of rail spinning end over end came scything through the air with a piercing whistling sound and impaled both Rudi and his pony before finishing like a quivering lance vertically in the ground. Simultaneously, the landscape was swathed in brilliant white light followed with scant pause by a deafening clap of thunder. A wind rose and immediately sheets of driving rain dredged across the veld.

Aileen screamed and tried to dismount to go to her friend. Craven who with one glance knew both pony and rider were beyond all help grabbed her pony's trailing reins and shouting "Hold fast" took off at the gallop down the river bank. The danger evident in galloping at full pelt across the darkened veld was clear to Craven but danger from the Boers even more so. After a mile he risked stopping to determine if the Boers were pursing.

The two horsemen in flight caused a furore among the blaster group. The deluge made it hard to be heard and Cauley had difficulty in restraining his men from following.

"Leave it. Come back," he roared at the trio who had actually started out after the riders. "Worse thing you could do is to go hammering into the dark after sods who could be waiting for you. And for what? Leave it and let's get back in the dry."

CHAPTER TWENTY-SIX
Safety

Aileen sat astride the Basuto with slouched shoulders and hanging head. Her eyes were blank and unseeing. It would be pointless giving her the reins back. Craven sighed and turning Remus into the wind led Aileen's pony to continue southward. The going proved hard and both animals had stumbled several times giving rise to the fear of broken equine bones. Remus had fallen heavily once but appeared uninjured. The storm had just shown signs of abating when the Basuto and its rider tripped and rolled heavily into a hidden donga.

Craven dismounted and scrabbled hurriedly down into the gully. There was at first no sign of Aileen and the Basuto was struggling in the pool of water. He caught sight of her face down, like a bundle of clothes, on the surface and wading across lifted her face clear of the water. Although conscious she remained inert and made no effort to stand. Craven pulled her toward the edge. Devoid of expression she remained in the position he put her and gazed sightlessly into the growing light.

He waded over to the Basuto still in the water struggling unsuccessfully to stand. It floundered on one side with its head raised to look at him. He saw the shattered fetlock as the bone ends jutting through the animal's skin shone white. He knelt in the water beside the doomed pony and murmured words of comfort as he held her head steady and placed the muzzle of his pistol in her ear.

Despite his strength, it was no easy task. He struggled to carry Aileen's limp form up and out of the steep, slippery sloped donga. He placed her against Remus' side and conveniently she remained standing as he mounted. Reaching down he pulled her dead weight up and onto the saddle in front of him grateful that she was wearing trousers. He reached behind him and unfastened his bed roll which he placed around her shoulders. There was little or nothing he could do about her sodden clothes and soon she began to shiver violently as he held her close. He nudged Remus into movement and walked into the coming dawn.

Aileen was treated by Methuen's medical officer then put into the care of one of the nurses attached to the accompanying Field Ambulance. Craven tried to see her but was told Lord Methuen wanted to see him before he did anything else.

The pale opaque eyes viewed the Colonel with frosty disdain.

"Colonel I won't mince words. I don't know if *your* General will be satisfied with what you have accomplished here but I am certainly not.

Once you have passed on any intelligence you may have from your escapade you are free to return to Frere. There are despatches personal for General Buller that you will deliver. Dismissed."

Craven controlled the impulse to smile. He stood, replaced his hat, saluted and with a curt "General" he left the tent.

He found the doctor as he was finishing his rounds and leaving one of the tented wards. After a hurried greeting Craven asked about Aileen.

"She has concussion and all the signs of fungal pneumonia. Her fever is rising rapidly. My hope is it will have stabilized by tomorrow. The hospital will be moving forward any time now and I want to get her to Wjnberg as soon as possible. I'll be sending her down on tomorrow's train. I'm glad you are here because I need to examine you before we do anything else."

Craven proved to be free of infection and as he dressed, he made his mind up to board tomorrow's train, make sure Aileen was in good hands and then travel north report to General Buller. But before he departed, he had one more thing to do.

Colonel Rimington was out on an extended reconnaissance with his full complement of Tigers. Craven would have liked to have seen them before he left but that was not to be. The fact they were all out in the field as a unit was significant. The battle that the General Lord Methuen considered to be the final push in the relief of Kimberley was obviously about to take place.

Craven wanted to accompany Aileen on the train to Cape Town but the Medical Officer for the train was adamant that he could not. The likelihood that her pneumonia was contagious. was high.

He readied Remus for the journey south and waited for the train.

BATTLE OF MAGERSFONTEIN

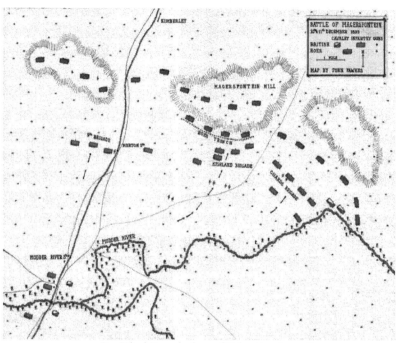

By Kind Permission of John Fawkes of
https://www.britishbattles.com

CHAPTER TWENTY-SEVEN
Magersfontein

De la Rey was a commanding figure. His aquiline nose, deep-set eyes, and neatly trimmed beard, unlike the full-face adornments of his fellows in arms, gave his presence dominance in any company. Added to this, his total command of language, together with the art of dramatic pauses, ensured complete attention from any audience. His proven military talents imbued with fresh, original thinking. added to his stature among the Boers. This was not to the liking of General De Cronje, hero of the First Boer war, and his superior. They frequently disagreed and the plans to bar the British progress to Kimberley would cause yet another clash.

"It is ludicrous to keep fighting from the tops of kopjes and even worse to try to defend so near to their objective of Kimberley. We must be prepared to defend every inch and inflict so much damage they pay dearly for each one gained."

De Cronje's attitude and tone revealed patronising derision when he asked in response,

"We have agreed our strategy, but will you tell us your plan, please, General Koos?"

"It is our last chance to stop them. Our weapons should be surprise and decisive volleys of fire. Their artillery hammers our defences because they know where we will be. We know their reconnaissance is feeble and believe the weakness should also be to our advantage."

224

He spent the next forty minutes outlining his plan, which he admitted differed vastly from their previous mode of defence. De Cronje was not convinced. De la Rey left the meeting but immediately contacted President Steyn, who, after conferring with the ailing President Kruger, received support for the proposal to go personally to see and hear for himself. He arrived and ordered a new war council speaking with De Cronje and De la Rey at length. The younger General forcibly put forward his plan again. The upshot was the proposed battle plan would be implemented.

It was no easy matter to effect the changes, but De la Rey exercised the dynamic control only he could bring to bear. The first step was to abandon the defensive positions at Spytfontein and move four miles nearer to the British to Magersfontein. The ubiquitous labour force of African labourers began work, at a furious rate, on the ten-mile crescent shaped line of trenches. The curved line of trenches had an additional feature. Each represented a wavering S shape so if a fortuitous shell landed in one end the occupants at the other would have an earth work protection. These short ditches could hold six riflemen spaced so they did not form a straight line easily detected by the opposing side's scouts. Six days later they were complete.

Methuen's plan to march by night to the attack positions lacked originality. It also did not pass the notice of the Boers. Yet again, intelligence was so weak as to be non-existent. The Tigers who had reconnoitred the area had been successfully stymied by Boer sharpshooters and had failed in spying out the land in front of Magersfontein. They reported there was evidence of the Boers but had no numbers and certainly no precise idea of the Boer positions. Methuen had turned down the use of a spotter balloon sent up the line by Buller.

The British artillery rained hundreds of lyddite shells on the sides of Magersfontein and its subsidiary kopjes—the deserted, empty, Boer free sides. The effect of the barrage did little or no damage but served as a thunderous warning to the Boers that an attack by infantry was imminent.

The night prior to the battle lightening flashed down and across the veld. The silhouettes of the surrounding kopjes sprang into focus then disappeared until the next blitz. Sharp splinters of sleet stung as well as drenched the soldiers marching to the front in the dark trying to avoid, the ant hills, holes and thorn bush impeding their passage. Ropes, knotted at regular intervals to maintain cohesion in the dark, were not altogether efficient.

The dawn before the battle opened dark, wet and windy. Then the sky cleared and the outline, then the solid shape, of Magersfontein became visible. With the British finally in position a thousand yards from the hill the order to advance rang out.

The crack of the first round from the Boer side was a clarion call for the host of Mausers to fire in unison and chop the Highland Brigade down where it stood. The violent torrents of bullets sweeping the plain felled all in their path. The strategy De la Rey had devised and implemented was diabolic in its logic and simplicity.

Magersfontein was not invested by the Boers. Their stand would be made several hundred yards forward of the hill. Trenches, dug to a depth facilitating upright firers, hidden by frontal camouflage of rocks, wattles, scrub, and grass, would provide cover for the riflemen. Two additional advantages of this positioning was to eliminate the hit and miss occasioned by firing down-slope at advancing troops. With this method the level flight of the lead had a strong possibility of hitting a following target should the rifleman miss the first. Also the low trajectory of the bullet retained more force at greater distances. The advantage of smokeless rounds was already well known to both sides. Before the enemy had time to recover from his initial surprise it would be all over.

De la Rey had factored in the knowledge this special positioning of his burghers would also deter the less brave Boer combatants from leaving the front prematurely since many of them no longer had mounts.

The British had no time to waver. The herd instinct, this time flooded with thought blocking panic and confusion, took hold. The ranks broke and for many even the automatic reflex action to drop to the ground or duck, failed. The fusillades continued to pour into the mêlée of disoriented kilted warriors. Bemused by the suddenness of the onslaught and the conflicting orders given by their equally befuddled officers and NCOs some crawled forward, in the vain hope, of bringing the fight to the unseen enemy. Others sought a measure of shelter behind the anthills and rocks. Many attempting to flee to the rear were brought down by a deadly wall of Boer fire. Almost miraculously some sense of order reasserted itself and the clusters of men reformed into recognisable groups, but these remained in a state of checkmate and incapable of further forward movement.

The sun rose. The light from the blazing rays conspired to pin each man in position, a display of petrified moths, on the open plain. Any movement or even a wounded twitch drew the merciless Boer fire; an attempt to scratch, to lift a water bottle to parched lips or even easing position in an attempt to divert the corrosive heat from bare legs prompted a withering fusillade. Naked skin erupted into painful rashes and vesicles from the burning intensity of the sun. Each Highlander was a small rudderless boat becalmed on the sea of the African veld. The air held the relentless heat for the next seven hours.

The participation of the British field guns which moved into rifle range offered a glimmer of hope to the beleaguered Scottish troops. Lord Methuen, in a cart close to the winches, ordered the aerial reconnaissance balloon into the air. Communication was by a telephone line extended hundreds of feet down to earth. Although the extent of the Boers defensive line was now evident the knowledge could do nothing to change the status quo. This time the Boers signature ploy of hit and run was not put into the action. Firmly entrenched, the Boers line would hold and continue to dominate the field.

As the day wore on and the balloon's shadow extended the shade over Methuen's wagon his thoughts also darkened. Mentally he tried to compose his despatch to Buller, but the day had not yet delivered the final humiliation for the unfortunate 1st Division. The stillness, heavy with underlying tension, among the trapped soldiers had developed into forced ennui. Suddenly, orders to move forward rang out but had an adverse effect. The subjugation of communal fear which had enabled them to hold fast splintered and hundreds took to their heels and fled the battlefield. Officers with pointed pistols and kicks ineffectually threatened and cajoled the men into some return of order but disarray reigned.

The collapse was seized upon by the Boer rifles and many of the Highlanders were shot in the back as they ran helter-skelter to an out-of-reach safety.

From his headquarters on a hill their General watched the rout impassively. His assured victory had evaporated with the destruction of his redoubtable Division. His hope that during the night the Boers might re-group elsewhere and allow his advance toward Kimberley to continue was proved feeble and fatuous. De la Rey with his Boers firmly entrenched and with minimal casualties had no intention of withdrawing. Badly mauled, Lord Methuen relinquished the field.

CHAPTER TWENTY-EIGHT
Before Colenso
Fergal

I sat on a bench outside the schoolhouse with General Botha and watched General Meyer, only recently his superior officer, arrive in the company of two other commanders General Erasmus and General Kock. I was not there to attend the meeting and would not be in the room with Commandant General Piet Joubert. I had travelled with Botha as he wanted to move against the British as soon as possible after the conference. I felt a flush of pride when I learned he continued to value my newly found expertise in the levelling of bridges and destruction of rail lines.

The greetings between the generals were hearty and obviously the recent victories buoyed everyone's morale. Like their men they wore no uniforms, so their badges of rank were not material but had to be in the eyes of the beholder. They had to exude leadership by posture, intelligence, and example. Previous demonstrations of personal courage helped. My impression was they were all worthy of the trust placed in them by President Kruger and the Boer nation. In the last few weeks mistakes had been made but lapses by the enemy nullified most of them as the British proved to be vulnerable despite their reputation of infallibility. And in defence of the Boers there was little a newly baked general could do when hundreds of his men broke ranks, mounted up and en masse fled well prepared defence bastions. In the face of a baptismal barrage from the deep throated guns of the British many other armies had crumbled. Lyddite shells could shake many a man's nerve. Something I knew personally.

The small but growing gathering of commandos parted and gave way to two riders on lathered horses. One, recognising the General, did not dismount but handed down a letter to Botha who on reading it said

"General Piet has been delayed. They are resting for an hour or two. We won't be in session for a while yet. Why don't we use the time to share our views so we will not be ignorant of the opinions held by each of us? I suggest a jug of coffee and we take our places inside.

This is Menheer Fergal Boyle who is with the Irish Brigade out of Johannesburg. He's proving to be an asset. You can join us, at least until Oom Piet arrives." I nodded to the group and smiled my thanks at General Botha. Minutes later, after chatting informally, all took their places at the table. I occupied a chair in a corner and considered myself an observer. I obviously could not follow everything said since my knowledge of the Taal was basic, but I managed the gist of most of it.

Botha opened the discussions.

"I'd like to offer a word of praise, in his absence, to Commandant General Joubert, for his foresight in having organised the detailed mapping of the territory soon to be our stalking grounds for the months ahead. I can't see the British being so well equipped."

"And for ensuring most of us will fight in the area we come from," put in General Meyer

"It is an advantage we should maintain. We need to concentrate on preventing their scouts' intelligence gathering. Make it ineffectual by shooting down each and every one."

They carried on covering many aspects of the coming hostilities that were news to me but made it clear all were thinking men. Their appreciation was wholehearted, when it was pointed out by Botha, the initial delay in the invasion was justified as a logistical decision, since it provided sufficient time for the seasonal growth of grass thus allowing ample grazing for their ponies.

Outside the noise of the crowd, eager to see the Commandant General, was growing. When cheers erupted it was evident he was in sight. We all got up as one and left the room to stand in the playground to welcome our chief. An exuberant but not raucous chorus of the Transvaal national anthem filled the air as the General rode among the hat waving multitude.

Piet Joubert appeared tired and did not look well. I had not realised he was so old. His visage was grey, and his huge spade of a beard did little to hide it. The journey from Modderspruit, a good day's ride from the school, would tire a younger man, but was not, I was sure, totally responsible for his tiredness and the obvious signs of ill health. Although not invited my curiosity prompted me to return with the others and go back to my chair in the corner. My presence was not remarked upon. Once he was seated the others took their places. He opened a satchel, removed some papers, and began.

On the ride back to the Krugersdorp commando Botha was quiet. I assumed he was unhappy about the overall strategy Joubert had set out. The complete plan of action was one of defence and allegedly motivated by the older man's determination not to sacrifice his men unnecessarily. He had categorically refused to allow the Commandos to pursue the British. He considered the recent successes the will of God but believed to go further was challenging fate. His subordinate Generals were all for following up and breaking through to Durban to capture the port facilities and thus establishing their supply line to the outer world. Before General Joubert made his position clear, Botha may have been overly jocular by saying he could eat bananas in the city within a week. The revelation the strategy would be to enforce the siege of Ladysmith and abstain from offensive action dumbfounded his listeners.

"Has the General lost the will to wager total war, do you think, General?" I asked to break the silence.

Botha shot me a look of undiluted savagery.

"You know nothing of his worries and troubles," he snapped. It was some time before he spoke again, in a more conciliary tone.

"He is deservedly one of our heroes. When he was in his prime, he fought in the first war and trounced them at the Hill of Doves and Laing's Nek. He was a founder of our Republic. He loves our land and genuinely wishes our borders could be expanded. We owe our armaments and Mausers to his preparedness and dedication when he was in charge of the Transvaal's War Department. I supported him when he was openly against the rush to war and believed further negotiations could achieve acceptable results without bloodshed."

He lapsed back into thought.

"I believe he still thinks we can bring them to the negotiating table by showing we have the will, determination and can conduct a war of independence. No one wants peace more than we do. And we would share it with them."

He paused again then said,

"Our hatred for them is not as fierce or unrelentless as yours."

I was not shocked but rather subdued into silence by the explanation.

"At least not yet." he finished.

BATTLE OF COLENSO

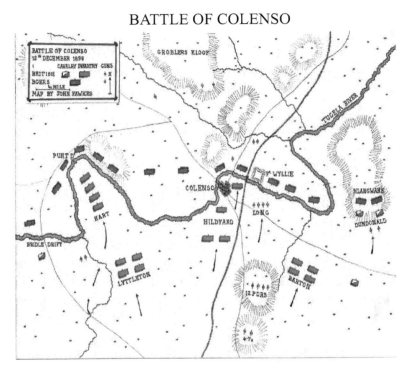

By Kind Permission of John Fawkes of
https://www.britishbattles.com

CHAPTER TWENTY-NINE
Colenso

Botha, sitting in the back of the 'spider' put down his coffee and stepped to the rear of the wagon to watch the approach of the rider.

"Commandant, a message from the President."

Botha leaned out and took the folded paper from the youth.

"Thank you. Rest your horse and get some refreshment."

The rider still waited.

"There will be no reply."

Botha at thirty-seven had proved his worth as General Meyer's deputy. The young general, already second in command to General Joubert, had been expecting this telegram, ever since the older man's horse had nearly crushed the life from his elderly body. In the first few lines Botha read he was now in command of all Boer forces in the invasion of Natal.

He had proven himself to be an energetic and resourceful officer and now he would be able to use his talents in pursuit of the war as he saw it. His main task would be to halt the British attempt to reach Ladysmith. He knew the route they would take, and he knew the most natural barrier on which to stage a defence. He would lose no time in doing so. Further reconnaissance to identify every detail of the lie of the land and preparation of defences were only part of the huge task ahead. The line in the sand where the Imperialists would be halted was not too distant from his present location.

The Tugela River.

It could scarcely be categorised as a village or even a hamlet, with a total of three houses and a bed-and-breakfast masquerading as a hotel. Its location on the Durban to Ladysmith railway line, and the arrival of General Buller, gave Frere, this mote of corrugated metal, an unexpected prominence. The Stationmaster's house had been looted and desecrated by the Boers who had occupied Frere previously. Cleared and refurnished it became General Buller's Headquarters with his Army of four brigades. The associated hustle and bustle of twenty thousand men, infantry, mounted troops, and support units, including the naval gun and searchlight crews, changed the location from a nondescript backwater to an armed urban centre.

There were no chairs in the converted dining room. The commanders and the second in command of each Brigade were gathered round the dining room table. Buller entered and went straight to the map spread on its surface.

"Gentlemen, good morning. My news for you this morning is I have decided not to pursue a crossing at Potgieter's. A despatch from

238

Magersfontein has influenced the change but there are other severe disadvantages associated, mostly logistical, for crossing there. A bridgehead at Colenso will be no easy accomplishment but it will be the lesser of two evils. I won't engage your time itemising them but will go directly to assigning your Brigade's tasks for forcing a passage at Colenso. Now, look at this map."

All eyes were directed down onto a Field Intelligence Map. This was a one-inch to one-mile blueprint spawned from faulty and incomplete intelligence gathered under extreme conditions, a rough draughtsman copy of a rail maintenance map, and a minute map on rice paper courtesy of a carrier pigeon from Ladysmith. Large areas were annotated 'These empty spaces do not show flat ground but rather lack of detail.' Buller stepped back from the table.

"Yes. It is virtually useless. Our intelligence gathering has been on par with this rubbish. The Boers have been bird dogging our scouts very closely. Many have not returned." He returned to the map.

"It shows, however the location of possible crossings essential to our success. The Tugela forms a formidable defensive line. There are several miles of flat open ground in the approach on the southern side. This is augmented by a line of kopjes, in close proximity to the river bank, on the northern side. The banks on that side are steep. There are five fords or drifts where crossings can be accomplished. There are two bridges; the railway bridge, now defunct since the Boers have demolished it and the road bridge which is still standing. The river creates a salient here at this point." A thick index finger traced the northerly pointing curve of the promontory. "Gentlemen, the Tugela is not an impregnable obstacle. Not easy but not impossible. Now, my two flanks will be protected by Colonel Burn-Murdoch on the left and Colonel Lord Dundonald on the right. General Hildyard, with the support of Colonel Long's 12 pounders, you will cross here." He pointed to the Old Wagon drift holding Hildyard eyes until the General nodded and murmured "Sir."

"General Hart, will carry out a left flanking movement here, crossing this."

Hart leant closer and read aloud, "Punt drift," then nodded saying, "Understood."

"The heavy artillery, the naval guns, will lay on from the rear."

The gigantic task of fortifying the line of the mighty Tugela began. Although an obstruction impeding movement, the fast-flowing Tugela in of itself would not bar the progress of a determined Army. Fifteen miles of gun emplacements, both real, and false as decoys to draw fire, camouflaged trenches for riflemen, again actual and pseudo, and all created through hard digging among the boulder clusters on the hillsides.

Although both sides had tacitly agreed to limit the fighting to white participants, a more fluid position was taken by each combatant to the free use of black manual labour. A myriad of African labourers dotted the northern kopjes for fourteen days of intense preparation fortifying the Boers position. Sandbags and broken rock were used for the defences in the kopjes and zig-zag camouflaged trenches on the flat ground at the bottom of the hills. Botha deployed his burghers on the northern side of the river and invested the commanding Hlangwane Mountain, the only Boer position on the southern side, with two Commandos.

In the early hours of the December night the Boers observed flurries of light which implied movement in the British camps. When dawn broke, they saw the British contingents were forming in the small hills five miles from what was to be the front line.

The opening of the battle provided one of the aberrations determining defeat or victory and emphasised the narrow margin of fortune between them.

Hlangwane, with its own defence of miles of impenetrable thick scrub covering the surrounding approaches, was not to the liking of the Orange State burghers. The dense vegetation would impede a rapid withdrawal and their compatriots were on the other side of the

Tungela. With the opening barrage of the battle by the British naval guns the defenders of Hlangwane took flight and abandoned their position and crossed to the opposite side of the river. Botha was furious but the disciplinary system of the Boer forces, based on free will and independence of the individual, were such he could not order them to hold. It was a blessing for the Boers the British were unaware the mountain was devoid of defenders. At this point Botha contacted President Kruger by telegraph and the answer exhorting the Boers to re-occupy and hold the mountain at all costs worked beyond Botha's hopes. The recalcitrant burghers returned to their former posts. Buller had lost the opportunity of using Hlangwane for enfilading fire on the Boers' left flank.

The guns of the Boers did not respond to the barrage causing doubts that they still constituted a presence across the river. Botha had been adamant. Not a shot would be fired until he gave the order when the British were within easy rifle range. His plan was not purely defensive. He intended, at a suitable stage in the battle, to turn his two outlying flanks inwards like a Zulu 'horns of the buffalo' pincer movement. When the British were on his side of the Tugela pushing on his centre, the extremities would converge and destroy them completely. He envisaged his enemy crossing the wagon bridge, deliberately left standing, and forming en masse to his front and centre.

On the three-hundred-foot kopje next to the platform of a 5-inch howitzer, courtesy of Krupp, General Botha watched the advance of the enemy. The Boer trenches and gun emplacements already knew the signal to open fire would come from this German armament. An integral aspect of the battle plan was to lure the British into pockets or traps from which they would be able to escape only with great difficulty.

Buller and a small group, including, General Clery and the Senior Medical Officer sat astride their horses on the slight rise to the left of the mound which accommodated two 4.7 naval guns. Through their glasses it was becoming clear the vaunted lyddite shells, because of their constrained area of impact, were not effective against the defenders' widely spaced positions.

A further series of more deadly errors dogged the British advance. Four thousand men were tightly bunched as the guide with the leading elements of Hart's advancing troops veered away from Bridle drift, the intended ford on the left, and led them instead toward Punt drift in the loop. Within minutes the British ranks were decimated by the three-sided maw of hundreds of Mausers unleashing a deadly cross fire. Those still upright received the brunt of the Creusot shell which landed in their midst. The final indignity was those men who had managed to reach the intended ford were ordered back into the maelstrom by Hart.

Botha, three miles away watched in flabbergasted surprise as, leading the advancing infantry by hundreds of yards, was a group of limbered field guns, jockeying into position to fire from short range. These were led by a brave, impulsive but foolhardy Irish colonel. Botha, realising the immense damage to his defences they would cause immediately jettisoned his original plan and ordered the howitzer to fire. His riflemen, who had been champing at the bit and were silently willing him to give the signal, opened a devastating volley directly into the artillery crews and their horses. The Light Horse, who had advanced on the right were chopped down by a murderous enfilading fire from Mount Hlangwane. The cries of the wounded were drowned by the screams and terrified neighing of the butchered steeds.

The indiscriminating whine of bullets added to the blood-soaked fracas. The remaining men still standing struggled to prevent the rearing and terror-stricken animals bolting from bedlam. All failed.

"I can't understand what the hell he is doing?" Buller said aloud. Damn!"

Colonel Long's men fought on, but they could not be re-supplied with shells and retreated to the shelter of a nearby donga. The General Lord Dundonald was stymied at the base of Hlangwane and although Hildyard had broken through to the village of Colenso the Boers field of fire on two sides made it an impasse or hollow achievement. The naval guns, which had followed the doomed gunner, though a relatively safe distance to the rear, were still in action but pinioned to immobility by the carnage that had destroyed their horses.

Botha was moving up and down the line shouting encouragement to his burghers and frequently returning to the gun positions. From this vantage point his attention was drawn to a close group of horsemen behind the British lines. The fire of the majority of his men was directed at the abandoned guns on the salient. He joined the men on the Krupp 5-inch howitzer and called to the master gunner.

"Gerrit, the group on the mound, the horsemen. Near the heavy artillery."

"Got them, General."

"Can you lay a sight on them and drop one in their midst?"

"We can do one close if not exactly."

"Do so. Now."

The gunner ran back to the howitzer, adjusted its angle of trajectory and prepared to fire.

I can't order men into this meat grinder. It's voracious. A bloody tragedy of my own making. Not evaluating the competence of my commanders before entrusting them—

Both he and his horse seemed to rise clear of the ground as all around him men and mounts were bludgeoned by a gigantic invisible sledge. The surface of the ground exploded upwards, vomiting and scattering earth, flesh and rags in all directions. For seconds he was transported back to the lower meadow on the estate at Crediton, where when seeking shelter under the oak from the rain, lightning flared slicing the huge trunk in three burning staves. The ground had shook then, the accompanying thunder added to the terror and he was thrown from his shying pony.

His deafened eardrums created a ringing silence. The numbness from the hammer blow to his torso deadened his senses. He looked around him slow to realise a Boer Krupps had found the group with devastating effect. A direct hit.

His glazed eyes took in the grotesque figure on the ground to his right astride two halves of a horse. Somehow his blunted senses relayed the sight to his brain. It was of his physician. He only knew it was Doc Hughes because he recognised the boots. The captain's head and one shoulder were missing. Sluggishly, he looked down and just as slowly his brain interpreted the significance of the rent in his tunic made by shrapnel from the shell.

The problem of the guns remained. The value of the lost guns to the Boers would be great but the associated shame would be immense. Added to the failure of the attack, his attack, the recriminations from members of his staff, and he could see them plainly in his mind, and of course his voluble critics in the press at home, would be severe. He would be finished.

Buller gave the order to withdraw. It appeared to him further bloodshed could not outweigh any meagre advantage gained. He accepted on this occasion the Boers were immoveable. He mounted Biffin and rode forward to join Hildyard and attempt to retrieve the guns.

Dismounting causes an involuntary grunt which helps to stifle the pain in my ribs. I go over to the cluster of junior officers and men from Hildyard's command. The strangest feeling courses through me. Close to happiness, joy. . . euphoria!.

It's my wound – and surviving death that's triggered it. The doubts are gone, those crushing moments of doubt, delaying every decision, vacillating and re-thinking each command. The fear dominating my actions has disappeared. The funk prompting the "What if?" scenarios is no longer with me.

"Right lads, this is the last chance to rescue those guns. Where are my volunteers?" I point to the sad cluster of cannon. The only sign of life out there is from the few pitiful creatures, whose escape from the terror traumatising them, is prevented by the tethers that shackle them to the limbers.

247

Six other ranks, the senior a corporal, leave their companions and come over. They won't be enough. I turn to my surviving staff but before I can say a word, three junior officers step forward. I thank them for volunteering. My plan is to recover the guns two at a time and they understand at once then busy themselves for the recovery. The other ranks hook up two teams while the officers hold the horses' heads then back them into the limbers.

They waste no time. It worries me that young Roberts has volunteered. We've kept him away from direct action. He was due to go to Ladysmith but that was before the Boers sealed the place off. Clery has him on his staff but since the General, with his men, is part of the order of battle, here he is. It's a conundrum because if I pull him out of this action it will be blatantly obvious then, that who he is and who his father is, guarantees special favours. No, he's checkmated any idea of side-lining him.

Looks quite chipper there with no obvious sign of concern for what happens next. Fooling around and looking positively joyful.

Captain Congreve mounts one of the horses. Freddy Roberts is nonchalant and jocular to the point of idiocy but the veterans among us know it's a form of fear control and acceptable under the circumstances. Freddy is always jovial and carefree. He is accepted as a good "brick" by his fellow officers and although he's known to be a featherweight his family ties do not appear to affect his actions. His attempt at the recently formed Staff College examinations resulted in abysmal scores scuppering any serious progress much beyond his present rank. Wolseley made a grudging concession to General Roberts. Should Freddy show extreme courage in action that bravery might offer another chance. Roberts senior reluctantly accepted this but did not forget he had had to grovel to Wolseley with whom he shared a mutual hatred. Field Marshall Lord Roberts is not of a forgiving nature.

They're off and Freddy is looking back over his shoulder at Schofield laughing and twirling his stick in imitation of a jockey at Ascot. Young fool.

In the Boer trenches it was obvious the British are about to try to recover the guns. Hundreds of rifle bolts pushed rounds into breeches and enemy cheeks nestled against cold metal. Sharp eyes selected targets which are predominantly horses as riders could be brought down later at leisure.

The firing started immediately the rescuers left safety. All round the galloping horses thousands of spits and spurts of dust erupted from the dry veld. The fire intensified and the firers achieved greater accuracy.

Despite the nearness of the guns, I have difficulty in making out the figures through the haze and dust as they approach their objective. My vision clears as Freddy is struck and falls from his horse. Congreve is hit too and his horse crashes to the ground. He is thrown just short of the guns. I see Freddy writhing, obviously in pain, but thankfully alive. Two of the guns are limbered and come helter-skelter towards us. My last view of Captain Congreve is as he crawls toward the shelter of a donga and disappears over the lip. Freddy has stopped moving. I can't take my eyes away from the abattoir in the dust.

As expected, the Boers redoubled their efforts to deter or destroy any further attempts. The devil aided their efforts and the haze which had hampered them to a degree earlier lifted.

The next team out was blocked. A further try was made with three teams, but twelve horses were downed, one rescuer killed and five wounded. Buller refused to allow any more attempts. His reluctance to sanction more savagery overwhelmed him. He could not accept any recommendations to attempt the recovery after dark. Enough was enough.

The General stayed on the battlefield until he felt sure the last of the troops had withdrawn safely. The news of the further failure of trying to take Hlangwane, through the waist high thorny scrubs, and its rocky nether slopes by Dundonald's mounted troops was yet another blow.

Unfortunately, not all of survivors had left the abattoir of Colenso. Surrounded by maimed horses and butchered bodies of men Congreve, despite the wound in his leg and the wounded Freddy whom he found unconscious and dragged, reached a small donga. It was already occupied by twenty or more soldiers. He shaded Freddy's head with his coat. His friend had been shot in the stomach and had two other wounds.

In the late afternoon, a group of Boers approached the donga and from a distance called upon the occupants to surrender. The senior officer present refused, and a fire fight erupted. Then during a lull, the Boers, under a white flag, suggested a short truce while the wounded were cleared to safety. During the negotiations, and unseen by the men in the donga, about a hundred Boers with levelled rifles came up behind. The commander and all the unwounded were taken into captivity while the wounded were allowed to leave in the care of the medics who had arrived.

Despite Captain Congreve's efforts on behalf of his friend, Freddy Roberts died of his wounds. He was the recipient of a posthumous award of the Victoria Cross, recommended by General Buller, for his conspicuous gallantry under fire from the enemy.

Long's impetuosity would cost him his life and the attempt to recover the abandoned guns would be filled with dashing but fruitless bravery and death. Only two of the twelve guns were recovered, and the ten remaining became the property of the Boers whose gunners would use them against their foe in the not too distant future.

Botha's undoubted victory, with minimal losses, his undeniable talent for war, his intelligence, energy, and inherent wiliness would ensure his place among the heroes of his people. Aspects of his approach to the strategy and tactics of war, of originality, freshness and application were talents that were sadly lacking in the British leadership in the field. The British dogma that wars can be won by numerical superiority and unlimited supplies was no longer infallible. Its result here, as in the coming World War, would never be swift and the price invariably high. Some lessons are never learned.

CHAPTER THIRTY
The Wounded

The hospital was to move. They helped the loading of the hospital equipment and medical stores onto the wagons and then, after a short distance, their removal to the train. Tents, panniers, boxes of all sizes, motley sacks represented the hospital in its unassembled form.

As the last wagon rolled away Greta, together with Daisy and Sister McCaul, who despite her new friendly disposition did not allow the use of her first name, climbed onto the scotch cart. The mule studiously ignored them. Greta looked over the now empty expense of veld. Although deserted there was ample evidence of the Army that had occupied the space before her. The site of each of the thousands of tents was delineated by a pale rectangle of suffocated grass. No doubt it would revive and grow quickly hiding the scars of occupation. It would take longer for the recovering veld to hide the litter and debris of ripped and crushed cardboard boxes, rusty cans, and crumpled biscuit tins which stretched as far as the eye could see.

As the nurses boarded the train the boom of the cannon, complemented by the echo, as they shelled the Boer trenches across the Tungela, rolled like spasmodic thunder. It seemed far closer than it was although the guns were sited miles away.

The nurses occupied the one solitary passenger carriage with two of the senior surgeons while everyone else, officers, men and orderlies found places on the open wagons among the stores.

The oppressive heat hung relentless and heavy in the compartment despite the open windows. Conversation dwindled to a halt in the carriage as mouths and nostrils dried. Nurse McCaul passed round a bottle of tea which was welcome to the other occupants.

Shouted news of obstructions on the line ahead was relayed by the engine driver explaining the cause of the delays. The existence of the hindrances evidenced the proximity of the Boer and caused a stir among the officers and soldiers.

Then the exodus continued as the train built up steam and pulled out of Frere to begin the haul to Chieveley. After ten miles they clattered over the trestle bridge and the talk which had started after the tea stopped abruptly as they looked down at the wreckage of an armoured train. This was their first sight of the reality of war. The train climbed the incline to the town's station, they could hear the rapid thuds of pom-poms adding to the incessant boom of the guns and the persistent crackle of rifles. The Senior Medical Officer (SMO) looked grim and voiced the opinion the action could not be going well.

The train halted outside the station of Chieveley. There was shouting outside, and they realised it was calls for the SMO who was to report to the battlefield. He grabbed his haversack and jumping down from the train was given a saddled mount and left quickly in the company of the messenger. The remaining surgeon got out of the train but remained close by. He was soon joined by another doctor who imparted the news the fighting was severe and going badly, guns had been lost and scores of wounded would be coming in.

The nurses arrived at the hospital and reported immediately to the operating surgeon in the nearest marquee. There were four, each with an associated cluster of bell tents forming a row below the naval guns on the ridge. He assigned each to a marquee. They were soon at work as the field ambulances, carts and wagons arrived filled with human wreckage. Each vehicle, filled to overflowing, arrived with men with all manner of wounds and degrees of severity to be treated. There were sitting wounded to be helped down and other unfortunates on stretchers to be unloaded. The nurses quickly assessed the nature and extent of the wounds and directed where they should be taken. Some were stretchered immediately to an operating table under the canvases of the marquees or to a line waiting to be seen by the surgeons. There were also those whose wounds were not life threatening and those who no longer needed medical attention. Tourniquets, lint and bandages amply applied still failed to staunch much of the blood. Unforms, bodies and the ground were saturated with gore. Lanterns and lamps were lit as darkness encroached but still the wagons came with the small, ragged red cross pennant fluttering beside the driver and his cargo of moaning torn bodies.

Greta worked tirelessly under the direction of the surgeon at the table, awash with blood, as he rapidly performed amputations and she struggled to keep pace cauterising stumps of arms and legs. The screams, at first piercing her eardrums and throwing her into a mental turmoil, eventually became background noise which her brain reluctantly accepted. Dawn broke and still they came. Just after daybreak the Boers agreed an armistice for the stretcher bearers to collect the wounded unhindered by Mauser bullets.

And the flow of the broken continued.

The one-day cease-fire which General Botha had offered expired the next morning. All the British wounded had been recovered from the field. Military operations on both sides would commence. The Staff thought the hospital at Chieveley might be shelled, deliberately or accidentally, by the Boers. In either case the result would be the same, so it was decided to evacuate all the wounded from the battle zone to a place of safety.

Early next morning a hospital train pulled up alongside the field hospital while moonlight still held sway over the night. By first light the worst cases were loaded.

Greta stood erect and eased the ache from her back by stretching. The soldier had drunk his fill from the cup. She leaned over and lifted the half-filled bucket to move to the next stretched when she heard someone call her name.

Janet, who had become closer and more friendly with Greta since Aileen's departure, hurried over from the small group in earnest conversation in the shadow of the train.

"Greta I've got to take over the duties of Train Nurse."

"Why?" asked Greta as she placed the bucket down and wiped her face with the back of her hand. Her face had blanched at the news. She had never made friends easily and it seemed as though Fate was determined she should be friendless. And depressed.

"Nurse Canning has gone down with enteric fever and is now a patient here. She is too ill to be moved."

"When do you have to go?" Greta was obviously troubled by the news. Another familiar face departing.

"I have to collect my things and be back by ten to go with the train to the base at Cape Town."

"Is it just for one journey?" She strained to keep the disappointment out of her voice and tried to sound hopeful. The news must be as bad for the sister.

"I certainly hope so, but they haven't said. Let me grab my bits and pieces and I'll get back here as fast as I can." She took Greta's free hand and gave it a consoling squeeze before walking off as briskly as was possible on the rough ground. Greta's eyes filled with tears she could no longer contain. They ran freely down her cheeks as she moved on to give water to the wounded.

Wide walkways between each stretcher and the neighbouring one on both sides separated the lines of wounded. Ambulatory and lightly wounded soldiers carried the detachable bunks from the train to lay them on the ground next to a soldier. It took seconds to lift and transfer him to the train with his original bedding. Not one experienced disagreeable shocks when the occupied bunk was placed in the innovative sliding system on the train.

All carriages held medical supplies and fresh bandages for any contingencies occurring en route to the Cape. Meals for the patients and staff came from the cookhouse at the rear which could be accessed by the corridor which ran the length of the train.

The two nurses stood at the steps of the carriage where its door stood open. Janet had collected her baggage but, on her return, had been unable to join Greta straightaway. Called to the presence of the PMO and she had not been free to talk with Greta until the engine started up prior to leaving for the base. Both could not speak. As the train's whistle blew Greta helped her departing friend board then handed up her bag. She stepped back and closed the carriage door.

Wordlessly she lifted her hand and waved feebly as the train shuddered then the engine leaned into the pull and the wheels began to roll. Janet leaned out and reached for Greta's hand but only the tips of their fingers touched as the train separated them.

CHAPTER THIRTY-ONE
The Plan

"Hey, Jonge! Luke! Wait up!" The youth, on his way to the field kitchen for supper, with his rifle in the crook of his arm, stopped and looked toward the caller walking briskly toward him.

"Luke, as soon as you've eaten, your father wants to speak with us."

"What about?"

"Ah, Luke, this is one of the few times the Commandant hasn't confided in me. I'll get him to tell me what's it all about next time. Promise."

"All right Jan. Genug." Both grinned good-naturedly. They had grown from boyhood together and had joined the commando on the same day. Back in Kerkenhof they competed against each other in the frequent shooting competitions; Jan Peeters was an excellent shot, an undisputed marksman, but without fail Luke, Commandant Trichardt's eldest son, would win the trophy. Their birthdays were only two days apart and at seventeen years of age they were considered mature adults and looked after the younger members of the commando the youngest of whom was thirteen. Jan's father, who had lost a foot to a female lion, and his uncle, injured in a harvesting accident costing him the use of his right hand were also in the commando.

They rinsed their metal plates after the meal, which both had hurried but each tried to hide his excitement from the other by remaining unconcerned. Together they walked across the centre of the laager to the wagon belonging Commandant Trichardt who was seated with someone who both were sure was not a member of their commando.

"These are the two who will be with you. If they agree." said Trichardt around his pipe.

Fergal nodded and eyed the approaching two young men critically. Both carried the ever-present Mauser, the Widow Maker.

"Commandant." said the taller of the two.

"Luke, Jan." he replied in acknowledgement. "Sit down, both of you, this may take a while or maybe not, if you refuse." he said in Afrikaans.

Both crossed their ankles and sank to the ground with their rifles across their laps.

"This is Mijnheer Boyle. He was with the Irish Brigade and I think highly of him and his men. He has produced a plan General Meyer thinks might work." He switched to English. "This is my eldest son and his friend. Both have seen service."

"You speak English?" Fergal addressed Jan.

"Yes. I do. My brother's wife is Irish and taught me." Fergal smiled. The pleasant lilt of the young man's English would not be amiss in Dublin.

"Go ahead, Mr. Boyle, tell us again of your plan." said Trichardt.

"A moment, please," Fergal replied, nodding at his pipe. He gathered his thoughts as he filled, tamped, and lit the briar. Behind the cloud he began.

"The aim is ludicrously simple — sorry, quite simple. The doing of it not so much. I intend to assassinate the leader of the British Army, General Buller. I realize he will be replaced immediately. However, the effect this action would have on the morale of the Khakis would be devastating. It would also prove this land really is ours, showing we can go anywhere and deal out our justice to those who commit crimes against us.

"I believe the surest way for this to be successful is to use our strongest skill, which is marksmanship, coupled with a Mauser.

Commandant Trichardt has told me you are the best men possible to fulfil this plan." Fergal returned the pipe to his mouth and waited for either of the two to comment. Both remained silent and returned Fergal's gaze with expressionless stares of their own.

"He would be the leader in this action?" asked Luke in Afrikaans without taking his eyes off Fergal. "What has he done for our freedom?"

"Fair questions," answered Trichardt, "But you ask him. Go ahead." He knew Luke would not be hesitant with his questions, and totally accepted the premise; if you were to be led by a stranger, then you would want reassurance they were capable. This was the Boer credo. Every individual had the right to question and then act in accordance with their own desires and will.

"Mr. Boll," began Luke.

"Boyle. But best call me Fergal," the Irishman interrupted with a smile which was not returned.

"Mr. Boyle, have you fought against the British?"

"Every day of my life, young man. Not always physically but I have made efforts in other fields to thwart their intentions. My country is under occupation by these bastards.

"As for actual fighting your brother and I were lying aside by side at Dundee alongside the Transvaal Staat Artillerie. You know we guarded the guns and kept them safe for Commandant Trichardt. Not all of us came out of those battles alive."

"Can you shoot? Can you ride?"

"Yes to both but qualified by not well for either. Which is why I need your help."

Luke looked in question at Jan who returned his look with a shrug. Luke nodded then turned to Fergal.

"We are listening."

Fergal was folding his meagre extra clothing and placing it in the duffel bag he had bought in Johannesburg when Luke and Jan called to him from outside the small tent the Boers had given him.

"Take this please," said Luke, handing over a set of pannier bags. Fergal opened one side. It was already packed with assorted items. A shirt, a long-sleeved undershirt, and socks together with a sheath knife were in that side and he did not open the other as he belatedly thought it bad manners to be so curious. At Fergal's surprised thanks Jan said, "They belonged to a friend. He doesn't need them anymore." Astute enough not to enquire about the friend, Fergal gave a serious nod.

"Did you ever live outdoors in Ireland? Maybe when hunting?" asked Luke.

"No, never. Never hunted or lived in the open in Ireland. But in Canada, yes."

A look passed between the two youths, but Fergal was undecided on how to interpret it.

Early next morning, in the light mist and the night's lifting darkness, Fergal's small party, mounted on Basutos, with a mule and loaded panniers, left the circled wagons.

Fergal had made it clear the previous night he respected the two young Boer's greater expertise in all things African. He conceded it was right they take the lead in deciding what, where, when, and how in all matters of travel and self- protection. He expected them to set the pace with proviso they should reach their destination while the General Buller was still in his rear echelon headquarters.

The panniers on the mule had been filled with dried biltong, mealies, biscuits, belts of rifle ammunition and a medical kit. Each of the three had cross-bandoliers of 7x57mm Mauser ammunition. Luke and Jan had sheath knives while Fergal had a Luger pistol. All three had British issue short gabardine waterproof coats which the Boers had looted when they captured Dundee and raided the Army stores.

With Fergal riding in the middle of the trio they made substantial progress the first day over the veld toward Colenso. Luke said they had covered thirty miles and suggested they camped for the night while it was still light. He chose a dip in the side of a kopje where it was possible to lie or sit and was deep enough so the flames of their fire could not be seen. He was confident the training of the ponies was sufficient so they could be left unfettered to graze in the evening then sleep during the night without wandering off. The pack beast was a different story, so he was pegged with head ropes. They removed their saddle bags and stopped Fergal from unsaddling his mount.

"We never do, on the veld," Jan explained, "We might need to move quickly."

The party dined on biltong and a tin of salmon with rough slabs of bread. Fergal had to admit the coffee brewed by Jan was excellent. Rolled in the blankets, around the dying ashes of the fire which Luke had damped down with the dregs of the coffee, they were soon asleep.

Next morning they rose at dawn, and Fergal followed suit as they shook the night's dew from their blankets, before folding them. Next to their ponies they ate bread, and each drank from their water bottles before mounting and continuing toward Colenso.

The clouds rolling in from the Indian Ocean were quickly building into banks which filled the sky and the day darkened. As they were putting on their coats the first deluge fell. In seconds they were drenched but they leaned into the rain and continued. As with most rainfall on the veld it was heavy and persistent but with equal alacrity it stopped. The sun broke through and they rode through the clouds of vapour rising from their drying bodies.

"We Irish have a great respect for what you are doing to throw off the British yoke." He had to explain to the boys what "yoke" meant and all three were soon laughing at his antics as Fergal tried to mime the meaning of the word.

Jan, leading the way but sitting half turned in his saddle, to share in the merriment, took the fatal shot in the throat. Fergal, whose pony jumped forward at the crack of the rifle caught Jan and prevented him from falling from his horse. Luke had immediately lifted both hands in the air and somehow had found a light-coloured neckerchief to wave. Two more shots followed, but fortunately went wide, then he edged his pony nearer to Fergal.

"Put your hands up."

"They'll hang me." said Fergal

"They're not khakis. They're Transvaalers."

Fergal raised his free hand while holding the unconscious Jan in his saddle and upright. Seven or eight hundred yards away, three horsemen were galloping toward them. Luke jumped down and came round to ease Jan down from his horse. He laid his wounded friend on the ground but even from on his horse Fergal could see the damage to the lad's throat and knew Jan wouldn't breathe again.

The horsemen drew nearer but had their rifles levelled. They dismounted fifty yards away and weapons still aimed at Fergal and Luke shouted for them to keep their hands in the air. They came closer and seeing the dead Jan whooped and congratulated the one who had fired the shot. Luke immediately leapt forward and slapped and punched the marksman all the while shouting Afrikaans curses and swearwords. The other looked in surprise and dawning recognition. Not one was older than thirteen.

The three boys had taken part in a skirmish the day before against British infantry. Before the British could bring their field guns to bear, they escaped. They did not believe they would be needed by their commando for two weeks as they had lost twenty or so men in the battle. It would need to rest up and regroup with new reinforcements. They would use the stand-down to leave their commando and go home for the wedding celebrations of an older brother.

One of them said the soldiers were wearing the same coats. They apologised profusely but maintained, half-heartedly, they thought they were shooting at British soldiers as the coats were not what they knew as Boer clothing. Their spyglass was an ancient piece of equipment good for detecting shapes in the distance, but its utility ended there.

They helped to scrape out a trench which Luke ensured was deep enough for his friend's resting place and for it to be undisturbed by any scavengers. The group gathered rocks and stones to cover the freshly turned earth. All stood bareheaded and with bowed heads as Luke said a prayer over Jan's makeshift grave. Without a further word, he gathered some small rocks to make a marker for the grave. He felt no compunction to be gracious toward the three young commando members and curtly told them, with underlying venom, "Go home."

As they drank their coffee, they watched the others mount who, with chagrined faces and muted voices, said goodbye then swiftly booted their ponies into a gallop. Luke threw his coffee dregs onto the small fire and returned the tin cup to his saddle bag. Silently he mounted then looking down at Fergal said,

"The General?"

Fergal nodded then swung into the saddle.

They had ridden for hours in silence without break unless it was to relieve themselves.

"Fergal," said Luke using the Irishman's given name for the first time, "What does the General look like?"

"He's tall. Exceptionally tall. For a soldier you would expect him to stand up straight, but he is even more erect than most. Ramrod straight. He is also a big man; I mean broad shoulders and heavy."

"Where will we see him? To shoot."

"Their headquarters are in Frere and he will not be difficult to identify."

They reverted to silence and rode on for twelve miles or more before Luke spoke again.

"Does he have hair on his face? Moustache? Beard?"

"He has a big moustache but no beard."

At dusk they called a halt for the day and put the horses and mule out to graze. They unloaded the panniers to eat the tinned beans and rice and to use the bags as pillows. Their evening repast over, Fergal lit his pipe as Luke cleaned his weapon. Fergal would have liked to converse, but he could see Luke was preoccupied. He decided to sleep and unfolded his blanket and wrapped it around his body. He positioned the pannier so they could sleep head to head and said goodnight.

He awoke and listened. He could see the outline of Luke's head and shoulders. He too must have heard the noise. The voices, faint at first, grew louder. Luke thumbed the safety catch forward and as quietly as he could cocked the rifle. The voices were clearer now.

They were English.

Luke had chosen their site carefully, being mindful of the need to make a quick escape if the enemy were to stumble upon them. He had chosen a bivouac near the top of a kopje under an out crop of two large overhanging rocks where there was a shelf before the ground fell away. Should they be discovered by others on the crest of the hill they could retreat down the slope. Should they be approached from below they could traverse the slope for a short distance then had only a short climb to the top to flee down the reverse slope.

They remained still as they listened. The voices were raucous and gave no sign the owners expected problems. The crude banter and shouted obscenities evidenced the consumption of alcohol. One started a corrupted version of "We're off to Dublin in the Green." The voices, heckling and crudely calling for silence, were Irish. Fergal realised they were in danger of discovery by members of an Irish regiment. Luke, sensing his apprehension, put a restraining hand on his arm. They lay still and during the next hour the voices dwindled in frequency as each of the soldiers on the kopje retired and fell asleep. Luke whispered to Fergal,

"We stay here quiet. No sudden moves."

For the next hour they waited and were about to leave when they heard scuffling footsteps above their heads. Too late they interpreted the grunts. There followed a fart and a loud sigh of relief. The stream of urine arched its way outwards to splatter on the rock above their heads and shower them both. They endured the discomfort, felt the warmth, and smelt the alcohol as the effluence soaked their hair and ran down their faces. Both remained flat as they heard the soldier stumble to his bed.

After agonising long minutes of suspense, they gathered their trappings together and edged down the slope before, feeling sure they were not observed, stood up to retrieve their animals. They walked the mounts for a quarter of a mile before mounting and riding into what remained of the night.

CHAPTER THIRTY-TWO
Desolation

Luke pointed. "Grobbendonk. It's small. My father once sold three bullocks to 'n Engelsman there." Fergal strained to see the buildings, but his sight failed him. He could make out only a misshapen blur. They rode on and soon the shapes morphed into four bungalows. They dismounted in front of the first one. Its desolation was proof it was no longer occupied. The unknown fate of the occupants added to the disquiet felt by both men.

The shards of a trampled picket fence and the small clumps of wilted plants among the hoofprints of tethered horses evidenced a tender care sadly long extinct. Crushed Barberton daises and broken blue rhododendrons provided a slash of dying colour. Muddied items of a child's clothing, strewn on the path to the house, showed the extent and heartlessness of the larceny. Shutters of wood hung like broken wings in front of each broken window, and the front door was missing. They left the Basutos with trailing reins and entered.

"Careful where you walk," said Fergal in a subdued voice pointing to the first of the human excretions they were to see. The hostility in the destruction was hard for him to stomach. Even the evictions back home had never undergone this level of loathing. Everything capable of being looted was gone. What could not be removed had been ruthlessly wrecked beyond repair. Books, torn in two lay half burned in remnants of a fire in the centre of the room, while other paper littered the floor. The bookcase once shelving them lay splintered and in pieces. Cupboards with doors ripped asunder, drawers torn out, rifled, and thrown to the floor, among clothing sliced apart, and widespread filth showed a savage vandalism. The total was evidence of a fiendish malice. From among the fragmented chairs and crockery Luke picked up a trampled photograph of a child and stared down at it. Fergal moved to his side and in commiseration said "Bastards. Vile bastards."

"Who?" asked Luke looking up.

"The British. The fucking soldiers."

Luke smiled at him without mirth. "This wasn't them. They haven't got this far."

"Who then?" asked Fergal with surprise.

"Us, my friend, us. Probably, the Johannesburg Commando." he smiled sideways at the older man. "Or perhaps one of the Uitlander brigades?"

"You think it's probable?"

"I'm sure of it. It's useless to look for food in here," the young Boer went on, "Let's try the other houses."

The was no moon. Rolling clouds, ever lower heavy with rain. like grey, dull, misshapen cushions, darkened the sky and swept ever closer appearing soft but ominous. The air chilled so they prepared to stay for the night. They led the animals to the next house, which had a sizable lean-to against the nearest wall. They tethered the animals, unsaddling the horses and unloading the mule.

"We need forage for the beasts. I'll go looking if you light a fire."

Fergal went back to the first house for firewood. He looked at the shutters and sighed. While ripping them down he convinced himself it was pragmatic and not vandalising as it was when the others before them did it. As he returned the first rain fell in plum sized drops and he barely made it to the second house before the deluge vented its wet cascades on the hamlet.

He was placing the kindling in the fireplace when Luke returned.

"I've fed the horses and mule. Let's eat." From a knap sack, he must have found while foraging, he took out five tins, bare of labels.

Luke saw his surprised and questioning look.

"The other three houses are farmer's homes. In the old days there were always emergency stocks of food hidden nearby in case of Kaffir attacks. I just knew where to look."

Beside the roaring fire, which held the chill of the African night at bay, they feasted on beans, rice, and potted chicken. Fergal filled and smoked a night time pipe and they drank the hot tea together. Rolled in their blankets, feet warmed by the dying embers, they slept fitfully through the night.

Dawn broke. Luke made the morning brew as Fergal readied the horses, placed the bedroll behind each one and loaded the mule with its panniers.

Minutes later they departed the dismal shells of the ravaged houses. Within an hour the warmth of the sun changed to the uncomfortable swelter of summer on the open veld. Fergal who had been nodding in the saddle jerked upright as the Basutos quickened their pace unbidden. Minutes later he heard the sound, which increased as they went on. They had smelled water.

"We're near the Tugela." said Luke. Fergal saw the change in the veld's grass, thicker, longer, and lush as they neared the bank of the yet unseen water. He could hear but not see the river. Mimosas and clumps of bushes stretched thickly in both directions before them. Moments later he looked down from the higher northern bank onto the wide expanse of the fast-flowing Tugela. Luke leaned forward in his saddle.

"Na ja. That's what we have to cross but there are more open spaces down river where we can get down to the water. Down there the undergrowth is too thick." After a thirty-minute ride Luke found a suitable descent, through a break in the thorny undergrowth, to the edge of the water.

276

He dismounted. As he undressed, he said, "Make sure you pack your bundle tightly in your oilskin. And put your boots back on. The bottom can be uneven." He waded into the fast-flowing torrent.

"The bottom's firm. Rocky. We should be good to cross here." He noticed Fergal's apprehension.

"I can't swim," the Irishman said defensively.

"Neither can I, but we don't have to." He nodded at the animals. "They can. Just don't let go," he laughed. Fergal could not join in.

With Luke in the lead and Fergal gingerly following behind, holding the lead rope of the mule, they waded into the water. Less than ten yards in the level reached the men's waists and moments later the girth of the horses. The horses leaned into the water and heads held high struck out for the opposite bank. Both men had their hands deep into the tail hair of their horse which towed their rider through the rushing water. The pull of rope on the mule became heavier and Fergal realised the animal was balking. He pulled tighter only to find it obdurate and stronger than he was. He felt his grip on his pony's tail weakened and in desperation almost cried out. He bit down. His hand and arm on the rope went numb. He felt his fingers slacken. He couldn't close his fingers. The pull of the panicked animal behind was too much. Its weight and the drag of the water increased. Fergal gave a shout of despair as the beast spun round in the flood. The last image he had was of the huge whites of panicked eyes and bared yellowed teeth as it brayed frantically. It snorted water and struggled fruitlessly against the relentless drag of the Tugela as it rushed to the sea. Fergal desperately tried to hold on but failed. He lost his grip, his arms flailed, he tried to shout but he went under. He surfaced briefly then the river filled his mouth choking off his cries before pulling him down to disappear below the surface

Luke had reached the southern bank of the river and waded ashore still holding his horse's tail. He turned and saw Fergal's predicament but could only watch helplessly. Fergal's head bobbed up again, yards down the flow, as he ran along the bank.

Four hundred yards downstream the rush of water hurled Fergal headlong against an outcrop of rock. A blizzard of varied but intensely bright flashes exploded in his head. The current pressed him against the stone but simultaneously pulled him along its rough surface before releasing him violently back into the mainstream. Seconds later something inflexible under the water clamped his ankle. The ever- present flood twisted him with ease in a complete turn while the underwater vice held his foot. He did not hear the fracture but every nerve in his body reacted to it. He screamed. The next instant his leg was free. His boot bobbed to the surface with his sock. Both stayed in view for seconds then vanished in the swirling eddies gathering him up and bearing him away into the main current.

There was no respite and he slammed into a solid object. Whatever it was it remained immovable. He realized it was a partially submerged tree. His hands feverishly tried to get purchase and hold. The pressure of the current was his saviour as it pushed hard against his back and pinioned him in place. His head was above water and as he gulped air the pain from his chest was excruciating. He managed to get an arm around the waterlogged trunk of a fallen Jackalberry and as his eyes cleared, he realised the roots had remained fast in the bank, providing a support for him to drag himself along to dry land.

Hand over hand he edged along the trunk of the tree, slowly, as the pangs of intense pain forced him to gasp with each movement of his arms. His feet found solid footing and he crabbed his way toward safety. Drained of strength and every breath a burning agony he collapsed half in and half out of the water. He lifted his head and saw double figures approaching before blackness cloaked his consciousness and the earth of the bank cushioned his drooping head.

When consciousness returned, he struggled for air as he tried to breathe. It eased as he lifted his chin from his chest. He rasped for breath before falling sideways from his seated position against the bank. He fought off Luke's hands as the youth tried to get him back to an upright posture.

"I can't breathe. Can't… air into..."

Luke stared at him then, as realisation dawned that Fergal had suffered a chest injury, grasped him firmly by the shoulders and pulled him to a lying position. The pressure on Fergal's chest eased and despite the initial thrash of pain his intake of air improved. The young Boer strode over to his pony and loosened the girth-band to pull out the square of blanket from under the saddle. He quickly slashed the material into strips then rolled one strip into a pad.

"Which side is it? Here, under your hand? Right move it away." He used the other strips to band the pad in place. With the chest bandaged Luke turned his attention to Fergal's broken leg. With the Irishman's rifle as a splint he bound it to the leg with more strips of blanket, not without moans and the occasional shriek from Fergal.

Fergal caught glimpses of Luke's endeavours between periods of closed eyes. Any attempt to watch met with the blurriness of double vision and an aching head and nausea. He dry-wretched. An overwhelming fatigue made consciousness a weight, pressing down on his eyelids, and tugged at him to sleep. Luke tried but could not keep him awake and he slid downwards into a fitful sleep.

During the night he awoke and was distressed to realise the double vision had not cleared. He watched the blurred silhouette of his companion against the light of the dying fire.

He cleared his throat and spoke.

"Luke. I'm thirsty."

He fumbled with the water bottle the Boer had uncapped and drank deeply.

"Fergal, are you able to talk? We need to discuss what we are going to do."

"Yes. But I'm finding it hard to think."

"Then don't. Just listen. Then worry about it." The young fighter sounded angry.

"First, you are not fit to continue. But I am. You weren't taking the shot, I was. So, it can still be done but only by me. You won't be able to ride in the condition you are in. So, I go alone."

Fergal ignored Luke's remarks and asked,

"Why are you angry, Luke?"

"I am angry because I thought you were stronger and more capable than you are. This whole effort, including Jan's sacrifice, is at risk. We have lost our supplies. And you are no longer fit to play a part. And why? Because holding onto a pony's tail is beyond you." Fergal did not reply. It was pointless to do so. The Boer was right.

To lessen the bitterness of his remarks Luke went on.

"My people cross rivers often and never does this happen. I should have known you could

281

not do it, but I didn't. I am angrier with myself."
He paused. "I saw the mule this evening at the
river. On the other side. Laughing at me."

"Perhaps, if he is still there, it would be
worthwhile trying to get him back?"

"Why? The panniers are no longer there. The
food and extra ammunition are no more. Lost in
the Tugela. And what would I do with a stupid
empty donkey?

"Anyway, I think it best if you stay here. I'll
change the splint so you'll be able to use your
rifle should you need to. There is plenty of water,
but no food," he shrugged. "But I will be back as
soon as I can. I return for you after I have killed
the General."

He lay just below the crest of the kopje.
There were no obstacles between his position and
the darkened entrance to the marquee dominating
the scores of smaller brown tents. The camp
covered a wide area and he had spent the best part
of the previous day searching the hills for this
vantage point. It surprised him the Army had not
posted lookouts or sentries on this or the other
high ground commanding the area of their
bivouacs.

His Mauser rested on the small cluster of
stones he had prepared and the rock outcrop to
his right provided a defensive shadow. He bit into
the biltong and chewed as he considered the
situation. To the entrance of the marquee and the

pennant, with its occasional flutter in the light breeze, was seven hundred yards. Although there was no wind up on his hill the movement of the pennant below, dictated he should factor the zephyr into his shot. He smiled without mirth at the anomaly that they had abandoned the differences in uniform distinguishing the officers from the ordinary soldier to prevent the commissioned ranks being singled out for special attention by Boer marksmen. And yet they flagrantly signposted the location of their general with a flag! His spyglass would have been ideal for this work in hand, but it had gone south with the panniers. He tried but failed to suppress a fleeting thought that this was a jinxed action but not before the cost ran through his mind. Jan, the Irishman, the food, and the mule; an exorbitant price to pay with nothing yet accomplished.

"Na ja!" he said aloud. "This I will change."

After three days of hard riding, well into the falling darkness of each night, he reached the Tungela. He rode straight to the thorn tree where he had left the incapacitated Irishman. There was no sign of Fergal but a mass of hoofprints, and a set of wheel indents evident in the area, showed a large contingent of horses had been there. From the freshness it had not been long ago. With relief he recognised the prints of Basutos which presaged welcome news. Men of their own side had discovered the injured Uitlander. A closer search around the base of the tree revealed a strip of paper, part of an envelope, held in place by a strip of bark half cut to form a rudimentary clip. The sliver of paper bore the word 'Colenso."

After following the tracks upstream for an hour he found the ford where the party had crossed. If only he and Fergal had found this crossing place!

It was not the most comfortable journey he had ever made. It was decidedly the worst. The pain, from his fractured leg, agitated by the bumps and bounces of the wagon, which unfailingly found every rock, depression, and uneven surface in the one hundred and twelve miles of veld was unremitting. The original splint had worked its way loose and he felt what seemed to be the rough ends of the broken tibia jarring together. He suffered nausea and bouts of dry retching during each mile travelled. Now it was over.

The driver pulled out the restraining pins on the heavy tailboard and let it swing free, unsupported. The thud, as its downward swing was halted by the frame of the buckboard almost, but not completely, drowned out Fergal's agonised yelp. The driver heard it and grinned maliciously. He pulled himself up on the floor of the wagon and grabbing two handles of the makeshift stretcher pulled it roughly toward the end of the wagon. Another Boer appeared beside him and helped to lift the litter and the injured Fergal from the body of the cart. With sudden deliberation the driver let go of his end and this time the jarring crash caused the injured Irishman to scream. Through the mist of welled up eyes occasioned by the physical distress he heard the two men arguing and then there was a total change in the driver's attitude toward him. From the second man's explanation he understood the driver thought he was a captured British soldier. Both he and the corporal of the group, which had found and rescued him, spoke English when the leader questioned Fergal.

While working in and around the mines near Johannesburg Fergal had picked up many Afrikaner words and had a superficial understanding of the language. This smattering increased because of conversations he had with Luke in the time they shared. The great difficulty occurred when he tried to learn more by speaking Afrikaans with Boers who had knowledge of English. They would all without exception become impatient with his fledgling efforts and pre-empt, or steam roller, his attempt by replying in English. He had more success with those Anglophobic Boers who knew no other language than their own and would not consider speaking the accursed Engelse taal. The Ermelo Kommando, to which the corporalship rescuing Fergal belonged, had no Uitlander participants. The thirty-two Boers, who were its members, were extremely parochial. And dour. Laughter was scarce and smiles even rarer. Part of this, Fergal realised, could well be because the Commando had no particular successes in the two engagements in which it had taken part. Its losses had been severe and the small group where Fergal now found himself had lost eight men. Their bravery in the face of superior odds and the tenacity with which they twice held the line to allow others to withdraw to safety was renowned throughout the command. Fergal soon realised even those who showed consideration and toleration toward him displayed a coolness his Gaelic intuition interpreted as distrust. His mobility limited by his leg injury, he depended on his companions to meet his everyday needs. He could not join the line for his meals, without help he could not reach the latrines, he could not even play his part with light duties around the camp. He had been assigned to the vleiskorporaal, who was responsible for provisioning and to maintain the records of food supplies by accounting for the receipt and consumption of rations. He had the distinct impression this group was the only one operating such a system.

He had bouts of near depression triggered by his thought of not being able to accompany Luke to the final scene of their mission. Failing. His feelings of helplessness descended into despondency when he thought of the Irish Brigade; the camaraderie, the conviviality and sense of brotherhood that he missed.

There had been no news of the success -or failure of their shared mission to kill Buller. He did not know if Luke was alive. A probable cause for the present antipathy to his existence was that he enthusiastically, if not boastfully, told the corporal, and those within earshot, of the plan he had devised. Luke's absence, most likely because he was dead or captured, and he, the foreigner, was still in this world, would be grounds for them to not warm to his presence.

The days passed slowly as did the return of the use of his leg. The splint had been replaced by the group's medic, a veterinary surgeon, and the result had been more than he could hope for. There would be no deformity, there was a limp but best of all no permanent weakness. Capable now of contributing, he completed tasks with zest and the enjoyment of being whole again. His wellbeing was made whole when he saw Luke dismounting and reporting to the corporal. About to go over and greet the returning marksman he held himself in check at the thought of his previous eagerness and the reaction of the Boers to it.

He waited impatiently while Luke reported to the corporal. He could barely restrain himself when they both sank cross-legged to the ground and smoked together. Thirty minutes later, at long last, finally Luke stood and nodded to the corporal. He turned and seeing Fergal grinned and hurried toward him his arms held wide. They hugged, then Fergal broke away.

"Come. We have much to talk about."

They went to the kitchen area and collected two mugs of marula coffee then moved to the shade of a squat, thick-trunked baobab. With their backs against the tree they sipped the scalding substitute coffee. Luke was grinning and he could hold his silence no longer.

"Ik heb het gedaan! I did it!!" He threw the mug to one side and awkwardly reached around to clasp Fergal by the shoulders.

"We did it!"

Fergal anxiously asked Luke to describe the shooting again.

"How many more times, Fergal? I think you don't believe me." Luke could not keep the irritation from his voice. "Three times should be enough, even for an Uitlander!" He said the last jovially trying to lighten the atmosphere.

"Luke, I need to be sure before I can report this -this success to the Commandant. Luke, please, once more."

"Alright. It was still daylight when I reached the kopje overlooking the British base near Chieveley. I left my pony at the bottom and taking my rifle and water, because I expected a long wait, I got down on my belly and inched my way to but not quite the edge. I lay just to the right of a large boulder." Fergal filled his pipe without taking his eyes away from Luke. Luke took a breath and continued.

Movement in the foreground to his right caught his eye. It was the General, he was sure, accompanied by escorts and aides. Back from a reconnaissance? Dismounted they milled around outside the marquee, waiting for the grooms to lead the mounts away. Three, including the General, disappeared into the gloom of the large tent. Relieved he had seen the General and could now identify him Luke now felt sure this mission would succeed.

As the sun passed its zenith the heat was uncomfortable. The activity, and stress, of the past few days took their toll. Despite the excitement he felt at what he was about to do, drowsiness dulled his senses and he caught himself nodding. There was little activity taking place below. The shadows grew longer and as the air cooled then chilled darkness fell. He pulled his blanket toward him and allowed sleep to come.

He awoke with a start. It was daylight and the veld shimmered already with the growing heat. A moving horseman below attracted his attention. Mounted on gigantic, majestic charger much larger than a Basuto or any other African horse this rider was his man! The General riding toward the encampment. He must have been for an early ride. *He still has half a mile before he's back in the camp. It's now or never.* Luke set up for the shot.

To aim down at a target could cause an unexperienced rifleman to underestimate the distance. He was confident he would have no such problem. He taken such shots before with complete success against big game and humans. This would be no different.

He stabilised his lower half by spreading his feet wide and turning his knees inward, so the inner sides of his heels were on the ground. He brought the rifle into the aim and set his elbows. The pennant moved to the same degree as the day before, no more, no less. The horseman was at the camp's perimeter and seconds later he would be in shot. The target dismounted and handed the reins to a soldier then turned to enter the marquee.

Luke had drawn in a deep breath, taken up the slack of the trigger, then releasing half a breath, fired. He stayed motionless in position until he saw the panicked soldiers running toward the fallen figure of his strike. There was no movement from the fallen man. A hit by a soft nosed bullet rarely allowed anyone to walk away. Six or seven men picked up the huge officer and carried him into the tent. Satisfied and elated Luke inched back from the edge then stood and loped down the reverse slope to the waiting pony.

When Luke finished Fergal reached over and clapped him on the shoulder.

"Couldn't wish for better. Our reputations will be golden when Botha hears of this."

"Maybe so," said Luke non-committal." He had lost the excited lift the killing had initially given him and wondered if Jan's sacrifice was worth the result. It was plain the Irish man had no such doubts. "He was just one soldier but maybe you are right, if he was so important."

"I need to report our success to your father and want you to come with me."

Both collected their mounts and Luke helped Fergal to saddle up. With rations from the cook they set out for Commandant Trichardt's Commando.

Trichardt was having a midday meal to the lee of one of the Commando's wagons. The huge transport provided a welcome area of shade to relax in. He looked up as his son and the Irish man approached. After wiping his lips with a kerchief, he beckoned them forward. His smile was open and wide for them both, but it was obviously Luke who prompted its warmth.

"Commandant, may we report the result of our operation?" Fergal asked.

"Naturally. Here, sit" A young man offered two folding chairs, opened then set them opposite the Commandant.

"Some refreshment, perhaps? No? A glass of Jenevre?" He filled a glass as Fergal accepted and passed it to him. Luke had shaken his head at the offers and waited for the protocols to be over and the report made. Fergal reported on each stage of their journey together up to the disaster at the Tugela and asked Luke to continue the narrative. Trichardt continued with his meal, occasionally nodding but asking no questions.

"And so, there was nothing to report on the ride back. It was uneventful." Luke finished.

"So, you are convinced we no longer have General Buller to contend with?" the Commandant asked in neutral tones.

Both Fergal and Luke answered enthusiastically in the affirmative.

"Heeren, I have to tell you we know Buller is alive and well, with his troops, heading north to Ladysmith. Our scouts have made independent corroboratory reports of several sightings, in fact three of them only yesterday."

Fergal's jaw hung open and he looked to Trichardt then to Luke and back to the Commandant.

"I'm sorry," said Trichardt, "but whoever was shot by my son, it was not Buller."

CHAPTER THIRTY-THREE
The Killing

The train slowed as the whistle sounded. Craven lowered the window and looked ahead and saw the platform of Chieveley Station in the distance.

"We're there," he said to the other occupants. He pulled his pack and rifle down from the rack before circumventing the other passengers who were standing and reaching for their luggage. "Enjoy your stay," he said, joining the laughter before setting off down the corridor to the end of the train. The smell of horse manure, not unpleasant to a cavalry man, wafting through the corridor, indicated the presence of the horse boxes. Remus whinnied and eagerly looked over his shoulder toward him.

"There, old man," Craven murmured, "soon be on terra firma." He patted the curve of the muscled haunches before picking up the saddle blanket from the nearby shelf. Good naturedly, but firmly, pushing against Remus' hind quarters so he could get past into the box he threw the covering on to the charger's back and saddled him. From choice he had retained the Namaqua rifle bucket as opposed to the general issue short butt version. He holstered the rifle then waited with Remus, as they were joined by other members of mounted infantry, as they were not first in order to leave the train.

The horse box stopped before the start of the platform. He heard the hiss of steam as the driver jettisoned the surplus, followed by the shouts of the Kaffir porters as they placed the wooden ramps in position. Doors slid open and the first mounts clattered down, their riders ducking as they left the train.

Before mounting he checked with a waiting cavalryman for the location of General Buller's headquarters. In less than two minutes he had left the environs of Chieveley and was in open country. He slowed Remus to a trot, and both enjoyed the sunshine. The vastness of the veld never ceased to amaze him. The clear unpolluted air allowed visibility in detail almost to the horizon unless a heat engendered haze rose to diminish focus.

He saw the camp from three miles out and nudged Remus into a canter. The horse opened its stride and Craven knew the animal was enjoying the run. They headed for the pennant hanging limp in the morning air and were acknowledged by the sentries. Two of the three had functioned as waiters during the evening meals aboard the RMS Dunottar Castle and recognised the Colonel. He handed the reins to the waiting groom and turned to enter the shade of the headquarters marquee.

The force of 7x57mm Mauser bullet slamming into his body, shredding flesh and bone as it barrelled through, spun him around and dropped him as though poleaxed. He was fortunately unconscious before toppling over as his head hit one of the white painted rocks at the side of the tent entrance. Four privates assigned the duties of company runners while the General was on site, and waiting outside the marquee, rushed across to gather up the fallen giant and carry him into the tent. One left the group as they lowered him to the ground and ran off to fetch the Medical Officer. Within minutes the MO, kneeling beside the comatose Craven, had cut his uniform jacket away and applied a tourniquet, close to his armpit above the torn flesh. The act of ducking and half turning to avoid the low hanging canvas, as he entered the tent, changed the point of intended impact and the long round soft-nosed bullet ripped into his upper arm as opposed to the back of his skull.

Greta had been present in the operating theatre tent when the MO was called to the General's tent. She had heard the furore. Sighing she set about preparing the operating table and checking the medical tools for cleanliness. The standard items were laid out on the sheet covering the subsidiary table next to the operating table; the capital bow saws, catlins or doubled edge straight amputation knives, bone forceps of diverse sizes, suture needles, and scalpels. Prepared dressings and tourniquets completed the array ready for use by the surgeon. The sawdust bucket had been refilled and she positioned it under the foot of the operating table. Greta had just tied back the rolled canvas of the door when six orderlies puffed and panted their way into the operating theatre with the stretchered body of a tall man. His head lolled and his unconscious face turned toward her. Her first thought was,

"I know this man."

She studied the patient more closely when he was lifted on to the operating table and she helped her colleague to cut away the remnants of his uniform jacket. While the rest of his face was tanned the skin colour covering the orbit of one eye was pale. He had obviously worn an eye patch though the artifact was no longer evident. The theatre nurse trundled the cannister of nitrous oxide over to the operating table while Greta brought the liquid ether. She stepped back as the surgeon leaned over the unconscious Craven and the theatre nurse positioned herself to pass the called-for implements.

"Well, Colonel, it looks as though your arm or what is left of it has to come off," the SMO said to the oblivious Craven who stirred.

"Put the cone on. Then put him under." The junior surgeon busied himself with the mix then started the application of the anaesthetic. "Pass a new tourniquet and as soon as I get it in place loosen and remove the one already there." The tourniquets were exchanged in co-ordinated movement by the theatre nurse and the surgeon.

With the canvas straps tightened the procedure began.

"The long catlin then stand by with the saw," ordered the SMO. With the double-edged amputation knife, he skilfully made a circular deep cut on Craven's shattered arm, followed by a tour de maitre just as quickly. He held his hand out for the saw, and within minutes had removed the damaged flesh and shattered bone. With little ado the removed arm was dropped in to the sawdust. With the sutures the arteries were closed and the flaps of skin, created when cutting through the flesh, were folded over and stitched in place.

"Apply the dressings, but not too tight. You know what to do." He stripped off his rubber gloves then said, "Get the orderlies back here and have the Colonel taken to the recovery tent. Make sure he regains consciousness in the next forty or so minutes. Any problems send for me."

Craven spent three days in the recovery tent before he was moved. Greta had asked she be responsible for his care as he had been a friend of hers. This was not strictly true, but she felt an affinity for Craven as a Klondiker and because he had helped them when he had faced down Dawson's most prominent rogue.

Craven, after seventeen hours in the twilight world, before the anaesthetic wore off, awoke and tried to sit up. He failed. The realisation he had no left arm filtered through his mental haze and he fell back and stared at the canvas above his head. His recall of what had happened ended at the entry to General Buller's tent. He became aware of the presence of someone else in the tent and saw the nurse with the covered dish and a mug on a tray.

"Good morning, Colonel," she said placing the tray on the locker beside his iron bedstead. Craven attempted to get out of bed by swinging his legs out and, without bringing his left side into play, sitting then standing up. The space around him took on a life of its own and gyrated around his head. His eyes crossed and the nurse barely got to him. Strong and capable as she was, she could not hold him completely. His unconscious form slivered down her front. She called for help. With difficulty, and the assistance of two orderlies, Craven was lifted and pulled back into bed. He returned to consciousness almost immediately and gruffly asked for help to sit up. His one good eye stared balefully at Greta.

"Good afternoon, Colonel. Do you feel you can eat?" Craven detected an accent. "Do you think you can eat something?"

"A drink please and I'd like to know what happened," he replied.

"You were shot by a sniper as you arrived here."

Craven did not respond as he tried to process what she had said. He took the mug and drank thirstily.

"I came to see the General. I have information for him."

"He knows. They have your satchel. The General has left instructions he be informed as soon as you are awake. I'll tell them." Greta turned to go when Craven called to her.

"Nurse, please, a moment. I'm sure I know you. We've met before. Am I delusionary?"

Greta smiled and paused.

"No, we know each other. We'll speak later. The General will want to speak with you more urgently."

Greta told the lieutenant that Colonel Craven was awake and as well as expected. She waited as the young officer spoke with Buller. The senior officer, champagne glass in hand, looked over at her as his aide-de-camp passed on her message. The General stood up, removed the napkin and threw it on the table. Jacketless and red braces on display he strode over and curtly said, "Lead on, young lady."

CHAPTER THIRTY-FOUR
Recollections

Due to the exceptional care and attention devoted to his recovery Craven avoided the usual risks of infection and sepsis following radical surgery. During the days following he practiced with his sabre, dressed, and undressed, saddled and unsaddled Remus and devised methods by which he could accomplish the day-to-day tasks he had easily managed pre amputation. The charger seemed to be aware of the change in his master and was not quite so robust with his welcoming head nudges.

Craven rode Remus to the kopjes where he envisaged the Boer marksman had lain in order to bring him down. The Boers were recognised as good shots, and sniping was one of their universal practices. With the many excellent shots in their ranks it would foolish not to utilise such a skill in war. When a target of opportunity presented itself any Boer worth his salt would try to make the shot but would not necessarily go out of his way to select individual victims unless on the battlefield. Officers leading attacks on the battlefield were fair game but assassination of a run-of-the-mill individual officer not in the field was unlikely.

On the second day Craven found the place from where the Boer had taken his shot. A.

7.57mm empty casing glinting beside a clump of gorse caught his eye. He looked toward the camp and picked out the General's tent. As a professional soldier Craven could but admire the skill needed to hit him at that distance. It was little consolation, but the distance could very well have played a part in limiting the damage caused by the dum-dum that had brought him down.

"It was in Canada. Dawson City." Greta said as they sat on the folding canvas chairs outside Craven's rent. She was off duty and had joined Craven to re-introduce herself. He watched the smoke from his cigar spiral lazily through the still morning air. The sun was pleasantly warm and had not yet reached the highs of a summer day on the veld.

"The Valkyrie! Your saloon! And your friend?"

"She is in Wjnberg ."

Greta obviously did not know but there would time enough to reveal what should be a pleasant surprise for her.

"But how and why did you both come out here?"

"You'd better light another cheroot, it is a long story," Greta laughed. She would enjoy bringing Aileen to her, if only in conversation.

I enjoy talking with Colonel Craven. It's the most relaxing time I have had since coming out here. Even when Aileen was here, we were always busy and there was not time to sit and simply chat. This man from the past has made it possible. And for this I thank him.

I think, after he made the bluff and switched the gold in the Valkyrie, when Cromer tried to browbeat us into paying protection money, I always had a soft spot for him. He was a giant then, in physique, courage and his kindness but he paid a terrible price for defending us. And now here he is, severely wounded but in my care giving me the opportunity to repay him.

I can see the loss of the arm is troubling him. Not, I think, the pain or the change in his body but to have to learn whole new ways of doing things with one hand. Thank goodness he is right-handed.

"A penny for them, Sister Greta?"

His question brought me back from my musing and caused me to smile.

"Sorry. I was thinking of many things, Dawson City, meeting you, going to England, coming here, and many other things too numerous to mention." He picked up his cigar case and, with some fumbling, managed to extract one. I watched him struggle but realised helping would not be the right thing to do. I did however open the box of Vestas and struck one. As he leaned in to light it, I could smell his hair. The strong aroma of carbolic soap was not unpleasant, but I would think it something he would not use back in London.

302

Sitting back in the folding chair, his demeanour was such that I felt he had something to say but was holding back.

"So," he said, "I would like to know more."

"Yes, well I think you should.

I described how we met and became friends winding up as two of the most successful entrepreneurs in the Yukon. I did not dwell on our circumstances in Wales or why we had, naively now I think, volunteered as Princess Christian nurses. I did mention, I thought I needed to share, my brother fighting with the other side. I described how Aileen was assigned to Wjnberg which caused us to be separated. He was a good listener and asked only one question.

"Do you know where Aileen is now?"

That brought me back, I'm afraid, and I felt the sadness again. He noticed and apologised. I told him it was not his fault. He was about to say something, but I hurried on.

"I have written several letters to her but had no reply. I do know she is not at Wjnberg anymore." He was quiet as he drew on his cigar. We remained silent together. Then he broke the stillness.

"I met your friend."

I was thunderstruck, there are no other words for it.

"You met Aileen? Where? Is she well? How is that poss—"

303

He leaned forward and put his hand on my knee comfortingly and said quietly,

"Shush, Nurse Greta, let me tell you."

Craven finished. She was staring off into the dusk. He had never seen a woman so happy, gloriously overwhelmed by relief and joy. Her emotional response convinced him he had made the right choice to omit any mention of Rudi. Besides, as he related the story, he realised the need to process what he now knew about the relationship that had disturbed him so much and how he wrong he had been. Perhaps he might tell her later.

The sound of the bugle calling the soldiers to their evening meal reminded me I still had duties. I was on nights. I rose and wishing him "Good Evening," left to wash and change for my shift.

The night skies here are beautiful. Dark velvet with myriads of diamonds sprinkled in abundance, which increase in number the more you look. There is not a cloud anywhere although it is getting chilly out here even with my cape

I wonder if Aileen sees these skies. Ach, don't be childish, Greta, of course she does. In Cape Town they have the same sky! God, she must recover, please don't let her die. No, don't think that, of course she won't, she'll be fine. Soon, she'll be working just as hard as you are, probably even harder, and then she'll write. Now, for marquee eight and my forty soldier boys from

Liverpool. I hope young Lester made it through the day.

Schade! Private Mansfield's bed is empty, more than empty, it's stripped and only the bare white mattress to show. He'll be buried in the morning with the other boys who don't make it through the night. I must make a note to look up his next of kin address and write them.

As he heard the movement at the entrance to his tent Craven looked up from his book to see the General, magnum and two flutes in hand, ducking through the doorway.

"Don't get up m'boy. Sit." He turned to the soldier carrying the chair, "Put it down there, other side of the table. Fine. Beacon, thank you."

The general eased himself onto the canvas bucket then busied himself peeling the foil and opening the champagne. Before it could foam, he had filled the two glasses and placed one before Craven. He clipped two cigars, passing one over, then lit both.

"Right. Pleasantries first. How are you?"

"Well. sir. Anxious to get back into harness."

"Always seem to get such nonsense, from you young 'uns. Absolute nonsense. But I'll accept you are on the mend!" When Craven said he was, the General nodded. Suddenly, he asked,

"Why did he shoot *you*?" The question caught Craven by surprise.

"I was probably a target of opportunity."

"You think? Some happy go lucky Dutchman, miles from nowhere, risks taking a shot into a camp of thirty thousand soldiers. At someone who was standing in the entrance to my tent. And under my pennant." Craven quickly realised where the General's reasoning was taking him.

"They don't need to go about potting officers in the off season. We give them plenty of targets on the battlefield."

They turned their attention to their cigars. The General suddenly chuckled then broke into open laughter, "Probably wasn't a Boer. It was probably somebody Lansdowne sent!" Craven aware of the General's disgust at the War Office for its lack of real support understood the reference, laughed heartily.

Several nights later Beacon informed him that the General would appreciate his company. The sky was swathed with dark cloud as he made his way across camp from the hospital area. It was late evening. Craven ducked under the awning of General's tent. As befitting the rank the spread of canvas was larger than most. The General, in braces and shirt sleeves, was leaning over the map of southern Africa. He looked up then, placing a hand on the small of his back, grunted.

"Too old for this game, what?"

"No such thing, sir. Probably just the damp in the air."

The General grunted, this time in derision. He watched as the Colonel took his cigars from one of his breast pockets then almost gently took the case from his hand and took out two cigars. Both had already been clipped. He returned one to Craven. The General struck a Vesta and lit the other officer's cigar before lighting his own.

"If I didn't," he said good naturedly between draws to ignite the Monte Cristo, "know better, Nicholas, I'd say you were in sycophant mode." He returned his attention to the chart.

"Anyway, look at this and then tell me what you think. Here's the situation.

Both gave their attention to the rudimentary map which had the likely area for the next confrontation with the Boers highlighted with a large red circle. The name Spy Hill was prominent together with its Boer name that would in a few short days resound in British Military history:

Spion Kop

CHAPTER THIRTY-FIVE
Sister Greta

The blood bath of Spion Kop is over but the waves of human flotsam and wrecked bodies continued to flood the marquee. It is slightly bigger than a large tent. The operating table under the rows of panniers lining both side walls and holding the operating instruments shifts the focus. Underfoot the much trodden discoloured grass has not surrendered and still manages, in places, to raise a blade or two erect. There are basins and buckets galore. Room for personnel is at a premium with the surgeon and his assistant, the anaesthetist, and the other nurse. She stands with the others in silence as the surgeon calls for the next stretcher. The patients on the array of stretchers outside have all been examined under anaesthetic to alleviate the pain of the prods and pokes of discovery. The night continues with the fifty first operation taking place. Fresh layers of new blood on her hands makes it difficult to grip the limbs the saw and knife have pruned from the living bodies. The apron she used to provide a dry grasp on the amputated flesh was soon sodden and a fresh well of tears surged. This time it was frustration triggering them.

Shortly after two in the morning she is relieved by an Orderly, but her work is not over. She is called to the side of Senior Sister McCaul and allocated an area of stretchered souls to treat.

The sweat blinded Greta as she bandaged ruptured torsos, stitched gaping leg wounds, and applied tourniquets. She forced herself not to weep as the results of the carnage lay before her on the grounded stretchers. She was aware of an overpowering sense of inadequacy drawing tears and forcing her to use all her mental power to suppress them.

As dawn morphed into day the flow continued unbroken with the cries of the African drivers mingling with the creak of the wagons and screams of the mutilated. Beside each wagon forming a single file were the walking wounded. The majority just dragged their rifles, and many were unarmed. There were bandaged heads, tattered empty sleeves and some staggered blindly along, pitifully clutching the sleeve of one who could see. Then by late afternoon, when the medical staff were struggling to stay conscious the last ambulance was unloaded. Early evening saw the baptised-in-war sisters washing the gore from their faces and hands in a bucket under the shelter of their new home.

Typhoid fever seemed to be stalking the cadre of qualified nurses in the war zones and would strike again.

Greta took the piece of linen, her makeshift handkerchief, from her apron pocket and wiped her forehead before leaning over the comatose Highlander. She checked his pulse. His breathing was spasmodic and although unconscious the lines of pain were pronounced on his tanned face.

He was young, muscular but lacking a right leg and had three bullet wounds in his torso. She raised her head and looked at the Orderly at the other side of the bed who returned the gaze with a slight shrug of his shoulders. Greta removed the bloodstained rags and beckoned for the Orderly to pass the bandage she had prepared.

Quickly and efficiently she applied the strip of cloth of the makeshift dressing to the raw stump, fastened it and snipped the ends neatly with the scissors hanging from her belt. She deftly adjusted the dressing on the soldier's amputation relieved he had remained unconscious making the change manageable. As she straightened, he suddenly thrashed his arms about, rose to a half upright position then fell back. A trickle of blood ran down his chin onto his neck. Greta wiped the flow away then stiffened as she feared life had left the boy. She checked for the beat of a pulse for six minutes. There was no sign of one. She nodded to the Orderly and both pulled the single sheet over the dead soldier's head and shoulders. Greta closed her eyes briefly as she made the sign of the cross.

They walked to the trestle table at the entrance to the ward. As Greta was recording the death on the fatality's millboard the Orderly, who had been theatrically displaying his impatience for her attention, by loud sighs and scuffing his feet, asked,

"Can I go to my billet for my baccy. Sister. I forgot it." Greta sighed. She nodded but knew it would be at least an hour before he returned despite his sleeping quarters being in the second line of tents only yards away. He was not alone in being work-shy, idle, and ignorant. Among themselves the orderlies even had a word for their laziness. Skiving. The recalcitrance and surly responses had increased. News of the arrival of trained male nurses and orderlies from the recently formed R.A.M.C. was common knowledge. The present orderlies would be returned to their original units and once again be required to be soldiers.

She sat down to savour a rare quiet moment. She thought about Aileen and wondered when she would return. She pulled the jotter towards her and began to write.

"*Dear Aileen,*

First, let me apologise for not writing sooner but it has been head spinning hard labour with casualties arriving in their hundreds. It is one endless chain of maimed and dying men. I know you must be having the same daily intakes of wounded and sick. Here, the numbers of lads affected by enteric is increasing. The shortage of medical supplies is dreadful, by which I mean drugs, syringes, even bedding. Worst of all we have plenty of outdated and expired medicines but little of which serves a useful purpose"

Greta paused and wiped her brow with the back of hand and tucked back the lock of hair that had escaped the restraint of her cap.

311

"The dietary requirements for those, the majority, suffering from typhoid are virtually impossible to maintain. The provision of fresh milk is rare, as it is difficult to come by, but any advantage is lost by the orderlies failing to provide clean drinking utensils. The supply of new milk is then contaminated and becomes undrinkable.

Two weeks ago, I have learned of a large capture of wounded Boer soldiers who are being treated in the General Hospital in Cape Town. When I learned of this, I asked for a transfer there, but I couldn't give the real reason. I have heard nothing back. It doesn't seem you will be back here any time soon. I have what may be a forlorn hope of finding my brother but at least there is a chance there and hopefully I will be able to help more than just British soldiers. It is what I always wanted to do."

Greta blinked rapidly against the dryness of her eyes and the fatigue threatening to engulf her.

"I have to end here without telling you of the things I really wanted to say, as I have to get ready with the others as I can hear them assembling outside which means more patients are due.

Be safe Aileen. I miss you.

Deine Greta"

Moments later the exhortations African drivers and whip cracks sounded in the middle distance signalled the arrival of more wounded from the battle. The creak of leather and rattle of harness became clear as the oxen wagons came closer and she hurried to the tent opening to supervise the unloading of the damaged beings. She dreaded this part of her work as many would not have survived the jolting bone shaking nightmare on the flat bed of the bullock cart.

The column of wagons seemed unending as no sooner had one arrived and the indefatigable Indian bearers swarmed up into the interior and rapidly but carefully unloaded the wounded before another lurched forward to take its place.

"There must be over four hundred here," Greta thought, as her mind, by now, in the brief time she had been in Africa, was well versed in the analytical skill of estimating numbers of wounded purely by how tightly they were packed in the covered wagons.

Despite her training in England and her empirical knowledge rapidly acquired in these wards, she still experienced strong feelings of inadequacy in her ability to lessen the suffering of the young, mutilated warriors who entered this charnel house. Lack of medical supplies, bedding, beds, and even fresh water contributed as much, if not more, to the death rate as the actual injuries. The few military orderlies in attendance were woefully ignorant; hygiene and the concomitant danger of infection from filth meant nothing. The surgeon, Mr. Treves had initiated training to extend their limited knowledge on cleanliness. It had not been without antagonism on their part. It seemed to Greta they were attendants because they lacked the courage and skills of fighting soldiers but were also failing in this field because of ignorance.

CHAPTER THIRTY-SIX
Reunion

Aileen gazed out of the window at the flowering bushes in the Superintendent's garden. Movement behind her and the sound of the door closing signalled that Mrs. Carstairs had returned. Aileen stood as the other woman took a seat behind the desk.

"Please sit, Nurse MacLean. Recovered from your ordeal?" She smiled as though she expected none of her nurses to suffer such trivialities.

"No after effects from your pneumonia? Good. We were concerned about your chances and to see you safe and sound is gratifying. But I assume you are here for a reason other than announcing your well-being?"

"Thank you, Ma'am. Yes, I would like to request an immediate return to my old post before an assignment to any other location is made."

"Fortunately, your wishes fit in with my intentions so that will cause no difficulty. There is one condition, however. I could not allow you to leave our care without being sure you have indeed fully recovered. I would be obliged if you would remain on convalesce here with us for at least one more week in case a relapse occurs. Of course, I would want you to have a clean bill of health from Doctor Matheson before you depart."

She sat deep in thought on the bench. Around her was blanket of purple from the fallen petals of the jacaranda trees in late bloom. Reaching into her apron pocket she withdrew Greta's letter to re-read it for the fourth time. It had been sent more two weeks previously and had made slow progress through the system. The envelope bore the marks of its travail to finally reach her.

Her heart ached for Greta and she wondered if the one letter she had been able to write had reached her friend. The news that that she had met Rudi would certainly brighten her day.

Tomorrow she would embark for Durban then catch the train and they would celebrate being together again before getting into harness to work in unison once more.

Her voyage to Durban was pleasant and the weather was favourable. Sea voyages were not among her favourite and she did not need a second opinion to confirm she was a bad sailor. There was no reason to suspect that the Indian Ocean would be any kinder to her than the Atlantic. She had heard the horror stories of sailing in this part of the world where tropical storms would erupt with demonical ferocity. She had dreaded the possibility of such an occurrence but even if one did, nothing could prevent her return. The good news was a tempest was unlikely to occur at this late stage in the voyage. The outline of the Durban rooftops rose from the horizon and she went below to gather her things.

Sister McCaul surprised her by the warmth of her welcome. The once strict martinet smiled broadly and held her arms wide before enveloping her in a hug. Despite the warmth of the welcome her first thought was of Greta and she could not hold back. She asked where Greta was and if she were at work on the wards. The first inclination was the clouding then the disappearance of happiness from the sister's face.

She felt her legs buckle at the news. It was as if a boulder had crashed onto her abdomen, crushing the air from her lungs to suffocate her into the blackness. The older woman caught her before she fell. She came round with the thought that something terrible had happened but for the first few seconds could not recollect what it was.

She tried to rise but Sister McCall pushed her gently but firmly back on the pillows.

"Here, drink this," she said holding out a glass. She kept her hand on Aileen's steadying it and guiding it to her lips. She waited until Aileen reached to put the glass on the bedside table.

"How...what happened? Did she suffer. When was this . . ."?

Her older colleague hushed her and made her lie back before she began.

The flow of soldiers brought down by the severe and protracted fever filled the doctors and nurses with dread. There was no question of self-interest or self- preservation even though this disease was indiscriminate in its choice of victim. The fear was that the inadequate number of professionals and lack of resources would be unable to cope with predicted flood.

It was not long in coming.

The cause of typhoid fever was well known and documented but conditions in South Africa, where fresh water was inadequate to support the vast number of troops in the field, many of whom lacked the basic knowledge regarding hygiene and its importance to well- being. Much of the water came from indifferent sources; loops of uninviting stagnant pools formed by the remains of a weakly trickling stream. Water found in the bottom of dongas after a shower is the colour of mud and thirsty soldiers, who regard almost anything liquid as potable, refer to it as 'khaki and water.' The troops wash their socks and shirts in this coffee coloured soup, bathe in it with gusto and drink from these same puddles and worse do not believe in the efficacy of boiling. Inadequate sanitation and rudimentary latrines contaminating water sources increased the chances of endemic disease.

Soon, the number of typhoid sufferers outnumbered the wounded. The interminable hours devoted to the intensive care of the sick, with little time for recuperation took its toll of the nurses. Greta was one of the first.

She lost her appetite and did not go for breakfast for thirteen days thinking it was fatigue she felt during and after a shift. She slept badly. One morning while on the wards a severe headache and stomachache evolved into violent diarrhoea. On her way back to change, having been unsuccessful in reaching a toilet, she collapsed and was found unconscious by an orderly. Two nurses carried her to the ablutions where they undressed and bathed her. While one put her to bed and waited with her for the doctor the other washed the soiled garments and hung them out to dry.

Greta regained conscious but was delirious and asked anyone approaching her bedside,

"Aileen, are you here? Where have you been?" She said nothing else but seemed to be aware eventually Aileen had not appeared. She lapsed into silence until the next approaching figure reached her bedside when she would ask the question again. One early afternoon she had a substantial period of lucidity which impressed the doctor and was regarded as indication her health was improving. She drank some fresh milk which her body retained. Although still weak she asked for pen and paper. When it arrived, she appeared to slip back into unconsciousness but later, in the night she asked the duty nurse to prop her up and give her the writing materials. The nurse left a lit candle and retired to the table at the end of the marquee.

Sister McCaul broke off to take an envelope from her pocket.

"As you can see it was not addressed. We knew you had been taken by the Boers and could see no way of getting it to you. Somehow, though, I knew you would be back, and I held it for you."

"Liebe Aileen,

Ich Weiss nicht wie lange ... " It was obvious Greta had realised she was writing in her native German and scored out the words with spidery strokes.

"Dear Aileen,

I am ill and confined to bed. I have the dreaded fever but am sure I will be well soon. Even so, now will be an appropriate time to write you as I am, for sure, not busy. Please don't be concerned but remember where all my documents are at home.

I had never considered when we decided to come out here disease or injury might happen to us. We were nurses, invulnerable and strong, and able to give tender care to the poor wounded soldiers. I wonder where my Rudi is? Please tell me you are all right, please, please, please. . ."

The funeral took place the day after she died. Sister McCaul bathed her and clothed her in a fresh new uniform. Her coffin, with those of four young officers, was taken to Chieveley cemetery escorted by Sister McCaul and a replacement nurse who had not met Greta while she was alive. There was a short inclusive service over the five graves by the Chaplain. Sister McCaul stayed after the others had returned to the hospital and busied herself with the simple wooden cross she had brought.

"I'll get the trap when you feel able to go and see Greta. It is not far from here and we won't need an escort."

"Thank you, Sister McCaul."

"Please call me Fiona. We've been colleagues long enough and I consider you a friend now," said the Sister in an embarrassed rush as she left to make the arrangements.

In the cart going to Chieveley cemetery Sister McCaul was determined there would be no awkward silences and filled the time reminiscing and telling anecdotes about her time with Greta. Aileen listened listless and red eyed. Just before they reached the graveyard the older woman described Greta's grave and how to find it. She would not come with Aileen to the grave side since she was sure she would want to be alone. Aileen tried to smile her thanks, but it was a wan effort. Sister McCaul remained in the cart.

The cemetery was bare and surrounded by barbed wire. There were no trees and no adornments whatsoever. Aileen made her way to the site where Greta lay surrounded by dead warriors. She walked hesitantly and forced herself to read each of the names of the fallen soldiers as a means of delaying the incontrovertible truth, trying to hold off the finality that seeing the grave of her friend would bring. It became impossible to read as the tears flooded down her cheeks and she cried uncontrollably but silently.

She reached the simple cross that Sister McCaul had placed at the head of Greta's grave and dropped to her knees. Her heart sank as she could see from the freshness of the earth that she had missed seeing Greta by a day or two at most. Fiona had not mentioned when Greta was taken.

"I'm here at last my love. You are alone no more."

CHAPTER THIRTY-SEVEN
Mozambique

The heady days of telling victories were sadly in the past. The severe losses suffered by the British at the battles of Magersfontein, Colenso, and Spion Kop were gratifying but were now sadly insignificant in the overall scheme of the war. With diminishing resources there was little that could be done to halt, or even slow, the remorseless juggernaut bulling its way forward driven by the callous determination of Roberts and Kitchener. Reinforcements for the Irish Brigade were few and the calibre of the recruits did little to inspire confidence. Fergal did not consider himself to be a quitter. He believed however, that he was pragmatic, and the time was fast drawing close when it would be wise to prepare for the end. That is, the end as far he was concerned.

Most of the actions, as the Boer Commandos retreated further into their homeland, were inconclusive although not too damaging to the Boer War effort but Paardeberg had been a body blow. De Cronje's surrender had been too much for many Boers and only the cadre of younger Generals and their dedicated followers remained defiant.

Fergal stirred the beans over the weak flames of a damp wood fire. He could murder for a hot drink, but their meagre supply of tea had finished

323

at breakfast the day before. They had stretched the ration out by re-using the leaves two or three times, thanks to young Lester's ingenuity of wrapping a minute quantity in a piece of cotton kerchief, before immersing it in the boiling water.

They relied heavily on the local Boer populace to provide food and supplies but now things were so dire that there was hardly enough for the people's own needs. The situation had not been helped by some of the Uitlanders acting like mercenaries, instead of volunteers, and succumbing to looting and ransacking. There had been rumours of rape. The incidence of drunkenness among them was increasing and Fergal had to concede even his Brigade suffered from the malaise. Gradually the majority of the local populace were becoming more than indifferent to the plight of the volunteers.

Fergal heard whistling and looked up to see Lester retuning with a hessian sack which sadly was not bulging. Squatting beside Fergal he pulled out a round loaf and two battered tins without labels. He smiled at the older man as he took out a knife and began to shave the mould from the bread.

"This is the pits." said the young American chewing stolidly on the crust. "I'm thinking Delagoa Bay and home."

Fergal didn't answer but he had also been thinking along those lines. He did feel a reluctance to rush into a departure because the Boer leadership had been generous with praise if not with material goods. The Brits were closing in and it was not beyond doubt that they would block the recognised escape routes out of the country.

The sudden ear-splitting roar of cannon shots and their reverberations caused the two men to spring to their feet and lose all thought of hunger or thirst. They snatched up their weapons and ran to their ponies, mounting and riding out join the rest of the Brigade in flight. Catching up with the leading riders Fergal ordered everyone to head for the ruins higher up the slope.

An hour later having finally gathered his men together for roll call Fergal shouted out the names. The group was protected from view, and probable artillery or rifle fire, from the soldiers by one of the many sections of ancient walls that covered the hills around Machadodorp. The gaps in the register revealed that six men had not returned. They could still be at large and on their way in but for Fergal it was a reasonable assumption that they were now part of the haemorrhage of fighters calling it a day.

They had no sooner set up a new camp area behind the wall when enfilading fire from a Maxim wounded or killed several of the Brigade with its first belt. Before they could react by returning fire six or seven more were chopped down.

"Retire! Retire!" screamed Fergal who had sworn that the word 'Retreat" would never pass his lips. Lester was on his knees shrieking to the heavens with his arms clasped tightly around his lower abdomen. Fergal snatched up the reins of his pony and pulled it over to the Irish American. With much difficulty he lifted Lester onto the waiting pony then swung up behind him. The way of escape from the machine guns was open and free from obstruction and they galloped across the slope but with the insidious rattle of Maxim bullets behind them.

Below, he could see roofs of the houses making up the small town of Machadodorp. Lester's injuries were severe, and he had taken one shot four inches or so above his left groin and two through his right thigh. The sleeve of his jacket that Fergal had cut off to make a pad stemming the flow was now a sodden mess of blood and mucous. Its colour was unique to gut shot injuries. Fatal gut shot injuries. With care, he checked the tourniquet on the wounded thigh loosening it for a few seconds then re-applying the pressure.

He searched the streets once again and finally saw a sliver of the red cross pennant indicating a hospital or aid station. Lester had subsided into low guttural moans and his eyes would roll. Fergal hoisted his companion onto his pony, and they walked across then down the slope to the hospital.

While waiting for the news of Lester's condition Fergal heard the whistle of the train from Johannesburg as it approached Machadodorp on its way to Lourenço Marques.

It would stop for fifteen minutes taking on coal and water.

Fergal made up his mind.

CHAPTER THIRTY-EIGHT
RMS Dunottar

The Royal Mail Ship the Dunottar had docked the previous night and boarding was to begin at ten the following morning. The Colonel had little luggage as most of his possessions had been lost during the many moves of both Methuen's and Buller's troops. He was philosophical about the loss and was more concerned about reaching England and Haddington Hall.

Remus was decidedly unhappy when he saw the sling and even more so when it encircled his middle. He was not skittish but there was a flash of white when his eyes widened as his hooves left the ground and he was swung aboard. When he was safely below decks Craven returned to wait with the other first-class travellers, mostly military, in the VIP lounge. As he smoked a cheroot, he idly watched the stevedores. swarming over the quayside loading cargo for the return voyage. Later a steward from the Dunnottar at the doorway to the waiting room announced that boarding was about to begin and that passengers should make their way to the forward gangway. As befitting his new station in life special arrangements were made for his return to England.

The General had broached the news to him that morning. Craven had found General Buller deep in thought holding a message form in his hand.

"You sent for me, sir?"

"I did. Sit down, Nicholas. I have," waving the paper, "bad news for you. It would appear your father has died. He was in Scotland and had a stroke while grouse shooting. I'm sorry."

The colonel remained calm and unperturbed.

"Thank you for the news, sir."

"I imagine you will be required at Haddington to make the necessary arrangements?"

"I would believe so, sir. I'm sorry to leave you in the lurch."

"Think nothing of it. I just hope everything works out smoothly for you. Undoubtedly it will but we need to get you home as quickly as possible. Get your traps together and we'll get you out of here as quickly as we can."

"Yes, thank you, of course, sir. One more thing if I may? Can you issue an authority for Remus to travel with me? At my expense of course."

The General stood and put out his hand.

"Think nothing of it my boy. Fella deserves a ride home. Request noted. Unlike many of the animals when this do is over, sad to say. I am sorry Nicholas. Although, I think you are better off out of this. I won't forget you were the first to

offer moral support. Or what it is has cost you."
He indicated Craven's missing arm."

They shook hands and he returned to his tent.
He was surprised that he had not felt more
emotion at the news of his father's passing.

He was met by the captain on boarding
which was only one of the changes that his
elevation to the peerage would bring. In his cabin
he unpacked the few possessions he had then
went to the hold to check on Remus. It seemed to
Craven that Remus was resigned to his situation
as he munched on the hay in the manger. He felt
satisfied he was repaying his horse for its faithful
service. Remus would live out his days in the
stables and meadow at Haddington.

Back on deck there were a few officers at
the portside rail, and he joined them. Below an
area of the dockside had been roped off to form a
lane for embarking passengers. He watched as
the line moved forward. Among the boarders was
a small group of nurses. The figure of one, taller
than her companions, drew his attention. The
glint of auburn gold escaping from the side of her
nurse's cap confirmed the news that his good eye
had signalled to his brain.

He entered the lounge and crossed to a
vacant sofa. The waiter came over and asked
what he should bring. She entered moments later,

alone, and seemed preoccupied but on catching sight of him smiled and joined him.

"What would you like Sister?"

"It's no longer Sister, Colonel. I have resigned. May I join you in a coffee?" Craven lifted his arm to beckon to the waiter, but he was already crossing the floor with a second cup and saucer. Craven poured the coffee for both then sat back. Both looked at each other without unease in a comfortable silence. Aileen sipped her coffee then said, "I think we should talk and become reacquainted."

"Yes, a lot has happened since we were last at sea."

"I was thinking of a time before that. Before Canada. Before the veld. Haddington Hall, to be precise."

THE END

About the Author

I spent my boyhood on various farms on the east coast of Scotland as the son of an itinerant and argumentative farm labourer who could hold a job no longer than a few months. Intoxicated, one Hogmanay he was arrested and held overnight in the cells for 'being drunk whilst in charge of a bicycle'. I joined a boxing club to develop a way of avoiding daily beatings. A spin-off benefit of this was winning the Midlands of Scotland Bantam weight championship in my age group.

I left Caledonia at the age of fifteen narrowly evading Borstal to join the British Army where I spent two and a half years in Boys Service and was posted to adult service and on stand-by for the Suez Emergency. Fortunately, that ended albeit rather ignominiously and I shipped out to Malaya, at the height of the communist insurgency there. On the completion of three years my next port of call was Belgium, then the UK, where, after selection and training, I served with the airborne forces. I passed sometime in Belfast, Northern Ireland during The Troubles. Eventually I went to Germany where I narrowly avoided being court-martialled for punching out a fellow warrant officer who had rather overestimated his physical capabilities. Hong

Kong followed the Fatherland where I moonlighted as an extra and stuntman for Shaw Bros and Golden Harvest Film studios. I appeared, albeit briefly, in Bruce Lee and I, episode nine of Hawaii Five O, and a myriad of other features produced purely for consumption by the Chinese cinema goer.

Returning to Europe I was recruited by a head-hunter on behalf of the U.S. Government and after several courses in CONUS, I served in most of the European countries and Israel & Turkey.

In my free time I managed to obtain two degrees from the University of Maryland off-campus further education project and travel extensively on mainland Europe moonlighting as a tour manager for a holiday firm concentrating on American clientele. With the downsizing of the U.S. presence in the European theatre, a friend offered me the job of Convoy Leader ferrying humanitarian aid to the beleaguered cities and towns of Bosnia-Herzegovina. This was under the auspices of UNHCR, during the conflict in the early nineties in the former Yugoslavia.

I retired to the UK and took up golf, wrote The Tuzla Run and offered my body, piecemeal, to medical science, which is currently in possession of three per cent of it, while I retain the rights to the balance — so far.

Connect with Robert Davidson:

authorbobdavidson.com

Other Books by the Author

The Tuzla Run (2011)

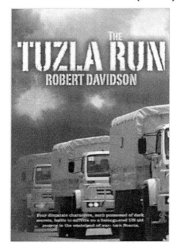

Amazon Customer:

"Davidson's descriptive details of the various geographic areas, and the war damage in the Tuzla region, comes across as personal experience rather than research. Once I started the story, I found it hard not to keep reading the next page and the next and so on, even at the risk of lost sleep."

Geoff Woodland Australia, Amazon Five-Star Review

The Yukon Illusion (2016)

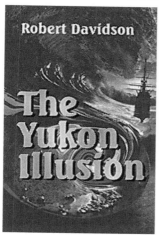

Amazon Customer Brendan Gisby
5.0 out of 5 stars No More Heroes
Reviewed in the United Kingdom on 28
September 2016
Verified Purchase
"For a whole host of reasons, I thoroughly
enjoyed this highly impressive saga of the quest
for riches in the Yukon of the late nineteenth
century. And here are but a few of those
reasons. The quality that struck me first is the
author's attention to detail. Davidson is not a
lazy writer. It's clear from the outset of the
novel that he has researched his material
thoroughly. So, when he describes the people
who set out for the Yukon, the way they speak,
the clothes they wear, the equipment they carry
and the landscape they must conquer, you know

that you're reading the real McCoy.

Equally authentic are the author's descriptions of the way of life back then. It's harsh, it's brutal, it's uncompromising – and Davidson doesn't hold back telling us that.

Another factor that more than contributed to holding the interest of this particular reader is the intricate weaving of the disparate lives of the three main protagonists; it's nothing short of masterly, in my opinion.

Above all, though, I celebrate the novel's absence of clean-cut, clean-shaven heroes. Davidson gives us real people, real characters, with all their weaknesses and vices plain for all to see. There were no heroes in that cruel, ruthless time and place.

I'll close my brief review with an observation for the author. I think there's plenty of scope for a sequel. I'd love to read one, Mr Davidson."

The Man From Armagh (2019)

Amazon Customer:
5.0 out of 5 stars Great Read
Reviewed in the United States on May 5, 2019
Verified Purchase
"Couldn't put it down. Action packed with all kinds of twists and turns. The story draws you into it and won't let go. This author has a style that I have not seen before. Can't wait for more of his talent to be shared in more of his works."

**Read reviews and buy the books on
Amazon.com / Amazon.co.uk**

338

Printed in Poland
by Amazon Fulfillment
Poland Sp. z o.o., Wrocław